Never had she dreamed she could look like this.

The evening gown flattered her with shades of creamy ivory and the softest shimmering green. Embroidery of darker green and a pale rose colour trimmed the round neckline and the low-cut bodice. The same colours were echoed in short slashed sleeves. A broad ribbon tied round the mid-level waist, and the ends trailed down behind her.

She stood there on the brink, transfixed by the beauty of it all. Mrs Dawson had truly outdone herself. Lush potted plants lined the dance floor and graced every flat surface, while garlands of fresh blooms draped the walls and twined gracefully up the pillars. Hundreds of glittering candles shone in three stunning crystal chandeliers. They cast their glow over a vast number of people—and they were all in motion. Even the air seemed to flow with the swell of the music and in time with the diaphanous drift of the ladies' gowns.

It looked a faerie world, unreal, like a glimpse into a shining, shimmering bubble. Such a fragile and delicate thing, to hold all her hopes and dreams.

Author Note

For many years the Dreadnought Seamen's Hospital provided health and welfare services to 'all distressed seamen' and the people who lived and worked in port communities. The hospital's very first home was on board *HMS Grampus*, afloat on the River Thames. Here a small staff dedicated themselves to those who made their lives on the sea. They took in their first patients in 1821.

By 1830 the hospital had outgrown the *Grampus*. The Royal Navy generously donated the ex-warship *HMS Dreadnought*, from which the hospital thereafter took its name. In 1870 the Dreadnought moved ashore in Greenwich. It became an important part of the local community, and treated sailors from all nations and locals alike until it closed its doors in 1986.

I admit to fudging the dates a bit in HER CINDERELLA SEASON, when I had the staff of *HMS Grampus* taking J. Crump in several months earlier than the hospital officially opened its doors. Once I knew Crump, and realised he was dying, I longed for him to end his days in a place of caring and dignity. I hope you'll forgive the poetic licence.

HER
CINDERELLA
SEASON

Deb Marlowe

 MILLS & BOON®
Pure reading pleasure™

First published in Great Britain 2008
Large Print edition 2009
Harlequin Mills & Boon Limited,
Eton House, 18-24 Paradise Road, Richmond, Surrey TW9 1SR

© Deb Marlowe 2008

ISBN: 978 0 263 20654 8

Set in Times Roman 15½ on 17¾ pt.
42-0209-83734

Printed and bound in Great Britain
by CPI Antony Rowe, Chippenham, Wiltshire

Deb Marlowe grew up in Pennsylvania with her nose in a book. Luckily, she'd read enough romances to recognise the true modern hero she met at a college Halloween party—even though he wore a tuxedo T-shirt instead of breeches and tall boots. They married, settled in North Carolina, and produced two handsome, intelligent and genuinely amusing boys.

Though she now spends much of her time with her nose in her laptop, for the sake of her family she does occasionally abandon her inner world for the domestic adventure of laundry, dinner and carpool. Despite her sacrifice, not one of the men in her family is yet willing to don breeches or tall boots. She's working on it. Deb would love to hear from readers! You can contact her at debmarlowe@debmarlowe.com

Recent titles by the same author:

SCANDALOUS LORD, REBELLIOUS MISS
AN IMPROPER ARISTOCRAT

For my Grandpap—
a real-life hero for the ages

Chapter One

Jack's hand held steady, his aim unwavering. His pistol was pointed straight at Hassan's evil heart. This time he would kill the bastard. This time he would.

But something moved in the shadowy dreamscape. A soft rustle sounded, impossibly close—just as his sleeping mind had known it would. Not Aswan. Smaller. Jack caught the faint scent of gardenias just a moment before he felt the press of cold steel at his temple.

A flood of fury and frustration swamped him. God damn it, now the innocent girl below him would die. *He* would die all alone up here in the pitch blackness of the Egyptian Hall gallery and an ancient treasure would fall into the worst of hands.

As it always did, night after night, an indescribable flurry of movement erupted as Aswan intervened. A woman's cry. A bright flash of light in the near darkness. And a searing pain that exploded in his arm and knocked him backwards.

Someone loomed over him. The sinister face swam in the darkness, but somehow he knew it was not the woman who'd shot him, nor was it the villain Hassan—it must be Batiste. Captain Batiste, the silent, invisible mastermind behind much of the plot to hurt his friends. The shadow began to laugh, and an old, cold rage burned deep in Jack's gut.

'So disappointing, Jack,' the figure whispered. 'I expected more of you.'

He scrambled backwards. It was not a stranger's voice reaching for him out of the darkness, but his father's.

Gasping, Jack jerked awake.

That damned dream again. He shook off the remnants of the nightmare and glanced at the clock on the wall—early afternoon. Had he fallen asleep in his chair? A heavy tome rested painfully against his injured arm. He tossed it on to the floor and scrubbed his free hand against his scalp, trying to chase away the fuzziness in his head.

That night at the Egyptian Hall had not been his finest moment. Perhaps that was the reason he relived it repeatedly in his dreams. He heaved a massive sigh. He didn't regret mixing himself up in Lord Treyford's misadventures, and yet…

Trey and Chione had taken their family back to Devonshire. Soon they would be leaving for Egypt, embarking on an adventure that Jack couldn't help but envy. He'd held his breath, hoping to be asked along, but Trey and Chione were occupied with each other, and caught up in the wonder of what awaited them.

Jack had been left behind and he'd found himself strangely unsettled. He pressed his good hand hard against his brow. His preoccupation with Batiste had grown, becoming something closer to obsession. The villain had slipped away on the tide, leaving Hassan and his other confederates to be caught up in Treyford's net. The man's escape nagged at Jack incessantly.

He stood. He was due to meet Pettigrew, to test those devilishly bad-mannered bays the baron was trying to sell. Jack cast a rueful glance down at his arm. This was not the most reasonable course of action, but, damn it, the man had baited him. At any other point in his life, Jack would have ignored the baron's desperate manoeuvre. Not this time. Instead he had risen like a trout to a well-crafted lure. A stupid response. Immature. And yet another maddening symptom of his recent erratic temperament.

Jack struggled into his greatcoat and decided to stop by White's and pick up his brother along the way. Charles was in town to further his reform causes before the Parliamentary session closed, and to conveniently avoid the domestic chaos brought on by a colicky baby. And since he had been the one to introduce him to Pettigrew, then riding along with a crippled driver and an unruly team was the least he could do.

As he set out, a chill wind began to gust. The cold blast of air made his arm throb like an aching tooth. Jack huddled a little deeper into his coat and rifled in his pocket for Pettigrew's hastily scribbled address. He stopped short. The baron's dire financial straits had led him to take rooms in Goodman's Fields. An unsavoury neighbourhood it might be, but it was conveniently located near enough to the London docks—where the offices of Batiste's defunct shipping company were located.

Jack quickened his step. This might not be a wasted day after all.

Lily Beecham glanced at her mother from the corner of her eye. Mrs Margaret Beecham had turned slightly away from her daughter, avoiding the brightest light as she concentrated on her needlework. Slowly, surreptitiously, Lily tilted her head back and directly into the path of the afternoon sunshine.

Though it wasn't the least bit ladylike, Lily loved

the warmth of the sun on her face. The burst of patterned radiance behind her closed eyelids, the brush of the breeze on her heated cheeks; it took her back, every single time. For a few seconds she was a girl again, in her father's arms, giggling like mad while he spun her round and his rich, booming laugh washed over her. Sometimes she could hear its echo still, the liquid sound of pure love.

Not now, though. Now she heard only the unnecessarily loud clearing of her mother's throat. 'Lilith, this is a public thoroughfare, not the back pasture at home.'

'Yes, of course, Mother.' Lily straightened in her seat. She glanced down at her copy of *Practical Piety*, but she'd read Hannah More's work many times over already and now was not the time to risk her mother discovering the thin volume she'd tucked inside. She got to her feet and began to pace behind the table they'd been asked to tend for Lady Ashford's Fancy Fair and Charity Bazaar.

The majority of the booths and tables in the countess's event had been strung along Rotten Row in Hyde Park, where they were sure to catch the attention of those with both the inclination and the wherewithal to purchase ribbons, bonnets and embroidered penwipes in the name of charity. The Book Table, however, along with the Second-Hand

Clothing and the Basketry tables, had been pro-
nounced more likely to appeal to the masses, and
had thus been placed outside the Grosvenor Gate,
right alongside Park Lane.

'It is somewhat frustrating, isn't it, Mother—that
we've sat here all day, just outside the most famous
park in London, and we've yet to set foot inside?'

'Not in the least. Why should such a thing vex
you? This park is full of grass and trees just like any
other.' Mrs Beecham's needle did not pause as she
glanced up at her daughter. 'We should count our-
selves fortunate to have been asked to help today. It
is an honour to be of service to such a noble cause.'

'Yes, of course you are right.' Lily suppressed a
sigh. She didn't know why she should be surprised
at the disappointments of the day. The entire trip to
town had been an exercise in frustration.

Long ago her father had talked to her of London.
He had perched her on his knee, run his fingers
through the tangle of her hair and spoken of great
museums, elaborate theatrical productions and the
noisy, chaotic workings of Parliament, where the
fates of men and nations were decided. He had spun
fanciful stories of her own future visits to the
greatest city in the world, and she had eagerly
absorbed every tale.

But her father had died before his stories could

come true and Lily's busy, happy life had been abandoned for sober duty and sombre good works. And so, it seemed, had her dream of London.

Her hopes had been so high when her mother had announced that they were to travel to town and spend the month of May. But over the last weeks, joy and anticipation had dwindled. She had trailed her mother from one Reformist committee to another Evangelical meeting and on to an Abolitionist group, and the dreadful truth had dawned on her. Her surroundings had changed, but her situation had not.

'Mr Cooperage will make a fine missionary, don't you agree?' her mother asked, this time without looking away from her work. Lily wondered if it was giving her trouble, so intent did she appear.

'He will if the fancy work inside the park proves more profitable than the Book Table. Even with the Cheap Repository Tracts to sell, we haven't raised enough to get him a hackney across town, let alone passage to India.'

Her mother frowned.

Lily sighed. 'I don't mean to be flippant.' She stood on her toes to peer past the gate and into the park. 'There does seem to be a bigger crowd gathered inside.'

Her mother's scowl faded as a young woman

strolling past on a gentleman's arm broke away to approach their table. Lily returned her friendly smile and admired the white lute-string trim on her violet walking dress.

'Good afternoon,' the young woman said brightly. 'But it seems as if you are out of A. Vaganti?' She nodded towards Lily's chair and the volume now peeking from the staid pages of Mrs More's work. 'I've already read *The Emerald Temple*. I was wondering if you might have the newest Nicolas adventure, *The Pharaoh's Forbidden City*?'

Mrs Beecham darted a sharp glance in Lily's direction. 'No, but we have several more improving works. Bowdler's Shakespeare, for instance, if fiction is what interests you.'

The young lady gave a soft, tinkling laugh. 'Oh my, no! Surely it is a shame to allow that man to chop apart the works of our great bard? What harm is there in Shakespeare? It seems I've read or seen his works from the cradle!'

She tilted her head engagingly. 'Forgive me for being bold, ma'am,' she said with a smile. 'How wonderful you are to give your day to helping Lady Ashford's good cause.' She dropped a curtsy. 'I am Miss Dawson.' She cast an encouraging glance at Lily.

Hurriedly, Lily returned the curtsy. 'My mother, Mrs Margaret Beecham.' She gestured and smiled back. 'I am Miss Beecham.' Something about the girl's friendly countenance had her blurting out, 'But please, you must call me Lily.'

'Beecham?' the girl asked with a frown of concentration. She eyed Lily curiously. 'You test my recollection of our ponderous family tree, but I believe we have relatives of that name. Might you come from Dorset?'

'Indeed, yes,' Lily replied. 'We are in town for a few weeks only.'

'It's a pleasure, Lily.' She looked over her shoulder as her companion called her name. 'Oh dear, I must run.' She leaned in close. 'That is my betrothed, Lord Lindley. We both adore A. Vaganti, but he would never admit to it in public.' She grinned and, reaching across the table, pressed Lily's hand. 'I feel sure we shall meet again.'

Lily watched the young lady take her gentleman's arm and head into the park. A little sigh escaped her. She might have been friends with a girl like that, had her father not died. She let herself imagine what might have been, for just a moment: friends, novels, walks in the park. Perhaps even she might have had a beau? She flushed and glanced at her mother, who regarded her with a frown.

'I hope you are not still mooning about participating in the social whirl?'

Lily took notice of the sharp note in her mother's voice and then she took her seat. She picked up her book, and gazed down at it for several long seconds. 'No, of course not,' she answered. A soft breeze, warm and laden with the green scent of the park, brushed her cheek. With sudden resolution, Lily pulled the adventure novel from its hiding place and opened it.

The heavy weight of her mother's gaze rested on her for several long seconds. Suddenly her mother let out a sigh that echoed her own. 'I do hope that young lady will buy something inside. Mr Cooperage's work is so important. Think of all those lost souls just waiting for him!' She resumed her needlework, then paused to knot her thread. 'We've had so little interest out here, I had begun to wonder if Lady Ashford might better have chosen the Hanover Square Rooms for her fair.'

'I'm sure it will all turn out well,' Lily soothed. 'You know the countess—she will have it no other way.' She smiled. 'And the crickets were singing away when we arrived, Mother. That's a definite sign of good fortune.'

Her mother's needlework went down, but her brow lowered even further. 'Lilith Beecham—you know how it upsets me to hear you spouting such nonsense!' She took a fortifying breath, but Lily was saved from further harangue by a shrill cry.

'Mrs Beecham!'

They turned to look.

'Mrs Beecham—you must come!'

'It's Lady Ashford,' Lily said in surprise. And indeed it was the countess, although clad as she was in various shades of blue and flapping a large white handkerchief as she sailed towards the gate, she resembled nothing so much as a heavily laden frigate storming a blockade.

'My dear Mrs Beecham…' the countess braced her hand on the table for support while she caught her breath '…it is Mr Wilberforce himself!' she panted. 'He has come to thank us and has brought Mr Cooperage along with him.' She picked up one of the Repository Tracts and began to fan herself with it.

Lily looked askance at her mother's stunned expression. William Wilberforce, the famous abolitionist and one of the leading members of the Evangelical movement, was Margaret Beecham's particular idol.

Mrs Beecham found her tongue. 'Oh, but, Lady Ashford—Wilberforce himself! What a coup!' She stood and pressed the countess's hand. 'How wonderful for you, to be sure.'

'And for you, too, Mrs Beecham,' Lady Ashford said warmly, recovering her breath. 'For I have told Mr Wilberforce how easily the charity school in

Weymouth went up, and how thoroughly the community has embraced it. It was largely your doing, and so I told him. I informed him also of your tremendous success in recruiting volunteers. He wishes to meet you and thank you in person! His carriage is swamped right now with well wishers and so I have come to fetch you. He means to take us both up for a drive and he'll drop you right here when we've been round the park.'

'A drive?' Lily saw all the colour drain from her mother's face. 'With Mr Wilberforce?'

'Come now!' Lady Ashford said in imperious tones. 'We must not keep him waiting!'

'Oh, but I—' Mrs Beecham sat abruptly down again.

'Come, Mother,' Lily urged, pulling her back to her feet. 'You've worked long and hard. You deserve a bit of accolade.' She smiled at the odd mix of fear and longing on her mother's face. 'It is fine,' she soothed. 'He only wishes to acknowledge your efforts.'

'We must go now, Mrs Beecham!' Lady Ashford had done with the delay. She reached out and began to drag Lily's mother along with her.

'Oh, but Lilith—' came the last weak protest from Mrs Beecham.

'The girl will be fine. The ladies from the other tables are here and she's not some chit barely out of the schoolroom. She'll know how to handle herself.'

'Goodbye, Mother!' Lily called. 'Do try to enjoy yourself!' She watched until the ladies disappeared into the crowd, and then took her seat, knowing the futility of that last admonition.

Traffic in the street ahead of her began to pick up. Shining high-perch phaetons wheeled through the Grosvenor Gate into the park. Gorgeously groomed thoroughbreds and their equally handsome riders followed. Ladies dressed in rich, fluttering fabrics paused at the tables, or giggled as they passed them by. Lily watched them all a bit wistfully. Surely they were not all so empty-headed and frivolous as her mother believed? Lady Ashford certainly thrived with one foot firmly in the thick of the *ton* and the other in the Evangelical camp.

She fought back a shudder as she glanced down at her plain, brown, serviceable gown. What did those men and women of society think when they looked at her? They could not see inside, where her true self lay. Did they see the girl who loved a bruising ride, and a thrilling novel? Could they conceive of her secret dreams, the longings that she'd buried so deep, she'd forgotten them herself? No. They could not. Why would they?

Lily straightened, shocked by a sudden idea. She'd been so excited to come to town, sure this was the chance she'd awaited: the long-anticipated sign of change and good fortune. But what if the sign had been meant for her mother instead? This disturbing thought kept her occupied for several agonisingly conflicted minutes. Of course she wished her mother happy. Hadn't she thrown herself into an attempt to please her for the last seven years? She'd done all she could to ease the blow of her father's loss. She'd settled down, acted the lady, given up all the rough-and-ready activities of her youth, all because she was eager to please a mother who had always seemed uncomfortable with and somewhat perplexed by her spirited daughter.

Only now did Lily realise how significant the prospect of change had become in her mind—now when the possibility appeared to be fading fast away.

'My dear Miss Beecham, here you are at last!'

'Mr Cooperage.' Lily shook off her disturbing train of thought and tried to rally a smile for the missionary approaching from the park. 'How nice to see you. I'm sure your presence is a boost to all of our volunteers.'

'Naturally,' he agreed. Lily tried not to wince. Everything about the missionary, from dress to manner, spoke of neatness and correctness. Yet Lily did not find him a comfortable man. His tendency to speak in pronouncements unnerved her.

'Will you step away a little with me?' he asked in

his forceful tone. 'I gave up my seat in my friend Wilberforce's barouche for your mother. What better recompense, I asked myself, than to seek out her lovely daughter?'

'I should not leave my table,' she hedged. 'I should not wish to miss a sale.'

He glanced significantly about. Not a soul appeared to rescue her.

'We shall not stray far,' he insisted. 'We shall stay right here near the gates.'

Lily sighed, laid a hand on the gentleman's arm and allowed him to lead her a few steps down the street.

'You, my dear Miss Beecham, are a fortunate young lady,' Mr Cooperage told her in the same tones he might use from the pulpit. 'I confess myself to be a great admirer of your mother's.' He took care to steer her away from the busy traffic in the street. 'Your mother, much like Wilberforce himself, has lived in the world. They each knew years full of frivolities and trivial pursuits. How much more we must honour them for having turned from superficiality to a life of worthiness.'

Lily stared. 'I must thank you for the compliment to my mother, Mr Cooperage, but surely you state your case in terms too strong?'

'Impossible!' he scoffed. His voice rang so loud that several passers-by turned to look. 'I could not rate my respect for the woman your mother is now any higher, nor my contempt for those who cling to a life of vanity and mindless amusement—' he flicked a condemnatory wave towards the park and the stream of people now entering '—any lower.'

Had Lily been having this conversation yesterday, or last week, or at any given time in the last seven years, she would have swallowed her irritation and tactfully steered the missionary to a less volatile topic. But today—there was something different about today. Perhaps she'd had too much time to think, or perhaps she had for some time been moving towards an elemental shift, but today the rebel in her—the one with the taste for adventure novels—had got the bit in her teeth.

She sucked in a fortifying breath and straightened her spine. 'Firstly, Mr Cooperage, I feel compelled to tell you that my mother has been worthy of your admiration, and anyone else's, for her *entire* life. Secondly, I would ask that you not be so quick to disparage the pleasure seekers about us.' She cocked her head at him. 'For is that not what today is all about—the happy mix of amusement and altruism?'

Displeasure marred his pleasing features, but only for a moment. He chuckled and assumed an air of condescension. 'Your innocence is refreshing, Miss Beecham.' He sighed. 'The sad truth is that if it would give them a moment's pleasure, most of these people would as soon toss their coin in the gutter as donate it to our cause.'

'But surely you don't believe that merriment and worthiness are mutually exclusive?' Her father's image immediately rose up in her mind. His quick smile and ready laugh were two of her most cherished memories. 'I'm certain you will agree that it is possible to work hard, to become a useful and praiseworthy soul and still partake of the joy in life?'

'The joy in life?' Mr Cooperage appeared startled by the concept. 'My dear, we were not put on this earth to enjoy life—' He cut himself abruptly off. Lily could see that it pained him greatly. She suspected he wanted badly to inform her exactly what he thought her purpose on this earth to be.

Instead, he forced a smile. 'I will not waste our few moments of conversation.' He paused and began again in a lower, almost normal conversational tone. 'I do thank you for your efforts today. However they are gained, I mean to put today's profits to good use. I hope to accomplish much of God's work in my time abroad.'

'How impatient you must be to begin,' she said, grateful for a topic on which they could agree. 'I can only imagine your excitement at the prospect of helping so many people, learning their customs and culture, seeing strange lands and exotic sights.' She sighed. 'I do envy you the experience!'

'You should not,' he objected. 'I do not complain. I will endure the strange lodgings, heathen food and poor company because I have a duty, but I would not subject a woman to the hardships of travel.'

She should not have been surprised. 'But what if a woman has a calling such as yours, sir? What then? Or do you not believe such a thing to be possible?'

He returned her serious expression. 'I believe it to be rare, but possible.' He glanced back towards the park gate. 'Your mother, I believe, has been called. I do think she will answer.'

Her mother had been called? To do what?

'My mission will keep me from the shores of England for a little more than a year, Miss Beecham, but your good mother assures me that there are no other suitors in the wings and that a year is not too long a wait.' He roamed an earnest gaze over her face. 'Was she wrong?'

Lily took a step back. Surprise? He had succeeded in shocking her. 'You wish my mother to wait for you, sir? Do you mean to court her?'

He chuckled. 'Your modesty reflects well on you, my dear. No—it is you who I wish to wait for me. You who I mean to court most assiduously when I return.' His eyes left her face, and darted over the rest of her. 'Your mother was agreeable to the notion. I hope you feel the same?'

Lily stood frozen—not shocked, but numb. Completely taken aback. Mr Cooperage wished to marry her? And her mother had consented? It must be a mistake. At first she could not even wrap her mind about such an idea, but then she had to struggle to breathe as the bleak image of such a life swept over her.

'Miss Beecham?' Mr Cooperage sounded anxious, and mildly annoyed. 'A year is too long?' he asked.

She couldn't breathe. She willed her chest to expand, tried to gasp for the air that she desperately needed. She was going to die. She would collapse to the ground right here, buried and suffocated under the weight of a future she did not want.

Her life was never going to change. The truth hit her hard, at last knocking the breath back into her starving lungs. She gasped out loud and Mr Cooperage began to look truly alarmed. Seven years. So long she had laboured; she had tried her best and squashed the truest part of her nature, all in the attempt to get her mother to look at her with pride. Was this, then, what it would take? The sacrifice of her future?

Lily took a step back, and then another. Only vaguely did she realise how close she had come to the busy street behind her. She only thought to distance herself from the grim reality of the life unfolding in front of her.

'Miss Beecham!' called Mr Cooperage. 'Watch your step. Watch behind you!' he thundered. 'Miss Beecham!'

A short, heavy snort sounded near her. Lily turned. A team of horses, heads tossing wildly, surged towards her. Her gaze met one wild, rolling eye. A call of fright rang out. Had she made the sound, or had the horse?

'Miss Beecham!'

Chapter Two

Jack Alden pulled as hard as he dared on the ribbons. Pain seared its way up his injured arm. Pettigrew's ill-tempered bays responded at last, subsiding to a sweating, quivering stop.

'I warned you that these nags were too much for that arm,' his brother Charles said. His hand gripped the side of the borrowed crane-neck phaeton.

'Stow it, Charles,' Jack growled. He stared ahead. 'Hell and damnation, it's a woman in the street!'

'Well, no wonder that park drag ground to a halt. I told you when it started into the other lane that this damned flighty team would bolt.'

'She's not moving,' Jack complained. Was the woman mad? Oblivious to the fact that she'd nearly been trampled like a turnip off a farm cart, she stood stock still. She wasn't even looking their way now; her attention appeared focused on something on the pavement. Jack could not see just what held her interest with near deadly result. Nor could he see her face, covered as it was by a singularly ugly brown bonnet.

'You nearly ran her down. She's likely frozen in fear,' Charles suggested.

'For God's sake!' Jack thrust the reins into his brother's hands and swung down. Another jolt of pain ripped through his arm. 'Hold them fast!' he growled in exasperation.

'Do you know, Jack, people have begun to comment on the loss of your legendary detachment,' Charles said as he held the bays in tight.

'I am *not* detached!' Jack said, walking away. 'You make me sound like a freehold listing in *The Times*.'

'Auction on London Gentleman, Manner Detached,' his brother yelled after him.

Jack ignored him. Legendary detachment be damned. He was anchored fully in this moment and surging forwards on a wave of anger. The fool woman had nearly been killed, and by his hand! Well, that might be an exaggeration, but without doubt the responsibility would have been his. He'd caught sight of her over the thrashing heads of the horses—standing where she clearly did not belong—and fear and anger and guilt had blasted him like lightning out of the sky. The realisation that his concern was more for himself than for her only fuelled his fury.

'Madam!' he called as he strode towards her. The entire incident had happened so fast that the park drag had still not manoeuvred completely past. People milled about on the pavement, and one florid gentleman glared at the woman, but made no move to approach her.

'Madam!' No response. 'If you are bent on suicide, might I suggest another man's phaeton? This one is borrowed and I am bound to deliver it in one piece.'

She did not answer or even look at him. 'Ma'am, do you not realise that you were nearly killed?' He took her arm. 'Come now, you cannot stand in the street!'

At last, ever so slowly, the bonnet began to turn. The infuriating creature looked him full in the face.

Jack immediately wished she hadn't. He had grown up surrounded by beauty. He'd lived in an elegant house and received an excellent education. From ancient statuary to modern landscapes, between the sweep of grand architecture and the graceful curve of the smallest Sèvres bowl, he'd been taught to recognise and appreciate the value of loveliness.

This girl—she was the image of classic English beauty come to life. Gorgeous slate-blue eyes stared at him, but Jack had the eerie certainty that she did not see him at all. Instead she was focused on something far away, or perhaps deep inside. Red-gold curls framed high curving cheeks, smooth, ivory skin gone pale with fright and a slender little nose covered with the faintest smattering of freckles.

And her mouth. His own went dry—because all the fluids in his body were rushing south. A siren's mouth: wide and dusky pink and irresistible. He stared, saw the sudden trembling of that incredibly plump lower lip—and he realised just what it was he was looking at.

Immense sorrow. A portrait of profound loss. The sight of it set off an alarm inside of Jack and awoke a heretofore unsuspected part of his character. He'd never been the heroic, knight-in-shining-armour sort—but that quivering lower lip made him want to jump into the fray. He could not quell the sudden urge to fight this unknown girl's battles, soothe her hurts, or, better yet, kiss her senseless until she forgot what upset her and realised that there were a thousand better uses for that voluptuous mouth.

He swallowed convulsively, tightened his grip on her arm…and thankfully, came back to his senses. They stood in the middle of a busy London street. Catcalls and shouts and several anatomically impossible suggestions echoed from the surrounding bustle of stopped traffic. A begrimed coal carter had stepped forwards to help his brother calm the bays. Several of society's finest, dressed for the daily strut and starved for distraction, gawked from the pavement.

'Come,' Jack said gently. Her steps wooden, the girl followed. He led her out of the street, past the sputtering red-faced gentleman, towards the Grosvenor Gate. Surely someone would claim her. He darted a glance back at the man who had fallen into step behind them. Someone other than this man—who had apparently left her to be run down like a dog in the street.

Lily was lost in a swirling fog. It had roiled up and out of her in the moment when she had fully understood her predicament. *Her life was never going to change.* Just the echo of that thought brought the mist suffocatingly close. She abandoned herself to it. She'd rather suffocate than contemplate the stifling mess her life had become.

Only vaguely was she aware that the stampeding horses had stopped. Dimly she realised that a stranger led her out of the street. The prickle of her skin told her that people were staring. She couldn't bring herself to care.

'Lilith!' Her mother's strident voice pierced the fog. 'Lilith! Are you unharmed? What were you thinking?'

Anger and resentment surged inside of her, exploded out of her and blew a hole in the circling fog. It was big enough for her to catch a glimpse of her mother's worried scowl as she hurried down from Mr Wilberforce's barouche, and to take in the crowd forming around them.

Her gaze fell on the man who had saved her from herself and she forgot to speak. She stilled. Just at that moment a bright ray of sunlight broke free from the clouds. It shone down directly on to the gentleman, chasing streaks through his hair and outlining the masculine lines of his face. With a whoosh the fog surrounding her disappeared, swept away by the brilliant light and the intensity of the stranger's stare.

Lily swallowed. The superstitious corner of her soul sprang to attention. Her heart began to pound loudly in her ears.

The clouds shifted overhead and the sunbeam disappeared. Now Lily could see the man clearly. Still her pulse beat out a rapid tune. Tall and slender, he was handsome in a rumpled, poetic sort of way. A loose black sling cradled one arm and, though it was tucked inside the dark brown superfine of his coat, she noticed that he held it close as if it ached.

His expression held her in thrall. He'd spoken harshly to her just a moment ago, hadn't he? Now, though his colour was high, his anger seemed to have disappeared as quickly as her hazy confusion. He stared at her with an odd sort of bated hunger. A smile lurked at the edge of his mouth, small and secretive, as if it were meant just for her. The eyes watching her so closely were hazel, a sorry term for such a fascinating mix of green and gold and brown. Curved at their corners were the faintest laugh lines.

So many details, captured in an instant. Together they spoke to her, sending the message that here was a man with experience. Someone who knew passion, and laughter and pain. Here was a man, they whispered, who knew that life was meant to be enjoyed.

'Lilith—' her mother's voice sounded irritated '—have you been hurt?'

Lily forced herself to look away from the stranger. 'No, Mother, I am fine.'

Her mother continued to stare expectantly, but Lily kept quiet. For once, it was not she who was going to explain herself.

Thwarted, Mrs Beecham turned to Mr Cooperage, who lurked behind the strange gentleman. 'Mr Cooperage?' was all that she asked.

The missionary flushed. 'Your daughter does not favour…' he paused and glanced at the stranger '…the matter we discussed last week.'

'Does not favour—?' Lilith's mother's lips compressed to a foreboding thin line.

Mr Cooperage glanced uneasily at the man again and then at the crowd still gathered loosely around them. 'Perhaps you might step aside to have a quiet word with me?' His next words looked particularly hard for him to get out. 'I'm sure your daughter would like the chance to…thank…this gentleman?'

'Mr…?' Her mother raked the stranger with a glare, then waited with a raised brow.

The stranger bowed. Lily thought she caught a faint grimace of pain in his eyes. 'Mr Alden, ma'am.'

'Mr Alden.' Her mother's gaze narrowed. 'I trust my daughter will be safe with you for a moment?'

'Of course.'

The crowd, deprived of further drama, began to disperse. Lily's mother stepped aside and bent to listen to an urgently whispering Mr Cooperage. Lily did not waste a moment considering them. She knew what they discussed. She remembered the haze that had almost engulfed her. It had swept away and left her with a blinding sense of clarity.

'I admit to a ravening curiosity.' Mr Alden spoke low and his voice sounded slightly hoarse. It sent a shiver down Lily's spine. 'Do you wish to?' He raised a questioning brow at her.

'I'm sorry, sir. Do I wish to what?'

'Wish to thank me for nearly running you down in the street while driving a team I clearly should not have been?' He gestured to the sling. 'I assure you, I had planned to most humbly beg your pardon, but if you'd rather thank me instead…'

Lily laughed. She did not have to consider the question. The answer, along with much else, was clear at last. 'Yes,' she said, 'even when you phrase it in such a way. I do wish to thank you.'

He looked a little taken aback, and more than a little interested. 'Then you must be a very odd sort of female,' he said. She felt the heat of the glance that roamed over her, even though he had assumed a clinical expression. 'Don't be afraid to admit it,' he said. He leaned in close, as if confiding a secret. 'Truly, the odd sorts of females are the only ones I can abide.' He smiled at her.

She stared. His words were light and amusing, but that smile? It was wicked. 'Ah, but can they abide you, sir?'

The smile vanished. 'Perhaps the odd ones can,' he said.

The words might have been cynical, or they might have been a joke. Lily watched his face closely, looking for a clue, but she could not decipher his expression. His eyes shone, intense as he spoke again.

'So, tell me…' He lowered his voice a bit. 'What sort of female are you, then?'

No one had ever asked her such a thing. She did

not know how to answer. The question stumped her—and made her unbearably sad. That clarity only extended so far, it would seem.

'Miss?' he prompted.

'I don't know,' she said grimly. 'But I think it is time I found out.'

The shadow had moved back in, Jack could see it lurking behind her eyes. And after he'd worked so hard to dispel it, too.

Work was an apt description. He was not naturally glib like his brother. He had no patience with meaningless societal rituals. A little disturbing, then, that it was no chore to speak with this woman.

She stirred his interest—an unusual occurrence with a lady of breeding. In Jack's experience women came in two varieties: those who simulated emotion for the price of a night, and those who manufactured emotion for a tumultuous lifetime sentence.

Jack did not like emotion. It was the reason he despised the tense and edgy stranger he had lately become. He understood that emotion was an integral part of human life and relationships. He experienced it frequently himself. He held his family in affection. He respected his mentors and colleagues. Attraction, even lust, was a natural phenomenon he allowed himself to explore to the fullest. He just refused to be controlled by such sentiments.

Emotional excess invariably became complicated and messy and as far as he'd been able to determine, the benefits rarely outweighed the consequences. Scholarship, he'd discovered, was safe. Reason and logic were his allies, his companions, his shields. If one must deal with excessive emotions at all, it was best to view them through the lens of learning. It was far more comfortable, after all, to make a study of rage or longing than to experience it oneself. Such things were of interest in Greek tragedy, but dashed inconvenient in real life.

Logic dictated, therefore, that he should have been repelled by this young beauty. She reeked of emotion. She had appeared to be at the mercy of several very strong sensations in succession. Jack should have felt eager to escape her company.

But as had happened all too frequently in the last weeks, his reason deserted him. He was not wild to make his apologies and move on. He wanted to discover how she would look under the onslaught of the next feeling. Would those warm blue eyes ice over in anger? Could he make that gorgeous wide mouth quiver in desire?

'*Mister* Alden.'

His musings died a quick death. That ringing voice was familiar.

'Lady Ashford.' He knew before he even turned around.

'I am unsurprised to find you in the midst of this ruckus, Mr Alden.' The countess skimmed over to them and pinned an eagle eye on the girl. 'But you disappoint me, Miss Beecham.'

The name reverberated inside Jack's head, sending a jolt down his spine. *Beecham*? The girl's name was Beecham? It was a name that had weighed heavily on his mind of late.

They were joined again by the girl's mother and the red-faced Mr Cooperage, but Lady Ashford had not finished with the young lady.

'There are two, perhaps three, men in London who are worth throwing yourself under the wheels of a carriage, Miss Beecham. I regret to inform you that Mr Alden is not one of them.'

No one laughed. Jack was relieved, because he rather thought that the countess meant what she said.

Clearly distressed, the girl had no answer. Jack was certainly not fool enough to respond. Fortunately for them both, someone new pushed her way through the crowd. It was his mother, coming to the rescue.

Lady Dayle burst into their little group like a siege

mortar hitting a French garrison. Passing Jack by, she scattered the others as she rushed to embrace the girl like a long-lost daughter. She clucked, she crooned, she examined her at arm's length and then held her fast to her bosom.

'Jack Alden,' she scolded, 'I could scarcely believe it when I heard that you were the one disrupting the fair and causing such a frenzy of gossip! People are saying you nearly ran this poor girl down in the street!' Her gaze wandered over to the phaeton and fell on Charles. He gave a little wave of his hand, but did not leave the horses.

'Charles! I should have known you would be mixed up in this. Shame on the pair of you!' She stroked the girl's arm. 'Poor lamb! Are you sure you are unhurt?'

Had Jack been a boy, he might have been resentful that his mother's attention was focused elsewhere. He was not. He was a man grown, and therefore only slightly put out that he could not show the girl the same sort of consideration.

Mrs Beecham looked outraged. Miss Beecham merely looked confused. Lady Ashford looked as if she'd had enough.

'Elenor,' the countess said, 'you are causing another scene. I do not want these people to stand and watch you cluck like a hen with one chick. I want them to go inside and spend their money at my fair. Do take your son and have his arm seen to.'

'Oh, Jack,' his mother reproved, her arm still wrapped comfortingly about the girl. 'Have you re-injured your arm?'

Lady Ashford let her gaze slide over the rest of the group. 'Elenor dear, do let go of the girl and take him to find out. Mr Cooperage, you will come with me and greet the women who labour in your interest today. The rest of you may return to what you were doing.'

'Lilith has had a fright, Lady Ashford,' Mrs Beecham said firmly. 'I'll just take her back to our rooms.'

'Nonsense, that will leave the Book Table unattended,' the countess objected.

'Nevertheless…' Mrs Beecham's lips were folded extremely thin.

'I shall see to her,' Lady Dayle declared. 'Jack, can you take us in your… Oh, I see. Whose vehicle are you driving, dear? Never mind, I shall just get a hackney to take us home.'

Mrs Beecham started to protest, and a general babble of conversation broke out. It was put to rout by Lady Ashford. 'Very well,' she declared loudly and everyone else fell silent. 'You can trust Lady Dayle to see to your daughter, Mrs Beecham. I will take you to fetch the girl myself once the day is done.'

She paused to point a finger. 'Mr Wilberforce's barouche is still here. I'm certain he will not mind dropping the pair of them off,' she said, 'especially since he has only just made you a much larger request. I shall arrange it.' She beckoned to the missionary. 'Mr Cooperage, if you would come with me?'

Everyone moved to follow the countess's orders. Not for the first time, Jack thought that had Lady Ashford been a man, the Peninsular War might have been but a minor skirmish.

With a last, quick glance at the girl on his mother's arm, he turned back to his brother and the cursed team of horses.

But Lady Ashford had not done with him. 'Are those Pettigrew's animals, Mr Alden?' she called. She did not wait for an answer. 'Take yourself on home and see to your arm—and do not let Pettigrew lure you into buying those bays. I hear they are vicious.'

'Thank you for the advice, Lady Ashford,' he said, and, oddly, he meant it. Charles stood, a knowing grin spreading rapidly across his face.

'Not a word, Charles,' Jack threatened.

'I wasn't going to say a thing.'

Wincing, Jack climbed up into the rig and took up the ribbons. Charles took his seat beside him and leaned back, silent, but with a smile playing about the corners of his mouth.

'The girl's surname is Beecham.'

Charles sat a little straighter. 'Beecham?' he repeated with studied nonchalance. 'It's a common enough name.'

'It's that shipbuilder's name and you know it, Charles. The man who is supposedly mixed up with Batiste.'

His brother sighed. 'It's not your responsibility to bring that scoundrel of a sea captain to justice, Jack.'

Jack stilled. A wave of frustration and anger swept over him at his brother's words. He fought to recover his equilibrium. This volatility was unacceptable. He must regain control.

'I know that,' he said tightly. 'But I can't focus on anything else. I keep thinking of Batiste skipping away without so much as a slap on the hand.' Charles was the only person to whom Jack had confided the truth about his wound and the misadventures that had led to it. Even then, there were details he'd been honour-bound to hold back. 'It's bad enough that the man is a thief and a slaver as well. But by all accounts the man is mad—I worry that he might come after old Mervyn Latimer again, or even try to avenge himself on Trey and Chione.'

It wasn't Charles's fault that he couldn't understand. Though he knew most of the story, he didn't know about the aftermath. Jack didn't want him—

or anyone else—to know how intensely he'd been affected. Charles must never know about his nightmares. He didn't understand himself how or why all this should have roused his latent resentment towards their cold and distant father, but one thing he did know—he would never burden Charles with the knowledge. His older brother had his own weighty issues to contend with in that direction.

'Would you like me to make some inquiries?' Charles asked.

'Both Treyford and I already have. Batiste has disappeared. He could be anywhere. All the Foreign Office could give me was that name—Matthew Beecham. A young shipbuilder—an Englishman from Dorset who moved to America to pursue his craft. Somehow he became mixed up with Batiste, and found himself in trouble with the American government. He's disappeared as well. The Americans have made a formal complaint against him. They want to question him and have asked that he be detained, should he show up back at home.'

'So? Does the girl hail from Dorset? Did you ask her if she has a relative named Matthew?'

'Not yet.' Jack watched Charles from the corner of his eye. 'I would dearly like to talk to the man. He's the only link I've been able to find. I'm not going to be able to rest until Batiste is caught and made to pay for his crimes.'

Perched ramrod straight now, Charles looked earnest as he spoke. 'You know, Jack, I've never known you to fall so quickly into something so… dangerous, as you did with Treyford.'

Jack bristled slightly.

'Now, forget that it is your older brother speaking and calm yourself,' Charles admonished. 'There must have been a reason for it, something that drew you into the fray.'

There had been, of course, but he was not going to share it with his brother. Once Jack had heard Treyford's story of a band of antiquity thieves menacing Chione Latimer and her family, he'd known he had to help. He and Charles were both all too aware of the difficulties of living with an unsettled sense of menace.

'Whatever the reason, I, for one, am happy to see you out from behind your wall of books.' Charles's gaze slid over Jack's sling. 'I'm sorry that all you appeared to get from your adventure was a bullet hole, but I would neither see you slide back into your old hibernating ways nor allow yourself to become embroiled in something even more complicated and hazardous.'

'What would you have me do, then?' Jack asked

with just a touch of sarcasm. 'Embroidery? Tatting?' He raked his brother with an exasperated glance. 'I've already told you, I have neither the inclination nor the patience for politics.'

Charles rolled his eyes. 'Why don't you just relax, Jack? It's been an age since either Mother or I have been able to drag you out of your rooms. Have a break from your work. Not everyone is fascinated with your mouldy classics.'

'They should be,' Jack said, just to tweak his brother.

Charles ignored him. 'Look about you for once,' he continued. 'Enjoy the Season, squire Mother to a society event or two.' He grimaced. 'Or if the thought of society is too distasteful, you can help Mother and Sophie with their charitable efforts. If you had paid attention, you would see that Mother is slowly becoming more and more involved with the work that the Evangelical branch of the Church is doing. This charity bazaar she is helping with is just a small example of their work. Their presence is only growing stronger as the years pass. Who knows? They might actually succeed in changing the face of society. And you might even find whatever it is you were looking for.'

'The only thing I'm looking for is Batiste.'

Charles sighed. 'Well, look again, little brother.' He

leaned back again, his grip on the side tightening as the bay on the left shied from a calling-card vendor.

Jack was forced to watch the pair closely once more. His mind was awhirl. Perhaps he should consider something different from his usual classical studies—and if his new path also brought him closer to finding information on Batiste, then so much the better. If this Beecham girl and his mother were both involved with the Evangelicals, then perhaps he could look into them as well. Charles could believe what he liked about Jack's need to find something he was missing. He knew the truth of the matter and it involved nothing so mawkish or sentimental.

And neither, he told himself firmly, did it have anything to do with the shine of red-gold hair or the taste of soft, plump lips.

Chapter Three

A stranger inhabited Lily's skin. Or perhaps it had only been so long since determination had pumped so fiercely through her veins, it felt as if it were so. But this was the old Lily—her father's daughter, sure and strong, confident that whatever she wished for lay within her reach. Almost as if it were happening to someone else, she watched herself talk, smile and climb into Mr Wilberforce's barouche. He and Lady Dayle were soon engaged in a spirited debate over reform. Fortunate, since this left Lily free to turn her rediscovered resolve to answering Mr Alden's troubling question: *What sort of female are you?*

She barely knew where to start, but she did discover that some aspects of the new Lily—her mother's daughter—were not so easily discarded. And all of them were firmly fixated on the sudden burst of light that had shone down on Mr Alden for one dazzling moment. Surely it had been nothing more than a stray sunbeam?

Perhaps not. Her nurse's superstitious Cornish wisdom had been a constant in her life and it had taken firm root in Lily's mind while she was still young. In recent years it had flourished into a guilt-ridden tangle.

So often she'd worried that she'd missed some forewarning of her father's tragic death. The storm that ultimately killed him had been immense. Nurse had moaned that his loss had been punishment for their failure to heed several unmistakable portents of doom.

Lily had vowed never to make another such mistake. But surely a bright beam of light was no portent of doom. Then what could it possibly mean?

With every fibre of her being, Lily wanted it to mean the change she longed for. It had touched on Mr Alden. Could it be that he would be an instrument of change? She flushed. Or was it possible that he might be something more?

'Lady Dayle,' she spoke up into a pause in the conversation, 'I fear that your son has re-injured his arm because of my inattention. I wish you would convey my apologies.'

The viscountess patted her arm. 'Do not fret yourself, my dear. Jack should not have been driving those cantankerous animals in the first place. I dare say his brother told him so. But Charles should have remembered that the instant he counselled against it, it would become the single thing in the world that must be done.'

Lily smiled. She'd grown up with her cousin Matthew and he had acted in just the same way. 'How did Mr Alden first injure his arm?'

Lady Dayle frowned. 'Oh, he got caught up in that trouble at the Egyptian Hall, at Mr Belzoni's exhibition. I haven't the faintest idea how or why—I had no inkling that Jack even knew Belzoni or Lord Treyford. It was just a few weeks ago—perhaps you heard of it?'

Lily shook her head.

'Yes, I heard of it,' Mr Wilberforce intervened. 'A ring of international art thieves, or something similar, was it not?'

'Something like,' Lady Dayle agreed. 'Jack will barely speak of it—even to me. And believe me, when her son is shot, a mother wants to know why.'

'Good heavens,' Lily said. She stirred in her seat. 'Shot? Mr Alden must lead quite an exciting life.'

'But that is just it! The entire thing was so patently unlike him. Jack is a scholar, Miss Beecham, and a brilliant one at that. At times he is all but a recluse. He spends more time closeted with his ancient civilisations than with anyone flesh and blood.' She shot Mr

Wilberforce a significant look. 'He is my inscrutable son, sir, and too reserved and detached from society to cause me much concern—especially compared to the rigmarole his brothers subjected me to.'

Mr Wilberforce laughed, but Lily fought back an undeniable surge of disappointment. A scholar? Inscrutable and reserved? It didn't fit the image she'd already built around that wicked smile.

But what did she know of men? An image of her father flashed in her mind. He dwelled heavily in her mind today—a natural reaction on a day when her past and her future appeared destined to collide. On the rare occasion she allowed herself to dream, the portrait she drew of a husband always shared important traits with George Beecham: twinkling eyes, a ready smile and a never-ending thirst for the next new experience. Never would she have conjured up a dry, dusty scholar who hid from life behind his books.

Lily had been hiding for seven long years. She'd done with it. She wasn't her father's little girl any more, but neither would she continue as her mother's quiet handmaiden. She fought back a surge of guilt. She didn't mean to abandon her mother, nor did she wish to give up the good works she had done along with her. She only wanted the chance to live her own life, while she worked to help others better theirs. Superstition would not make that chance happen. Neither, it seemed, would Mr Alden. She clenched her fists. She would find a way, and do it herself.

It was time she melded the two halves of her soul and finally answered that pesky question. It was time she discovered who Lily Beecham was.

Jack kept his senses alert, his eye sharp for movement in the roadway ahead. This was likely not the best time to be skulking about the East End, especially not on his own. But his eagerness for his brother's company had waned after listening to his admonitions and advice this afternoon. Charles would only have tried to talk him out of coming down here at all.

So Jack had dropped off his brother and then returned Pettigrew's nasty bays, and now he found his feet taking him towards the river, towards the reputedly abandoned shipping offices of Gustavo Batiste.

Little Bure Street was not exactly a hotbed of activity in the late evening. A pair of prostitutes propositioned him from a doorway, but he shook his head and continued on. No doubt anyone with legitimate business in these dockside buildings had long since gone home, but the full swing of the illicit enterprises of the night had not yet begun. It didn't matter; the alleyway he sought lay just ahead.

Jack slipped in and stood a moment, allowing his eyes to adjust to the deeper blackness before he moved forwards cautiously. He flexed his sore arm as he went. The narrow space was more a passage than a street, but it opened on to a small walled courtyard at the end. Opposite him a rickety set of wooden stairs led to an office. Across the doorway sagged a crooked sign: *G. Batiste & Co.*

Mervyn Latimer and Treyford had both warned him this would be a waste of time. The offices had been deserted for months. But Jack had a need to see for himself. He eased up the stairs, careful to keep his footsteps quiet.

The door was not locked. Jack pushed it open with his free hand and was forced to stop again and adjust his eyesight. It was pitch black in the small anteroom. It took several long moments for his eyes to adapt, but there was nothing to see once they had. A listing table, a couple of small chairs and dust lying thick on every surface. He shook his head. What had he expected? He was grasping at straws. His obsession with Batiste was not logical, his involuntary association of the villain with his dead father utterly without a rational basis.

From the back of the building came a thump and a muffled curse. Jack froze. His pulse began to race. Slowly he reached down and pulled a knife from his boot. He'd taken to keeping it there, since his mis-adventures with Treyford. It felt awkward and unbal-anced in his left hand, but it was better than nothing.

A closed door lay to the right of the broken table. He eased it open and found another narrow hallway. Several more doors were closed on either side, but the last one on the right stood cracked open, a faint light shining from within.

Who could it be? Silently he made his way there. He flattened himself against the wall and eased his arm from the sling. From inside the room came the sound of rustling papers and opening drawers. Grimacing at the strain, he placed his right hand on the doorway and gripped his knife tight with the other.

Thwang. Jack stared in shock and fascination as a wickedly vibrating blade abruptly sprouted from the opposite doorframe.

'I got another o' those,' a voice rasped from within. 'But this building's cheap and that wall is paper thin. I'm thinkin' it might just be easier to shoot you through it.'

The tension unexpectedly drained out of Jack, replaced by a rising flood of relief. He knew that voice.

'Eli!' he exclaimed. 'It's me, Jack Alden.'

The door flew open. The erstwhile sea captain turned groom stared at him in surprise. 'Jack Alden! What in blazes are ye doing here?'

'I might ask the same of you, old man!' Jack pocketed his own blade and thumped the grizzled old sailor on the shoulder. Eli grunted and crossed back to the desk he'd been rifling through. The rap of his peg-leg on the wooden floor sounded loud in the small office. Jack pulled the blade from the doorframe.

'How's the arm?' Eli asked. 'Ye look a sight better'n the last time I saw ye.'

'It's healing. But why aren't you in Devonshire with Mervyn and Trey and Chione and all the rest of them? They've all got to be busy, what with a wedding to plan and one hell of trip coming up.'

'Aye, 'tis a madhouse at times.' He held out a hand and Jack gave back his knife. With a sigh he slammed a drawer shut and sat in the seat behind the desk. 'Mervyn and Trey sent me up. Something's astir.'

'Batiste?' Jack asked, with a sweep of his hand.

'You know Mervyn's ways. He's got ears everywhere and hears every bird fart and every whisper o' trouble. He's got word that some of Batiste's men are on the move. Here. In England.'

Anger surged in Jack's gut. 'God, it eats at me, knowing he got away,' he said. The low and harsh tone of his voice surprised even him. He struggled again to rein in his emotion. 'I hate the thought of it—him sitting back, silent and scornful, manipulating us like so many puppets.' His eyes narrowed.

'After all he's done to Mervyn, he needs to be brought to justice.'

'What he's done to Mervyn's bad enough. But he's done others far worse. What worrit's me is the idea of him having time to stew. Revenge is his favourite dish and he'll be spittin' mad at how we foiled him.'

'So what do you hope to find here?'

Eli glanced at him. 'The same thing you were, I s'pose. Some hint o' where he might be hiding out. With the Americans after him as well as the Royal Navy, he's got to lie low for a while.'

'The bastard's got a ship and the whole world to hide in.' Jack sighed.

'Trey thinks he won't go too far. He didn't get what he wanted, and he thinks he'll try again. Like any man, he'll have a spot or two he goes to when his back is against the wall. Trouble is findin' it.'

Jack stood a little straighter. 'I might have a lead on that shipbuilder, Beecham. Perhaps he knows where Batiste would go to hide his head.'

'Do what ye can, man.' Eli sighed. 'I know Trey hates to ask ye—especially after ye got hurt the first time. But won't none of us be truly safe until that man is caught and hung.'

'I will. Tell Trey I will handle it.' He stared at the old man with resolution. 'In fact, I think it should be possible for me to begin right now.'

* * *

'Mr Wilberforce asked you to do what?' Lily's dish of tea hovered, halfway up. The evening had grown late. Lady Ashford and her mother had arrived to fetch her, and Lady Dayle had pressed them to stay for a cold supper.

'To make a tour through Surrey and Kent, speaking with local groups of Evangelicals along the way,' her mother repeated.

'Your mother has accomplished wonders in Weymouth, Miss Beecham.' Lady Ashworth accepted a slice of cheese from the platter Lady Dayle offered. 'She can share her methods and be an inspiration to many others.'

'Of course.' Lily's mind raced. This was just exactly what she'd wished for; a chance to travel, to see new places and meet new people. Her breathing quickened and her pulse began to beat a little faster. 'Mother, I'm so proud of you.'

'Congratulations, Mrs Beecham,' said Lady Dayle. 'You shall be one of the leading ladies of a very great movement. And to have the request come from Mr Wilberforce himself is quite an honour, is it not?'

'Thank you, it is indeed an honour.' Her mother looked exhausted. Lily felt a twinge of guilt. She'd spent a perfectly lovely afternoon with the viscountess and her mother had not even had a chance to celebrate her accomplishment.

'Will we be returning home first, Mother? Or shall we leave straight from town?' she asked. 'Either way, we must be sure that you rest beforehand. I can see you are quite worn out.'

An uncomfortable look passed across her mother's face. 'I'll be leaving from London in a few days, dear. Lady Ashford has graciously agreed to accompany me.' She met Lily's eye with resolve. 'You will be returning home.'

'What?' This time she was forced to set her cup down with shaking hands. 'You cannot mean that!'

'We've been away from home too long as it is. Someone needs to oversee the Parish Poor Relief Committee. The planning needs to begin now for the Michaelmas festival. We cannot abandon our duty to those less fortunate.'

'There are plenty of ladies at home willing and able to take care of those things,' Lily argued. 'Mother, please!' Resentment and disbelief churned in her belly. It was true that her mother had found less and less joy in life over the years. Her father's death had been a blow to them both. Grief and guilt were heavy burdens to bear, but Lily had been forced to cope alone. Sometimes she felt she had grieved twice over, for her quiet, reserved mother had sunk into a decline and a militant stranger had climbed out the other side.

Restrictive, distant, hard to please—yes. But Lily had never suspected her mother of deliberate cruelty before today. First Mr Cooperage and now—

She stopped, aghast. 'Does Mr Cooperage factor into this decision, Mother? Because I tell you now that I am not interested in his views on any subject!'

'Lilith!' her mother gasped. 'We will not discuss it further. This is entirely inappropriate!'

'Well then, it appears I have arrived at the perfect time,' an amused masculine voice interrupted.

Lily turned to find Mr Alden framed handsomely in the doorway. An instant flush began to spread up and over her. Was she doomed to always encounter this man at a serious disadvantage?

He advanced into the room and she tried to collect herself. Not an easy task. Poetic—that was the word that had sprung to mind earlier. Brooding was the one that popped up now. Darkly handsome and brooding. Though he had a sardonic smile hovering at the corner of his mouth, the effect was ruined by the rest of him. She just could not be entirely intimidated by anyone in that rumpled state. He looked as if his valet had dressed him in the height of fashion, in only the best silk and superfine, and then laid him down and rolled him repeatedly about on the bed.

She tightened her mouth at the image evoked and her flush grew stronger yet. A great many women, she strongly suspected, would enjoy rolling Mr Alden about on the bed.

'Jack, darling.' Lady Dayle rose to welcome her son. 'Do come in and join us. The ladies have only just finished with the fair and we are taking a cold supper.'

He kissed his mother on the cheek and made an elegant bow to the rest of the ladies. Lily shifted slightly away as he took the chair directly next to hers.

'I should thank you right away, Miss Beecham,' he said with a quirk of a smile in her direction. 'Usually I am the one for ever introducing inappropriate topics to the conversation. My brother informs me that virtually no one else cares for my mouldy ancients.' He leaned back. The seating was so close that Lily could feel the heat emanating from him. 'But you have saved me the trouble.' He raised a brow at her. 'Which distasteful subject have you brought to the table?'

'Never mind that, Jack,' scolded his mother. 'Mrs Beecham has been granted a singular honour. We are celebrating.'

Lady Ashford explained while Lily fumed.

'My heartfelt congratulations,' Mr Alden said to her mother when the countess had finished. He turned again to Lily. 'I'm sure you will enjoy the journey, Miss Beecham. There are some amazingly picturesque vistas in that part of the country.'

'I am not to go, Mr Alden.' Lily could not keep the anger completely from her tone. 'I am instead sent home like a wayward child.'

She noticed that he grew very still. 'Where is home, if I might ask?'

'In Dorset, near Weymouth,' she answered, though she did not see the relevance of the question.

'Ah.' He steepled his fingers and thought a moment. 'I suppose I can understand your mother's point of view.'

Irritation nearly choked Lily. She glared at him.

'You can?' asked her mother in surprise.

'Yes, well, it is only fair to consider both sides of the argument, and you must admit that travelling with an innocent young girl must always be complicated.'

'Innocent young girl?' Lily objected. 'I am nearly three and twenty and I have seen and done many things in the course of my volunteer work.'

'I do not doubt you, but the fact remains that you are a young, unmarried lady. As such you will most likely require frequent stops to rest, and special arrangements for private parlours to shield you from the coarser elements. If you stay at private homes, there will have to be thought given as to whether or not any single gentlemen are in residence. Not to mention that you will have to have a chaperon for every minute of every day. Without a doubt, two older, more mature ladies will travel easier alone.'

Lily gaped at him.

'You can see the logic of the situation.' He nodded towards her.

'There are so many things wrong with that litany of statements that I must give serious consideration on where to begin,' she responded.

'Do tell,' he invited. That lurking grin spread a little wider.

'I could refute your errors one by one, but instead I will merely ask you if you have any sisters, Mr Alden?'

'Nary a one.'

'Then I fail to see where you might have come by any experience travelling with *innocent* young ladies,' she said hotly. 'And if you are in the habit of consorting with other types, then I would only beg you not to equate me with them!'

'Lilith!' Her mother was clearly scandalised.

Lady Dayle, however, laughed. 'Bravo, Miss Beecham! You have routed him in one fell swoop. But now you are both guilty of introducing inappropriate topics to the conversation, so let us talk of something else.' She frowned at her son. 'Do not tease the dear girl, Jack. I believe it is a real disappointment for her.'

Mr Alden nodded at his mother, then spared a glance for Lily. Mortified, she avoided his eye.

Lady Ashford offered him the tray of biscuits. He took one and Lily saw him blink thoughtfully at the countess. '*Will* the two of you exceptional ladies be travelling alone?' he asked in an innocent tone.

'In fact, we will not,' the countess answered. 'Mr Cooperage will accompany us. We thought it possible to also raise money for his mission as we travel.'

'I knew it!' Lily exclaimed. 'Only today he informed me that he did not approve of ladies travelling from home.' She cast a disparaging glance at Mr Alden. 'I just did not expect to find other gentlemen in agreement with such an antiquated notion.'

'I said no such thing,' he protested. 'I said it was complicated, not that it should not be done. Is Mr Cooperage the gentleman from Park Lane, the one who was with you when you had your…near accident?'

'He is.'

'And he is an Evangelical, is he not?'

'He is. Why do you ask?'

Mr Alden drew a deep breath. He sat a little straighter. For the first time Lily noticed true animation in his face and a light begin to shine in his eye.

'I ask because I admit to some curiosity about the

Evangelicals. For instance, I find their attitudes towards women to be conflicting and confusing.'

'How so, Mr Alden?' Lady Ashford bristled a little.

'Hannah More argues that women are cheated out of an education and are thus made unfit to be mothers and moral guides. She advocates educating women, but only to a degree. Evangelicals encourage women to confine themselves to domestic concerns, but when their important issues take the stage—abolition of the slave trade, or changing the East India Company's charter to allow missionaries into India— they urge them to boycott, to petition, to persuade.'

'Women are perfectly able to understand and embrace such issues, Mr Alden.' Now Lily bristled at the thought of this dangerously intelligent and handsome man negating the causes she had worked for.

'I agree, Miss Beecham. In fact, in encouraging such participation, I would say that the Evangelicals have opened the political process to a far wider public.'

Understanding dawned. She cast a bright smile on him. 'Yes, of course you are correct,' Lily said, turning to her mother. 'You see, Mother, I have pe- titioned for change, educated people about the work that needs done and laboured myself for the common good. What is a little trip through Kent when compared to all of that?'

'That was not my point,' Mr Alden interrupted. 'On the contrary, I counsel you ladies to proceed with caution. People are noticing the good that you have accomplished. But if they begin to suspect that Evangelicals encourage women to rise beyond their station—not my words, by the way—then you could have a public uprising on your hands.'

'Like the Blagdon Controversy,' breathed Mrs Beecham, referring to the extensive public outcry against Hannah More's Sunday Schools as dangerous and 'Methodist'.

'It could be far worse,' Mr Alden said. 'Women do not rate any higher on the Church of England's scale than Methodists.'

'Thank you, Mr Alden,' Lady Ashford intoned. 'You have given us a great deal to consider. We shall proceed with care.' She fixed a stern gaze on Lily. 'You can see that it would indeed be best for you to stay home, Miss Beecham. Old warhorses like your mother and I are one thing. We would not wish to be accused of corrupting young ladies.'

Lily lowered her gaze. Hurt and dismay congealed in her throat, choking off any protest. She barely knew Mr Alden; it was ridiculous to feel this bone-deep sense of betrayal. But she could not stem it, any more than she could hold back the rising tide of anger in her breast. She raised her head and met Mr Alden's gaze with a steely one of her own.

'I cannot see where sending Miss Beecham home on the mail coach is any kinder or gentler than carting her around Surrey.' Mr Alden's eyes never left hers as he spoke. 'Clearly, the best thing for her to do is to remain here.'

Lily forgave the irritating man everything on the spot. 'Oh, yes! What a marvellous idea!'

Lily's mother sniffed. 'Well, I cannot see that a residence with a single gentleman in London is any less dangerous than one in Faversham.'

'But the Bartleighs, Mother!' Lily exclaimed.

Lady Ashford sent her an enquiring look and she hastened to explain. 'Very dear friends of ours, from home,' she said. 'They are due to arrive in London soon, for a short stay. Mother, you know they would not mind if I stayed with them.'

'Lilith Beecham,' her mother scolded, 'the Bartleighs are travelling to town to consult with the doctors here, not to chaperon you. I wouldn't ask it of them, even if they were due to arrive before we are gone, which they are not.'

But Lady Dayle was nearly jumping out of her seat. 'Oh, but Lily must stay with me! You need not worry, Mrs Beecham, for Jack has his own bachelor's rooms. I scarcely see him at the best of times, and now he talks of burying himself in his books for his next research project.'

Lily watched her mother and began to hope.

'It will be just Miss Beecham and I,' the viscountess continued. 'How perfect! She can help to introduce me to some of the worthy causes you ladies support, and I can introduce her a little to society.'

Lily's heart sank. That had been the absolute wrong thing to suggest.

'We are honoured by your invitation, my lady, but I do not wish for Lilith to go into society.' Her mother's mouth had pressed so tight that her lips had disappeared.

'Come now, dear Margaret.' The unexpected, coaxing tone came from Lady Ashford. 'It will not do the girl any harm to gain a little polish. She'll likely need it in the future.'

Her mother hesitated. Lily's heart was pounding, but she kept her eyes demurely down. The moment of silence stretched out, until she thought her nerves would shatter.

'I shall ask my dear daughter Corinne to help with the girl,' Lady Ashford said. 'You know that she and her husband are familiar with the right people. Although she is too far along in her confinement to take the girl herself, they will know just the events that a girl like Lilith will do well at.'

'Yes, of course, nothing fast or too *tonnish*,' said Lady Dayle in reassuring tones. 'Perhaps a literary or musical evening.'

Her mother heaved a great sigh. 'Very well,' she said ungraciously.

'Oh,' breathed Lily. 'Thank you, Mother.'

Lady Dayle was positively gleeful. 'Oh, we shall have a grand time getting to know one another, my dear.'

Lady Ashford knew when to call a retreat. She stood. 'Well, it has been a long and tiring day and I must still see to the tally of the day's profits. I'm sure that Mrs Beecham and her daughter will both do better for a good night's rest.' She inclined her head. 'Thank you, Elenor, for the tea and for your interest.'

The farewells were made. Lily returned the viscountess's embrace and agreed to meet to make plans on the morrow. She approached her son with a cautious step and a wary glance. 'Mr Alden, I scarcely know what to say to you.'

She flinched a little at the disapproval she glimpsed in his expression. But then she squared her shoulders. She had faced disapprobation nearly every day for years. Why should his stab any deeper?

'Thank you for everything that you have done for me today,' she said with a smile, 'Even though I'm sure some of it was quite unintentional.'

He bowed. 'I am very happy to have met you, Miss Beecham. It has been an…interesting experience.'

Once again he had donned that impenetrable mask. It saddened her, this barrier that she could not breach. Earlier today he had handled a difficult situation with humour and ease. But now he only looked worldly and cynical. How disappointing. He obviously possessed a great mind. She suspected he also possessed a sense of justice, perhaps even a thoughtful nature, but how could she know for sure?

This was her chance. Lily knew there would still be restrictions, but she could not suppress this glorious feeling of *freedom*. For a few weeks she would be able to relax, to give her true nature free rein. Perhaps if she was very lucky she might even find a position, or, she blushed, a suitor. Anything to supplant her mother's idea for her future.

Lily knew she owed Mr Alden for this chance, and, indeed, she was grateful. But staring into his closed countenance, she knew she had no time to waste on him.

'Goodbye,' she whispered. She turned wistfully away and followed her mother out the door.

Lady Dayle chattered happily for a few minutes after her guests had left. Jack listened to her, content to see her so excited about the coming weeks. When the servants came in to clear, he rose, kissed her goodbye and let the butler show him out. The door clicked closed behind him. Jack stood for a long moment on the step, breathing deep in the cold evening air.

The girl was from Dorset. He was going to do it—he was going to find Matthew Beecham, who would lead him to Batiste. He no longer knew if it was truly justice he sought, or some twisted sort of redemption. He no longer cared. He was going to quiet the roiling furore that had turned his existence upside down.

It would take some delicate manoeuvring, he was sure. He was going to have to proceed very carefully. He was more than a little disturbed by his own actions. Right now he stood, evaluating his options with reason and purpose. That had not been the case in there.

He'd done what he could to manipulate the situation in his favour. And he'd succeeded. But one minute he'd been speaking like a man of sense and the next Lily Beecham had been glaring at him with accusation in her lovely face.

It had done something to him. His brain had shut down with a nearly audible *click*. He had spoken up to fix the situation with her goal in mind as much as his, and with an overwhelming desire to remove the wealth of hurt in her eyes.

It was a very dangerous precedent. It had been an unthinking response, an action dictated by *emotion*. Clearly this was a very dangerous girl.

Yet having recognised his weakness, he was armed against it. He would proceed, as he always did, with logic and reason as his weapons. And a healthy dose of caution as his shield.

Chapter Four

Lily closed her eyes and let her heart soar with the music. Happiness filled her and she didn't even try to stem it—the ascending harmonies matched her mood so perfectly.

The last several days spent with Lady Dayle had been full—and incredibly fulfilling. The pair of them had shopped a little, and explored much of what the city had to offer. Lily had lost herself in fine art and turned her skin brown picnicking in the parks. They had encountered Miss Dawson again and Lily had struck up a fast friendship with the young lady, and she'd coaxed her into showing her all the fashionable—and safe—areas of the city.

Lily had laughed at the raucous prints lining the shop windows and lusted after the huge selections in the bookstores. Best of all, she had spent endless hours talking and talking with the viscountess.

Seven years of questions, comments and contemplations had bubbled up and out of her and Lady Dayle had matched her word for word. And though she did not share in it completely, the viscountess had not once chastised her for her boundless energy or curiosity.

Lily had not forgotten her end of the bargain either. She'd taken Lady Dayle along to several meetings of charitable societies and introduced her to the hardworking, generous people who ran them. The viscountess appeared happy to be wading into these new waters, getting her feet wet and judging which of the endless charitable opportunities interested her most.

Tonight, though, came Lily's first society outing. Lady Dayle had indeed chosen a musical evening. All about her sat people who took pleasure in each other and in the beauty of the music, and finally Lily felt the last of her restraints fall away. Her spirits flew free to follow the intricate melodies of the string quartet. Even the gradual darkening of the piece could not shake her enjoyment. The beauty of the mournful finish echoed within her and when the last haunting chord faded away she sat silent a moment, relishing it, and ignoring the silent stream of tears down her face.

'Oh, my dear,' Lady Dayle said kindly. She pressed Lily's hand and passed her a linen handkerchief.

Lily smiled her thanks and dried her eyes. She was attracting attention. Two ladies behind the viscountess smiled indulgently at her, but further away she could see others watching with their heads together or talking behind their hands. She raised her chin. 'That was absolutely beautiful, was it not, my lady?'

'Indeed it was,' agreed Lady Dayle. She got to her feet as the rest of the guests rose.

'I'd forgotten that music could touch you so deeply.' Lily sighed, following. 'Will they be doing another piece?'

'Before the evening is over they will. There is an intermission now, with food and the chance to mingle with the others.' Lady Dayle flashed a smile over her shoulder. 'Mrs Montague has asked that her guests also take part in the entertainment. Should you like to play? You mentioned the pianoforte, I believe.'

'Oh, no.' Lily laughed. 'It has been so long since I played anything other than hymns, and I doubt the company would be interested.'

'I think it would be very well received. This is the most fascinatingly diverse mix of people I've seen in a long time.' She gestured to a corner where a footman with a platter of hot oyster loaves stood surrounded by eager guests. 'Where else have you ever seen a bishop laughing genially with a patroness of Almack's and a banking magnate? Mrs Montague's acquaintances appear to come from nearly every walk of life.'

'I think it must be the extensive work she does for the Foundling Hospital,' Lily mused. 'It is easier to approach people when you do so for a good cause, and you quickly learn who is like-minded and who is not.' She took a glass of wine from a passing footman, and then stared at Lady Dayle. An odd smile had blossomed suddenly on the viscountess's face.

'There now, Lily, you must help me test my theory. Look over my shoulder towards the door and tell me if my son Jack has not just arrived?'

Lily started. A large part of her hoped that the viscountess would be proven wrong. She had not seen Jack Alden since the day of their first dramatic encounter. It was true that she had felt happier in the intervening days than in years, but too many times she had caught herself grinning at nothing, brought to a halt by a vivid recollection of that secret smile on his handsome face.

It still piqued her that this man—the first to awaken in her such an instant, physical response—should not also be the sort of man she could be comfortable with. She battled a sense of loss too, and a relentless curiosity. Why should Jack Alden—

who appeared to have every advantage—have grown so closed? What could have happened, to cause him to retreat so far into himself?

She would likely never know. But even though she knew that such a man was not for her, still she was plagued with sudden memories of the intensity of his hazel gaze, the heat of his touch upon her arm, the low rasp of his voice as he leaned close…

Stop, she ordered herself.

She took an unobtrusive step to the side and let her gaze drift towards the door. 'Yes,' she said. 'It is Mr Alden.' Her pulse tripped, stumbled and then resumed at a ridiculously frantic rate.

He stood framed in the doorway, casually elegant and annoyingly handsome. Though he focused on greeting their hostess, even from here she could see the cool remoteness in his gaze. He was the only man of her acquaintance who could manage to look both intense and aloof in the same moment. It irritated her beyond reason.

She stepped back, placing his mother between them so he was no longer in her line of vision. She cast a curious look at Lady Dayle. 'You are facing away from the door. How ever did you know that he had arrived?'

Lady Dayle laughed. 'A tell-tale gust of wind.' She nodded to the guests grouped behind Lily. 'Jack walks in and we are treated to a phalanx of fluttering fans, flittering eyelashes and swishing skirts. It is a sure sign when I feel a breeze tugging on my coiffure.'

'Is Mr Alden considered such a good match, then?' Lily asked. She grinned. 'I don't mean to offend; it is just that Lady Ashford indicated otherwise—and in quite certain terms.'

'Warned you off, did she? It's to be expected. She had hopes once, you see… Well, never mind, that's all ancient history.' She leaned closer. 'Jack is not approaching, is he?'

Lily carefully glanced over her shoulder. 'No. He's just moved past Mrs Montague. He doesn't look at all happy to be here, I must say.'

He looked across and met her gaze right at that moment. Her composure abruptly deserted her. Face flaming, she nearly took a step backwards just from physical shock. Reminding herself to breathe, she wrenched her gaze from his, concentrating on his mother once more.

'Good. Look at them.' Lady Dayle indicated the gaggle of girls who were focused subtly, and in some cases downright overtly, on her son. 'It's because he's so elusive, I suppose.' She sighed. 'It's a rare enough occasion that his brother or I can convince him to attend an event such as this. And with his name being bandied about lately after that contretemps at the Egyptian Hall, he seems to have become even more interesting.'

Lily stared thoughtfully at the hopeful girls. 'I assume Mr Alden enjoys the attention,' she mused.

'I wish he did,' Lady Dayle said flatly. 'Truthfully, I don't think he has the faintest notion of their interest. A fact that I believe sometimes spurs the young ladies on.' She sighed. 'He presents something of a challenge.'

Lily glanced carefully back in Mr Alden's direction. She might feel a bit of sympathy for him, if she could believe him to be as unmindful of them all as his mother thought. But her own experience had shown him to be intelligent and a keen observer.

She shook her head. She did not believe it. Mr Alden simply could not be oblivious to the fervent interest directed his way. Not even he could be so selfishly unaware.

Only consider their last encounter. Her desire to accompany her mother and Lady Ashford on their trip had been obvious, yet he had not hesitated to thwart her. The thought that he might toy with these girls in a similar fashion only fuelled her aggravation with him.

Lady Dayle had turned to glance behind her. 'Ah,' she said. 'Here he comes now.'

'Good evening, Mother. Miss Beecham.' Mr

Alden bowed low. Her heart thundering in her ears, Lily made her curtsy and tried not to notice the way the candlelight glinted off his thick dark hair.

'I do not have to ask if you ladies are enjoying yourselves,' he continued. 'Our hostess has already informed me and anyone else who would listen that Miss Beecham found herself transported by the music tonight. She is touting it as a sure sign of the success of the evening.'

Lily raised her eyebrows. 'Mrs Montague has no need of my approval, but I should be happy to provide it. The music tonight has been stunningly beautiful—I am sure I am not the only one to be so moved.'

'You were the only one moved to tears, it would seem.' He spoke politely, but Lily thought she caught the hint of disapproval in Mr Alden's tone. He looked to the viscountess. 'I hope that you warned her, Mother—'

'Warned me?' Lily interrupted.

He glanced about as if to be sure no one listened. 'I understand that you have been little in society, Miss Beecham—'

He got no further before Lily interrupted him. 'Pray do not concern yourself, Mr Alden.' She tossed her head. 'I believe we established your inexperience with women of my stamp during our last conversation.'

His mouth quirked. 'Your stamp, Miss Beecham?'

She glared at him over her drink. 'Yes, sir. My stamp. My education has not been limited to embroidering samplers and learning a smattering of French. Besides charitable work, my mother and I have duties to the lands my father left and the families upon it.'

'Very commendable, I am sure—' he began.

'Thank you,' she interrupted. 'Though you may smirk, you would be shocked at the lists of tasks that must be seen to on a daily basis, all while attempting to persuade the land steward that there is no shame in consulting a woman on crop rotation and field drainage. In the same vein, I have occasionally had to cajole proud but hungry tenants into taking a loan so that they may feed their families. I've been called to coax the sick into taking their medicine, persuade duelling matrons into working together on a charity drive and I have even spoken publicly against the evils of slavery. I think you can trust me to keep my foot out of my mouth at a musical evening.'

Mr Alden did not appear to be impressed. 'All quite admirable, Miss Beecham, but you've never before encountered London society, and that is a different animal altogether.'

'People are people, Mr Alden.'

'Unfortunately not. In society you will encounter

mind-numbingly bored people—arguably the most dangerous sort. You must understand, they are looking for something, anything, to divert them. I would not wish to see you targeted as a new plaything. Ridiculing a new arrival, painting her as a hopeless rustic, ruining her chances of acceptance— for many this is naught but an amusing pastime.'

Lily stared. Fate, chance and the heavens had finally conspired to set her free—at least for a few fleeting weeks—and he thought to tell her how to go on? It was the last straw. Jack Alden needed to be taught a lesson, and without a doubt Lily had enough of her old spirit left to be the one to give it to him.

She straightened her shoulders. When she had been young and in the grip of this determined mood, her mother had told her that she was worse than a wilful nag. Well, she had the bit in her teeth now. Jack Alden was a fraud. He showed the world a mask, exhibiting nothing but dispassion and uninterest, but worse lay underneath. He was as quick to condemn as the most judgemental of society's scandalmongers. Well, Lily would give him a taste of his own, and she highly doubted he would enjoy the flavour of either uninterest or censure.

'Jack, dear,' the viscountess spoke before Lily could. 'Do you really think I would allow Lily to do herself harm?' She cocked her head at her son. 'And in any case, I do not think you are in a position to speak to anyone about calm and rational conduct, not when you consider your own erratic temper over the last few weeks.'

He had the grace to redden a bit, but he ignored the jab at his own behaviour. 'Well, there is that old Eastern philosophy—the one in which a person who saves a life becomes responsible for it thereafter.'

'Let us not forget that you were driving the vehicle that threatened me,' Lily said. 'In fact, you saved me from yourself.' She raised a challenging eyebrow. 'What does your philosophy say about that?'

'Oh, dear,' Lady Dayle intervened. 'If you two are going to squabble like cats, then I am off to speak with Lord Dearham. He is a great lover of music…' she cast her son a speaking look '…unlike others I could name.' Patting Lily affectionately, she said, 'I shall meet you back at our seats when the music begins again, shall I?'

Lily watched her go before turning back to her victim. 'If you do not enjoy music, Mr Alden, then I confess I am curious to hear why you would attend a musical evening.'

He rolled his eyes. 'In fact, I do like music. But my mother will not forgive me for eschewing the operas that she so admires. I find that sort of entertainment too…tempestuous.'

'I see,' Lily said reflectively. 'Not having experienced the opera myself, I must reserve judgement. Still, one wonders if something other than the music drew your interest here tonight.'

He stiffened, obviously a little puzzled by her hostility. 'You are very perceptive, Miss Beecham.' He glanced after Lady Dayle. 'I find that I'm quite interested in the Evangelicals. I would like to know more about them.'

Lily lifted her chin. 'We are not specimens to be examined, Mr Alden.'

'Nor do I think so,' he replied easily. 'My brother mentioned their works and their intriguing notions on how to reform society.' He shrugged. 'I am here to learn.'

'You chose well, then. There are several influential Evangelicals here tonight.' She nodded across the room. 'Mr Macaulay, in fact, would be an ideal person for you to speak with. I dare say he can tell you everything you need to know.' She smiled ingratiatingly. 'He looks to be free right now.'

'Yes, he does indeed.' He smiled and she received the distinct impression that he was trying to win her over. 'But I came over here seeking a restful companion.' His gaze wandered briefly over her. As if he had physically touched her, Lily felt her skin twitch and tingle in its wake. She had to fight to keep him from seeing how he affected her. 'May I say,' he continued with an incline of his head, 'that I could not have found a lovelier one.'

'Thank you.' She kept her tone absent, as if his compliment had not set off a warm glow in her chest. 'I should think that this line of inquiry is very different from your usual research. Your mother tells me that you are a notable scholar.'

He nodded.

'You mentioned the ancients at our late supper a few days ago. Is that your area of specialty?'

'Yes, ancient civilisations.'

She eyed him shrewdly. 'I imagine you find it much easier to shut yourself up and study people of long ago than to deal with them in person. Real people can be so…tempestuous.'

That sardonic smile appeared. Lily's heart jumped at the sight of it. 'I do get out and amongst people on occasion, Miss Beecham. Thank goodness for it, too; I would not have missed making your acquaintance for the world.'

She ignored the good humour in his voice and let her gaze drop to his injured arm. 'Yes, but I do hope you did not strain your arm in doing so.'

'No, it is fine, thank you. I should be able to remove the sling in a week or two.'

'When your mother told me of your profession, I

asked her if you had sustained your injury in a fall from a library stepstool.'

Mr Alden choked on a sip of his wine. Lily saw his jaw tighten and when he spoke, his light tone had been replaced with something altogether darker.

'No. Actually I was shot—while helping to prevent a group of thieves from making off with some valuable antiquities.'

'So Lady Dayle tells me! I was quite amazed, and a little thrilled, actually.' She smiled brightly at his reddening countenance. 'You give me hope, you see.'

'Hope?' he asked, and his voice sounded only slightly strangled.

'Indeed. For if a quiet scholar like you can find himself embroiled in such an adventure, then perhaps there is hope for a simple girl like me as well.'

It was a struggle, she could tell, but still he retained his expression of bland interest. Curse him.

'Do you crave adventure, Miss Beecham?' he asked.

'Not adventure, precisely.'

'Travel, perhaps? A flock of admirers?' He was regaining his equilibrium, fast. 'Or perhaps you simply wish for dessert?' He flagged down a passing footman with a tray of pastries.

Lily had to suppress a smile. This oh-so-polite battle of wit and words was by far the most fun she had had in ages. She eyed the footman and decided to take the battle to the next level. She selected a particularly rich-looking fruit-filled tart. 'Travel,' she mused. 'That would be delightful. But since I have it on good authority that I am of no age or situation conducive to easy arrangements, I suppose I must wait until I am older.' She raised her tart in salute. 'And stouter.'

Her eyes locked with his while she took a large bite, only to gradually close in ecstasy. She chewed, sighed and savoured. 'Oh, I must tell your mother to try one—the burnt-orange cream topping is divine!' Breathing deep, she held her breath for several long seconds before slowly exhaling. She opened languid eyes, taking care to keep them half-hooded as she glanced again at Mr Alden.

And promptly forgot to take a second bite. That had done it. At last she had cracked his polite façade. He stared, the green of his eyes nearly obliterated by pupils dilated with hunger. It wasn't the tart that he hungered for, either. His gaze was fixed very definitely on the modest neckline of her gown.

'So if travel must be a delayed gratification...' he said hoarsely, then paused to clear his throat '...what will you substitute, Miss Beecham?'

'This,' replied Lily instantly, waving her free hand. 'Delightful company with warm and open-minded people. The chance to exchange ideas, enjoy music and good conversation.'

'I hear that Mrs Montague has opened her gallery to her visitors tonight,' he returned. 'She has several noteworthy pieces. Perhaps you will enjoy some good conversation with me while we explore it?'

Lily smiled at him. She popped the last bit of tart into her mouth and dusted the crumbs from her gloves. 'Thank you, Mr Alden…' she shook her head as he offered her his arm '…but I must decline. I see an acquaintance from the Foreign Bible Society and I simply must go and congratulate her on her gown.' She dipped a curtsy and, fighting to keep a triumphant smile from her face, turned and set off.

Flummoxed, Jack watched Lily Beecham walk away. This was not at all going the way he had planned. He'd mapped his strategy so carefully, too, and the troublesome chit had derailed him completely.

Aberrant—that's what she was. If it wasn't against all the laws of nature for one female to inspire so many conflicting reactions in a man, then it should be. She acted in a manner completely unpredictable. Her sharp wit and quirky humour kept him perpetually unbalanced—just as he desperately sought an even keel.

His nightmares had grown worse over the last few

days. He couldn't sleep and had no wish to eat. Worse—he couldn't concentrate on his work. The ability to form a coherent written thought appeared to have deserted him.

Things had grown so bad that scenes from his youth—memories of his father's disdain for his third son—had begun to haunt him even while he was awake. But Jack had not allowed his father's casual cruelty to touch him while he'd been alive, and he would be damned before he let the old codger torment him from the grave.

He'd focused all of his energies instead on the thought of capturing Batiste. One advantage Lord Dayle's 'damned bookish' son possessed was a wide correspondence. Jack had contacts all over the world and, though it had been a painfully slow process, he had been for several weeks laboriously writing and put them all on notice. If Batiste put in to port near any of them, Jack would hear of it.

His next step was to track down Matthew Beecham. The shipbuilder had had extensive dealings with Batiste, and he might just be able to lead him straight to him. But first Jack had to get through Lily Beecham.

He circulated amongst Mrs Montague's guests and tried not to be obvious in his observation of the girl. He'd taken note of her altered appearance straight away. She had a number of new freckles sprinkled across her nose, if he was not mistaken, and her red-gold mane had been tamed into a sleek and shining coiffure.

He thought he detected his mother's hand in the new style of gown she wore. She still dressed conservatively, but the gown of deep blue poplin represented a vast difference from the shapeless sack she'd worn when they met. The white collar, though high, served to draw the eye unerringly to her substantially fine bosom, and the soft and sturdy fabric snuggled tight both there and down the long, shapely length of her arms.

She looked quiet, constrained, the veritable picture of restraint—until she spoke. Then a man found himself either cut by the razor edge of her tongue or riveted by her marvellously expressive face. Nor was he the only one affected. She made the rounds of the room, talking easily with everyone she encountered, and laughing with uninhibited abandon. Clearly she had a gift. Every person she spoke with ended up smiling right along with her. The ladies gazed fondly after her and the gentlemen stared, agape and entranced.

Jack hovered across the room, in complete sympathy with the lot of them. Like a naturalist who had discovered a new species, he could not look away. The girl appeared perfectly comfortable conversing with strangers and seemed to be on the best of terms with Minerva Dawson, too. He'd heard some nonsense about those two being distantly related. They flitted about the room like a couple of smiling butterflies, one darkly handsome, the other shining like a crimson flame. Jack saw Miss Dawson's mother gazing fondly on the pair, but her companion—her sister, he thought— observed them with a frown. Well. Perhaps not everyone in the family was enamoured of their new connection.

Jack, watching closely as well, failed to see why. To his relief and chagrin, Miss Beecham never made a mis-step—until an elderly couple, arriving late, paused on the threshold of the room.

Obviously, she knew them. Mrs Montague had begun to herd her guests back to their seats in preparation for the music to begin again, but Miss Beecham struggled against the flow of people to fight her way to the newcomers. Her eyes shone and her sparkling smile grew wider still as she embraced them both with enthusiasm.

It looked to be a happy reunion. Jack watched surreptitiously as they talked. A few of the other guests had glanced over at the chattering threesome, but he thought he was the only one still paying attention when the older lady sobered, laid a gentle hand on Lily's arm and said something in a soft voice.

Jack stood too far away to hear the words she spoke, but he could see that they were not welcome to Miss Beecham. She paled, instantly and noticeably. All of the joy faded from her face and her hand trembled as she grasped the other woman's.

Mrs Montague chose that moment to notice her new arrivals. The little tableau broke apart as she greeted the couple heartily and began to pull them forwards towards the seating. Miss Beecham did not follow. Blank disbelief coloured her expression as she stared after the couple. She flashed a glance his way and Jack averted his eyes, pretending to be scanning for a seat. He looked back just in time to see her slipping away into the hall.

Jack's heart began to pound. She was clearly distressed and probably sought a quiet moment to herself, but this was it—his chance to get her alone and talking about her family. He had to take it. He edged towards the door and followed.

The tinkling and tootling of tuning instruments followed him into the hall. The few people left out there began to move past him, into the music room. Jack could see no sign of the girl. He glanced up the stairs. Several women still moved up and down, seeking or leaving the ladies' retiring room. No, not there. Instinct pointed him instead down the dimly lit hallway leading towards the back of the house.

He found her in the bookroom. Only a small pair of lamps fought the dark shadows here. Her head bowed, she stood, poised in graceful profile at the window. One hand stretched, holding the heavy curtain aside, but she did not look out. Jack's breathing quickened. Flickering light, reflected from the torches set up outside, danced like living flames in her hair. He stopped just inside the door. 'Miss Beecham? Are you all right?'

For a long, silent moment, she did not respond. Then she simply drew a breath and looked back at him, over her shoulder.

Jack, about to step closer, froze. There it was again, in her eyes. Pain, sorrow, loss. It had been the first expression he had seen on her face and it had struck him hard then. Now, when he could so closely contrast it with the joy and animation that had shone from her all evening, it hit him a staggering blow.

'Good God,' he said involuntarily. 'What's happened?'

She dropped the curtain. 'I…that is… Nothing, thank you. I am fine.'

The urge to know, the compulsion to help her, fluttered in his breast. He realised that it happened every time he was with her. She forged in him a disturbing and unfamiliar yearning for a connection. He had to ignore it, to find a way to remember his purpose. To regain control.

'Come, Miss Beecham, I'm not a fool. I can see that something has upset you.'

A china shepherdess graced the table next to the window. She avoided his gaze and touched the delicate thing with the lightest touch of her fingertips. Jack watched them glide over the smooth surface and swallowed.

'It's just…some disturbing news from a friend, I'm afraid,' she said, still not looking at him.

'I'm sorry to hear it.'

Now she looked up. She set the figurine aside. Her chin rose and the icy coldness of her glare held him fast. 'I should think you'd be happy to find that I am following your advice.'

'Advice?' Once again she had him at a loss. Ancient Sumerian was easier to translate than this girl's fits and starts.

'Yes. You see—here I am, hiding away, keeping my unsuitable emotions private.'

Stunned, Jack stared at her. Was this the reason for her hostility? Had *he* hurt her? He considered stepping closer, taking her hand, but he felt inept, clumsy. 'I do apologise. If you thought I meant to criticise… I hope you will understand, I only meant to help you.'

She crossed her arms defensively in front of her. 'Help me what?'

He took a moment to answer. 'Protect yourself, I suppose.'

Her arms dropped. Her eyes grew huge and some emotion that looked dangerously like pity crossed her face. 'Protect myself from what, Mr Alden?' She gestured towards the door. 'In there is a roomful of people come to pass a pleasant evening and enjoy some good music. It is not a den of monsters.'

She was so young. So naïve. Jack wanted to wrap her in swaddling and spirit her away, to somehow keep her safe in this pristine, happy state.

He took a step back. He was doing it again. *She* was doing it again. This was not why he had come here. He sketched a quick bow. 'I'm sorry. I did not mean to insult you.'

She inclined her head a little. He took what he could get and forged ahead. 'Your mother, she is well? I hope that was not the nature of your news?'

'Oh. No. Mother is fine. I had a letter from her yesterday. She and Lady Ashford appear to be enjoying themselves. They have met many new people and even approve of a few of them.'

'And the rest of your family?' he persisted. 'I hope they are well, also?'

'Thank you, but I have no other family. Mother and I have been alone since my father died.'

Jack's fist clenched. His breath caught. It could not be. Please. He did not want to have been wrong about her connection to Matthew Beecham. 'Just the two of you alone in the world?' he asked past the constriction in his throat. 'That is sad enough, in and of itself.'

'Just the two of us,' she said. 'Unless you count my cousin Matthew—but he lives in America now.'

Jack almost slumped in relief. Almost. He grinned at her. 'An American cousin? My brother's wife boasts such a connection. I hope yours is not so, ah, vibrant a character as hers.'

He'd actually drawn an answering smile. 'Oh, Matthew is a character, without a doubt.' She laughed. 'You would never believe me if I shared half the antics we used to get up to.'

'Are you close, then?' He held his breath.

She sighed. 'We were. Matthew lived with us for several years after his parents died. I was just a girl and I thought the sun rose and set with him.'

'I hope he returned the sentiment.'

'He did, or close enough to please me.' She smiled. 'He taught me the most unsuitable things! And I loved him for it.'

'Hmm, now he sounds like my brother Charles.'

'Oh, I've already heard a few of the tales about Charles.' She laughed. 'I don't think we could have kept up with him, even on our best days.'

'Nor could I.'

She glanced sharply at him and Jack wondered if he'd revealed too much.

'Matthew was special to me. Other than my father, I would say that he may be the only person in the world who has ever truly known me.'

Jack fought a twinge of conscience. He was too close to back down now. 'Was special? Do you not keep in touch any longer?'

'We exchange the occasional letter.' She grinned sheepishly. 'I confess, although I have altogether less to write about, I am far more likely to write him than vice versa. And though his correspondence has always been irregular and infrequent, it is always a delight when it comes.' She grinned again. 'American life has some rather droll differences from ours, based on his descriptions.' Jack watched, hopeful and more than a little enchanted, as a tiny frown of concentration creased her brow. 'But it has been months and months since last I heard from him. I don't think I realised until now just how long it has been.'

'And how does he find America, besides droll? Does he not miss his home?'

'Not at all, as far as I can tell. He's quite happy there. He's a shipbuilder and doing tolerably well.' She cocked her head. 'Perhaps his business has increased and that is what keeps him from writing.'

Disappointment and hope warred in Jack's chest. For a moment he considered telling her the truth, but cast the thought quickly aside. She obviously knew nothing of the trouble her cousin had tangled himself in. Matthew Beecham might just contact his cousin and ask for help. It would behoove Jack to stay close as well.

It was a sobering thought. She was damned perplexing. He didn't know if he could win her confidence, and, more importantly, he didn't know if he could keep a rein on his own unfortunate reactions to her.

He'd been quiet too long. She watched him, curiosity etched in her clear, fresh face. 'Well,' she said, 'thank you for distracting me from my sombre thoughts. I had best return to the music room.' She glanced at him again and made to move away.

'Wait,' he asked. His conscience still pricked him. He could not forget the earlier hurt in her voice.

She paused.

'About what I said earlier,' he began, stumbling a little over the words. 'I have no authority to dictate to you, or even advise you. Truly, I meant my words, as I said, as a warning. A friendly warning.' She'd stopped on her way out and stood very close now. The darkened room contracted around them. 'Perhaps you do not know, but my own family has shown a disregard for society's expectations in the past—and been persecuted for it. I just wish to spare you that sort of pain.'

Her face softened. Jack's gaze locked with hers. Her colour heightened and he noticed that those adorable freckles disappeared when she flushed. 'I begin to understand,' she said softly. Jack had the impression that she spoke as much to herself as to him. 'Perhaps you will scoff—' she spoke in nearly a whisper '—but we are very alike.'

A frown furrowed her lovely brow, and she caught that enticingly plump bottom lip with her teeth. Jack could not look away. Somehow the chit had turned the tables and was now worried for *him*. It was an intoxicating thought. Yet he was here with a purpose. He drew a deep breath and tried to clear his mind of anything else.

Her hand rose between them. Jack's pulse began to race. Small and uncertain, that hovering hand drove all thought of his objective from his head. For a moment, he felt sure she meant to draw it back. His gut twisted inside out as part of him longed to jerk away—and the other waited in breathless anticipation for her to touch him.

She did touch him. He saw the resolution in her eyes as she extended her arm and then he felt the butterfly touch of her fingers tracing a path along his jaw. His eyes closed. Her warm little hand slid over his shoulder and came to rest on his chest.

'When my father died, I thought just as you do,' she whispered. 'It is a very hard thing, to feel alone in a room full of people.'

But Jack's eyes were open again, and her words did not register. He could not think past the mix of empathy and desire swimming in the cool blue of her gaze, could not focus on anything but the movement of that tempting lower lip. Logic, his close companion all these years, screamed at him to stop, shouted a warning that, for the first time ever, he ignored. Her mouth beckoned. He had to taste it, mark it as his.

His gaze fixed, he mimicked her earlier movement, raising his hand and brushing the silky skin of her jaw. She gasped. He did not let it deter him. He ran his fingers into the smooth knot of hair at her nape and cupped her jaw. He leaned in, intent on his purpose—

'Miss Beecham?'

She jerked back, her eyes wide. Jack blinked. Then he cursed. Ever so slowly, awareness began to return. She stepped quickly towards the door, but the alarm in his head did not fade.

'Miss Beecham, there you are!'

It was one of the young pups who had drooled over her in the music room. He gave an extravagant bow and offered her his arm and a friendly grin. 'Miss Beecham, I've been sent to fetch you. Our hostess hopes you will entertain us all with a song on the pianoforte.'

She glanced uncertainly over her shoulder. The boy's gaze followed. His engaging smile faded.

Jack managed a grim nod. 'There, Miss Beecham,' he said, keeping his tone brisk. 'Perhaps this young man will take you back to my mother while I find the footman seeking me? Thank you for informing me of the message awaiting me.'

The boy's grin returned at the welcome request. 'I would be happy to escort you, Miss Beecham. Mr Bartleigh is but newly arrived, but he tells us you have more than a passing knowledge of many of the older broadsheet ballads. He's hoping you'll share your rendition of "Ballynamony".'

She hesitated. 'Perhaps I should not.' She glanced at Jack again, and this time there was a challenge glittering in her eyes. 'So many of the ballads are sentimental. I should not wish to expose myself to ridicule.'

'Never say such a thing! A lovely young lady such as yourself, in genial company such as this?

Impossible,' he scoffed. 'And should anyone dare to suggest otherwise, I will deal with them myself.'

Jack's jaw clenched. Miss Beecham smiled up at her young admirer.

He had to escape. Logic whispered fervently in his ear again and this time he paid heed. Logic stood correct and unassailable as always. He should feel grateful for the boy's interruption, not ready and willing to strangle both him and the baiting chit.

'Miss Beecham—' he could not look directly at her '—thank you for your kindness in coming for me. Please convey my farewells to my mother?'

'Of course. Goodnight, Mr Alden.'

He ignored the thread of steel in her voice and brushed past them into the hall. He did indeed go searching for a footman and sent the man off after his coat and hat.

He should be thrilled. He'd accomplished the first step and verified Miss Beecham's connection to his target. Now he only had to wait for him to communicate with her, or he might even prod her into discovering her cousin's whereabouts. She might even know more, such as where the shipbuilder might have gone when he disappeared.

He was not thrilled. The vague restlessness that had been plaguing him roiled in his gut, transformed into something altogether uglier. He'd had a narrow escape tonight, on several levels. This could not continue. He must control himself around the girl, no matter what tender emotions lived in her blue eyes and in spite of that damned tempting mouth of hers.

Control. Restraint. They were his allies, his support, as necessary to his existence as air. He breathed deep. He could do this. Hell, he'd already spent a lifetime doing this.

The footman brought his things. As he shrugged into his coat, the first few strains of a sprightly song began in the music room. Miss Beecham's bright, lilting voice wafted out and over him.

Wherever I'm going, and all the day long,
At home and abroad, or alone in a Throng,
I find that my Passion's so lively and strong,
That your Name when I'm silent still runs in my
Song.

Jack placed his hat firmly on his head and walked out.

Chapter Five

Lady Dayle's morning room shone bright and airy, as warm and welcoming as the viscountess herself. Unfortunately, Lily's mood did not reflect the serenity of her surroundings. She sat at the dainty writing desk, trying to compose a letter to her land steward.

Last night's conversation had triggered the idea. She'd spoken of her cousin Matthew to Mr Alden and she'd woken this morning with a sudden longing for one of his breezy, affectionate letters. She'd realised that it had been quite some time since she'd last heard from him and resolved to ask Mr Albright to forward any personal mail on to London. Perhaps a lighthearted, teasing missive from America awaited her even now.

She hoped it was so. She could use a bolster to her confidence. She'd thought she'd come to London to find culture and learning and to broaden her experience. She'd begun to realise, however, that what she was truly looking for was acceptance, the casual sort of recognition and approval that most people experienced on a daily basis. She had found it, too, and from some truly amazing and worthy people.

But she had not found it in Jack Alden. She had seen flashes of approval from him, to be sure, and flares of something altogether darker, more dangerous and intriguing. But there had also been wariness and reserve and something that might be suspicion. And it was driving her mad.

The why of it eluded her. Perhaps because she had spoken truly last night—they were alike in some deeply elemental way. They both stood slightly apart from the rest of the world. The difference between them was that he seemed perfectly content with his situation. But her reaction made not a whit of sense. She both wished to achieve such serenity and, for some reason, wished whole-heartedly to shake him from his.

She sighed. She very much feared that it was for an altogether more common reason that she found herself fixating on him. He had been on the verge of kissing her last night. She'd guessed his intent and her heart had soared, her pulse had ratcheted and she had waited, breathless, for the touch of his mouth on hers. When they had been interrupted she had been frightened, and wildly disappointed.

Later, though, in the privacy of her own room, she had been appalled at her own behaviour and angry at his. Was he so far removed from the world that kissing a young woman in a public venue meant nothing? But, no, then she had remembered how brilliantly—and smoothly—he had covered their almost-transgression. And when she thought further on it, she realised that in actuality she had goaded him into it. He wore his cynicism and reserve like a protective shell and she had not been able to curb her desire to pierce it. She knew she should have shown more restraint, but she'd been left vulnerable by Mrs Bartleigh's news. When he'd shown a bit of his own vulnerability she had overreacted. She'd taken the conversation to too intimate a level, pushed too far, got too close.

And he'd pushed back, struck out with his heated gaze and warm, wandering hands. Even now she couldn't help wishing she had discovered a few more of the weapons in his sensual arsenal.

'Good morning, cousin!' a voice rang out.

Lily started nearly out of her chair, an instant flush rising. She turned to find Miss Dawson advancing across the room towards her.

'Oh, goodness! Good morning, Minerva.' She

took up her still-blank sheet of paper and began to fan herself with it. 'You look lovely today!'

Minerva Dawson laughed, her eyebrow cocked as she clasped Lily's hand in her own. 'As do you, my dear. Something has put a beautiful hue to your cheeks. Do tell!'

'Oh, no, I am merely writing a note for my land steward.'

'So I see,' her friend said, glancing at the empty sheets in her hand and in front of her. 'Well, are you ready to shop? Mother gave me firm instructions. I am to find the perfect pair of gloves to wear to my engagement ball—elbow length and ivory. Not white, not ecru, but ivory.'

'I shall be ready to go in just a moment—if you would wait while I finish?'

Minerva rolled her eyes. 'Oh, if I must.'

Lily laughed. 'You know, Minerva, that I am thrilled that you found a familial connection between us, even if it is a distant relationship through marriage and largely born of your imagination—' she grinned to take the sting from her words '—but I do not think everyone in your family is as well pleased with such a link.' She gestured for her friend to sit and joined her in the comfortable grouping of chairs near the window. 'In fact, I think your aunt disapproves of me.'

'Oh, yes, she does,' Minerva returned cheerily. 'But Aunt Lucinda disapproves of nearly everyone without a title—including her husband.'

'Well, that does make me feel a little more sympathetic towards your uncle.'

'Don't let it,' her friend said flatly. She began to remove her gloves in a brisk manner. Leaning towards Lily, she lowered her voice. 'The man gives me chills. I don't care if he *is* my uncle.'

'I know just what you mean.' Lily shuddered.

'Well, you don't have to worry about them. I told dear Aunt Lucinda all about your vast lands in Dorset and the vaster amount of money you stand to inherit and that went a long way towards reconciling her to our friendship.'

'You are incorrigible.' Lily laughed.

'It is true.' Minerva sighed. 'But a little incorrigibility makes life ever so much more fun!' She waggled a stern finger in Lily's direction. 'And happily, there's a bit of it in you, too. Now don't try to bam me—you were mooning over some young man when I came in. Which one? That Mr Brookins, who waxed eloquent over your skills on the pianoforte?'

'No.' Lily abruptly decided to tell the truth. 'Actually, I was trying to decipher Mr Alden's puzzling behaviour.'

Minerva stilled. Much of the light faded from her smiling face. 'Oh? Do your thoughts lean in that direction, then?'

'No,' Lily said with a grimace. 'In fact, they travel in another direction entirely. I'm afraid Mr Alden does not like me much, and I was merely trying to work out why that is.'

'Hmm.' Her 'cousin' examined her closely. 'Lily, I am a very observant person, have I told you that?'

'Not that I've observed.' Lily smiled to defuse the serious tone Minerva had adopted.

'Ha. Well, I observed something interesting last night.'

'A sudden gust of wind?' asked Lily facetiously.

'No.' Her friend's brow furrowed. 'Whatever do you mean?'

'Nothing. Is this a game? Let me guess again. You observed…the immense number of prawns devoured by the bishop during the intermission?'

'Well, I did notice that. Shocking, wasn't it? I'd wager that he's not feeling quite the thing today.' The stern finger appeared again. 'But that was not what I meant. I observed Mr Alden and he was watching you very closely last night.'

'Probably because we quarrelled and I got the best of him,' Lily said sourly.

Minerva drew back, surprised. 'You bested him in

an argument? Well, I dare say that was a first for him. No wonder he looked so torn.'

'Torn?'

'Definitely torn. I swear, he alternately looked as he meant to devour *you*, or perhaps to bash you over the head.'

'No doubt he would prefer the latter.' She sighed, then got to her feet and wandered over to gaze out of the window.

Minerva pursed her lips. She sat back, levelling a stare in Lily's direction and drumming her fingers on the arm of her chair. 'Lily,' she began at last, 'you know that I only want what is best for you.'

Lily had to suppress an ironic chuckle. Minerva could have no notion how many times she'd heard *that* particular phrase in her life.

'Jack Alden is a very handsome man, in an intense and yet disarmingly rumpled way.'

'I know,' agreed Lily. 'Don't you have to stop yourself from straightening his cravat and smoothing out the line of his coat every time you meet him?'

Her friend stared at her. 'Well, no. But it is rather speaking that you do, my dear.' A gentle smile belied the slight crease in her brow. 'Just be careful,' she pleaded, her tone low and serious. 'Some men are amenable to having their neckcloths straightened and some are in no way ready to contemplate such a thing.'

'I understand what you are saying, Minerva, and I appreciate your concern beyond words.' Lily focused on the traffic outside in the street for a long moment. 'He's hiding,' she said abruptly.

Minerva heaved a great sigh. 'Yes, I know.'

'You do?' She spun around in surprise.

The corner of her friend's mouth twitched. 'I recognised the symptoms from personal experience.' She raised a questioning brow. 'As do you, I assume.'

Lily nodded.

'Well, then we both know that you cannot force him to stop. He will battle his own demons in his own time—just as everyone else must, sooner or later.'

Lily met her friend's gaze squarely. 'Would you consider me insane if I told you that I have been wondering…if perhaps I am meant to help Mr Alden?'

'No,' Minerva replied promptly. 'I would consider you the most generous girl with the grandest heart in all of England. But I would also warn you that Jack Alden is a man grown. He can help himself. You can go on enjoying your all-too-brief stay in London—as you were meant to do.'

Lily regarded her with affection. 'You are a very dear friend.'

'I know,' Minerva responded comfortably, 'but you deserve me.'

For several long moments Lily sat, silent. Her

thoughts swirled while her conscience struggled to find a balance between her wants and her needs. At last she sighed. She knew what she wanted, but she also knew what she must do.

'Minerva,' she said slowly, 'we will likely be seeing much of Mr Alden over the next weeks.' She grimaced. 'Tomorrow, for instance, Lady Dayle and I are to accompany him on a day trip to a friend's country villa.' She gestured helplessly about them, at his family's house which sheltered them. 'But I think it is best that I keep my distance—for all of our sakes.' Lily reached for her friend's hand and clasped it tightly when it came. 'Will you help me?'

'Yes,' Minerva responded slowly. 'I rather think I will.'

Whistling, Jack swept a brush down the muscled flank of one of his sturdy greys. 'Now this is a job for a one-handed man,' he said aloud. The doctor had agreed to let him leave off with the splint, but his arm still felt a long way from fully recovered. 'Let's finish it up, boys!' he called to the men polishing his brother's landau. 'Our ladies will be ready shortly. Let's be sure to give them a beautiful ride!'

He could see the vehicle, shining already in the early morning sun, and the grooms scrambling over the cobbled yard of the mews. His brother's voice rang out just then and Jack turned as Charles entered the stable.

Charles called for his mount and joined his brother, running a critical eye over the horse he laboured over. 'Morning, Jack. Your greys look to be in fine fettle today.'

'Perhaps not so flashy as Pettigrew's bays,' Jack answered, grinning, 'but they suit me well. Thank you again,' he added, 'for the loan of your landau. It looks to be a good day for our drive. I'm sure Mother and Miss Beecham will prefer the open air to a carriage and none of us would be comfortable squeezing into my cabriolet.'

'Remind me again where you are all off to?'

'Chester House. Lord Bradington has invited a select group to view his Anglo-Saxon collection and he's invited some scholars interested in the period to speak. I'm to read my paper on King Alfred's system of justice.' He shrugged. 'I had originally declined, but the day is fine and I thought the ladies might enjoy it. Miss Beecham seems to go in for that sort of thing.'

Jack grinned as his brother gave him the same sort of once over he'd just given his horse.

'You do seem to be in remarkably good spirits,' said Charles. 'I don't think I've seen you looking so relaxed in weeks.'

'Remarkable what a good night's sleep will do for

a man,' said Jack, continuing on with his brushing. He was in good spirits. In fact, he was vastly relieved and gloriously happy. 'It's all due to a grand bit of news, Charles. Do you recall Benjamin Racci, the fellow who had the apartments next to me at All Souls?'

He watched Charles grimace and search his memory. 'Vaguely. His area of interest had something to do with Muslims, yes?'

'Oh, you are good,' Jack said admiringly. 'No wonder you do so well in the Lords. Yes, in any case, Racci's obsession is Muslim influence on Western development. He's currently in Gibraltar, going over Moorish structures and mosques.' He paused, leaned on the back of his grey and smirked at his brother. 'And guess what he caught sight of in Catelan Bay?'

Charles's eyes narrowed as he stared at Jack a moment, then realisation dawned. 'Not Batiste?'

'Batiste, big brother!' Jack crowed. 'Racci got my letter, asking that he keep an eye and ear out, and then, wham! One morning he spots the *Lady Vengeance* riding at anchor in the bay. Racci sent a message off to the British Naval Commander, but she was gone before they got there.'

'So he's not been caught?' asked Charles.

'No, but neither did he re-supply. He's on the run, Charles, and for the first time I feel as if we truly might catch up with the bastard.'

His brother grinned. 'So that's why you are in such a good mood. Triumph of logic and reason over tyranny and villainy?'

'Perhaps not triumph, yet, but definitely a step in the right direction. And it was due to sound thinking and determination,' Jack corrected. 'As well as good contacts, of course.'

'Nice job, little brother.' Charles stepped back as his groom led his mount forwards. Another man came to take the grey and Jack savoured the feeling of his brother's approbation as he handed him over to be harnessed with his mate.

'I'm surprised you are bothering with poor Miss Beecham now that you've got Batiste on the run,' Charles teased as he swung up. 'Why bother taking her and Mother out if you no longer need to pursue her connection with Matthew Beecham?'

A small, cowardly piece of his soul had already whispered the same message in Jack's ear. He rebuffed his brother in the same way he had sternly talked to himself.

'The girl is Mother's guest, Charles, not a pawn in some game I'm playing,' Jack said reproachfully. He waved the groom away and checked his brother's girth strap himself.

'I know, I know, it was just a brotherly jibe.' Charles did not sound in the least repentant. 'I can't help thinking of what happened to me, though, last time Mother adopted a protégée.'

Jack froze. 'The situations are not at all similar.'

Charles laughed. 'I know. Just watch yourself.'

'Don't even joke about such things,' Jack said with shudder. 'What a wretched husband I should make, holed up in my rooms, losing myself for days on end in my papers and books.' He eyed Charles soberly. 'And we both know what a wretched husband does to a family. I have no plans to inflict such a fate on anyone.'

'You never know, Jack. Some day you might just meet a young lady who interests you more than your stale ancients.'

'Miss Beecham does interest me. She's a lovely girl, but I have no intention of making her miserable for the rest of her life. I give her the respect she is due as a friend of the family, but I'm not about to give up any other possible leads to Batiste.'

'Do you think the girl will co-operate, then?'

Jack shrugged. 'I won't know until I ask.'

'Best of luck to you.' Charles nudged his mount forwards. 'The vote on this bill comes soon, and then I'll be back to Sevenoaks for a few days.'

'I'm sure I'll see you before then.' Jack waved his brother off.

The landau stood ready, polished surfaces

gleaming, the horses prancing in anticipation. Dissatisfied, Jack climbed in. He much preferred to do his own driving. But he gave a nod of readiness to the groom and the team went wheeling after his brother. As the man eased them into the flow of traffic in the street, Jack steeled his nerves against the coming confrontation.

Despite his fine words to Charles, he knew his last encounter with Miss Beecham had been a disaster, start to finish. His shoulders hunched involuntarily. Especially the finish. He'd been sick at the thought of what he'd almost done and horrified at his own complete loss of control.

So close. His hand had buried itself in the glowing softness of her hair. Her breath had mingled, hot and sweet, with his. He'd stood mere seconds away from locking her within his embrace and ending her disturbingly empathetic conversation with a searing kiss.

After his escape he had waged a silent war with himself, wavering between his wish to stay as far away as possible from the dangerous chit and his need to ask for her co-operation in finding her cousin. She had every right to refuse him—to slap his face and order him to keep his distance. But he hoped fervently that she would not.

He felt better, more like himself, now. His success in finding a first trace of Batiste's whereabouts had taken the edge off of his desperation. He'd slept at last without being haunted by taunting visions of the captain and his father. He'd clamped down hard on his wayward emotions and taken a step back towards the equilibrium he craved.

This exhibition should be the perfect venue to help him get back in Miss Beecham's good graces. A gorgeous house, intellectual stimulation, fascinating antiquities, beautiful gardens—what more could he ask for? He could deal with her in his own milieu, impress her, charm her and get her alone where he could offer up his proposition and in no way act again like a weak-willed fool.

She was just a woman. One endowed with wit and beauty and a good deal of spirit, to be sure, but no longer a match for his discipline and determination. He could do this. If only she gave him the chance.

Traffic quieted as they made the turn on to Bruton Street. Jack stared as the landau slowed, approaching his brother's house. What was this? At first he tried mightily to hide his dismay. Then he gave up, gave in and simply laughed out loud. He had not granted the wily Miss Beecham enough credit. Give him the chance? Clearly she meant to leave nothing to chance.

Instead of a pair of ladies waiting patiently inside, a large group of people milled on the steps and on the pavement in front of the town house. Several vehicles waited empty in the street. He spotted Minerva Dawson and her betrothed, Lord Lindley. There stood Mrs Montague and—Lord, was that Sally Jersey? In the midst of them stood Miss Beecham. He caught sight of her as she gave a little jump and a wave.

'Good morning, Mr Alden!' she called. 'I hope you won't mind a few additions to your party!'

Chapter Six

Lily had succeeded in her ploy. She'd been unable to deny the twinge of satisfaction she'd felt when she'd glimpsed the surprise on Jack Alden's face this morning, but, she had to admit, he'd succeeded in surprising her, too.

A country villa? She turned round and round inside the incredible central hall of Chester House. Awestruck, she let her eye rove from the stone floor, over the magnificent plaster ornamentation and on to the high windows and the lofty dome overheard. Her jaw had dropped when they had pulled up to this gleaming neo-Palladian villa, but with her first step inside she'd fallen instantly in love.

Oh, how her mother would despise the place. A wealthy gentleman's playhouse. A hedonist's dream, replete with everything fanciful, ornate and overblown.

But so much more, as well. Like a light and airy treasure box, it showcased art and antiquities flanked by and contained within the most exquisite architecture. It stood testimony to man's capability for beauty, celebrated his sense of ingenuity and wonder. It spoke directly to Lily's soul.

Guests, laughing and boisterous, began to spill in behind her. Lily was swept along to an elaborate, tripartite gallery where, en masse, they were met by their host. In the midst of all the splendour, Lord Bradington looked short and somewhat ordinary, yet he stepped up to a lavishly inlaid marble podium and welcomed them with generous and open arms.

'The best way to properly see the collection is in small groups,' he announced. 'We will split up. Besides myself, we are fortunate to have several experts among us. They will be happy, I am sure, to share their knowledge and thus enhance your own enjoyment of the treasures on display. There will be plenty of time to see everything before we gather back here…' he gestured '…in the gallery, to hear our notable speakers and enjoy a light repast.'

Good-natured chaos ensued as people began to separate into groups. Lily took advantage of the confusion. She slipped behind a gilded pillar, anxious for a quiet moment to recover and take it all in.

This was it—what she had been anticipating,

hoping for, when she came to London. Not the riches that surrounded her, but the happy exuberance and simple joy to be found in sharing them, their history and the grand idea that they somehow connected every single person here.

Heart pounding, she leaned against the cool marble and peeked out into the crowd. Her eye unerringly went to Jack Alden, as it had done foolishly, repeatedly, all morning.

Why now? she wanted to cry at him. Why now, when she had reached her decision to stay away, made her resolution to avoid him, did he abruptly turn himself into the exact thing she hadn't acknowledged that she was looking for?

He'd had every right to be angry at her perfidy in inviting along Minerva and her fiancé, the Bartleighs, and a few others besides, to his outing. But he'd acted quite the opposite. He had taken off his hat, thrown back his head and laughed heartily at the sight of her entourage and she had been captivated by the sight of the breeze wafting through his dark hair and the green sparkle of amusement in his eyes. Even as she'd stared, he'd replaced his hat, and given her a jaunty salute, making her wonder if he'd guessed at the reason behind her strategy.

Nor had he objected when she had climbed up with Minerva to ride in Mr Brookin's flashy demi-landau. Instead, he had welcomed the Bartleighs into his own vehicle and, from what she could see, had spent the drive out chatting and charming them completely.

Now he gathered her friends into a group and then he raised his head and ran a searching gaze about the room.

'Lily Beecham?' he called. 'Miss Beecham must join us as well.'

The others echoed his cry. Lily breathed deep. There was no help for it. All she could do was join the group and avoid Jack Alden as best she could.

This, it turned out, was no easy task. In fact, she thought at one point that it just might be the hardest thing she had ever tried to do.

Gone was Jack Alden's veneer of cool reserve. Not once did she catch even a hint of worldly cynicism. Instead, he led their group on a private, informative, highly entertaining tour. The Anglo-Saxon antiquities on display throughout the house were fascinating and it seemed he knew something about every piece. He explained the incised decorations on a disc brooch, and pointed out the faint remains of tinning on a Saxon wrist clasp. He spoke at length and with enthusiasm about the theories regarding the Alfred jewel and the possibility that more might exist. He showed himself to be knowledgeable and passionate.

And nigh irresistible.

Lily was unceasingly aware of him all day. She felt attuned to his every clever remark and deep, husky laugh. She grew warmer every time she noticed that his relaxed manner only emphasised the strength of his form and his long-limbed grace. All day she watched him and her body hummed, head to toe, with a heated, shivering awareness.

And yet she forced herself to behave with complete indifference. She did not meet his eye, kept at least two others between them at all times, permitted herself only a distant smile so many times when what she really wished was to laugh out loud.

It was torture.

By the time the papers were read, the speeches given and the lavish spread of food consumed, Lily's head was aching. She was tired of fighting to keep her gaze from straying to wherever Jack Alden stood. When Mr Keller, another of the scholars invited to speak today, asked her to stroll with him through the famous gardens, she allowed herself one last fleeting glimpse, and then she took the other man's arm and allowed him to lead her away.

Jack Alden stood poised on the brink of madness. Ahead loomed naught but the chaotic pit and behind him lurked Lily Beecham, one tiny hand placed squarely at his back, urging him forwards to his doom.

He could not believe that it had happened again. He'd come with a plan and a purpose. He'd visualised how he would proceed. He'd anticipated and prepared for her every response. Except, it appeared, for this one.

She blended right in to the atmosphere of Chester House, as if she was meant to stroll amongst the beauties of the ages and enrich them with her own special appeal. He'd half-expected that. He'd expected her to be lively and vivacious. He'd hoped she'd be caught up in his own attempt at charm and charisma.

He'd been at least partly right. Good God—her allure was a nearly palpable thing. She had every man here in her thrall. But something had gone missing. She seemed interested, happy—and utterly indifferent to him.

Jack knew that he did not possess the renowned charm of his brother, but he exerted himself powerfully and did his best to channel Charles's effortless likeability—to no avail.

And just like that, all of his careful planning, and reason and logic, too, flew right out of the proverbial window. He could swear he heard his father's mocking laughter mixed in with the gaiety of the company. Her complete lack of interest triggered something alarming inside of him. He felt hot and reckless, and uncertain as well, as if he would do anything to get her to look at him the way she had at their first, eventful meeting.

He had a limited supply of self-control left, and it took every ounce of it to stay calm, act the perfect host, and exude amiability and unconcern. When he saw Keller take her into the gardens he breathed deep, squelched the urge to roar like an enraged bull, politely excused himself from his companions and followed.

He found them in the middle of the gardens, where a large, flat lawn had been created. The two of them strolled slowly along the western edge, admiring the border of alternating stone urns and cypress trees. At least, the girl appeared to be admiring them. Keller's attention was focused somewhere else altogether.

'There you are, Keller,' he called. 'Lord Bradington is looking for you, old man.'

'How nice,' Keller responded. His eyes never strayed from Lily Beecham's lithe shape.

'Yes, he's debating the dating on that collection of gold, die-struck belt mounts in the library. Apparently someone is arguing that they might be Viking-made.'

'What?' Now Keller's head came up and he looked back towards the house. 'That cannot be right. No, no. Those were clearly manufactured by early Saxons.'

'Someone's convinced Bradington otherwise. He's already talking of changing the placard and moving them in with the other Viking artefacts.'

'That will not do!' Keller exclaimed. He looked with regret at the girl. 'I'm so sorry, Miss Beecham, but I will have to go back and remedy this. Shall you accompany me?'

'No, you go in,' Jack interjected. 'Miss Beecham has hardly seen any of the grounds. I shall take her on. You can join us again once you have cleared up this travesty.'

'Perhaps I should go back,' she demurred. 'My friends…'

'Are all already strolling the gardens,' Jack said smoothly. 'I will help you find them.'

She said nothing further. Keller hurried back towards the house and Jack decided it would be prudent to move on.

'Have you seen the stone gateway?' He inclined his head at her. 'It is quite renowned as a place of good fortune.'

'No…' she gazed up at him with something that looked like exasperation '…I have not. Perhaps we should walk that way before poor Mr Keller discovers your ruse?'

Jack laughed. 'Was I that obvious?'

'Perhaps only to those already familiar with your machinations,' she said sourly.

He indicated the direction and offered up his arm. After a long searching look, she sighed and laid her hand lightly on his.

'A gate of good fortune, you said?' she asked. 'How does it work?'

'I couldn't say how the tales originated, but the legend says that you must pause on the threshold, thinking very hard on the difficulties of your life. You must concentrate and count to three silently while you swing open the gate and cross through.'

'And then?'

'And then your troubles are over.' He shrugged. 'The hardships you focused on will have disappeared.'

'Would that it were that easy,' she said wistfully. 'But I shall definitely write and tell my old nurse of it. She adores tales of superstition and fancy.'

The sun rode low in the afternoon sky. Its rays, filtered through spring leaves, painted the ancient statuary with a forgiving brush. Miss Beecham paused to admire the figure of Palladio. The soft light erased the harsh wear of time on his stern-faced visage, but Jack could not look away from the little fires it lit in the fall of her hair.

'I tried to get away earlier and ask you to tour the

gardens,' he said. 'I noticed that you looked a little pale and thought perhaps you'd welcome a quiet stroll with a restful companion.'

An ironic snort was her only answer.

Jack clenched his teeth. Even her sarcasm attracted him. When they resumed their stroll he allowed his gaze to run down the turquoise-and-ivory dress she wore and he briefly mourned the bosom-enhancing high waists that had lately fallen out of fashion.

He breathed deep and forced himself to focus. All of his work today had been leading to this.

'Hmm. I left myself wide open with that remark and you failed to take advantage of it. Forgive me, but you have not seemed yourself today, Miss Beecham,' he said. They'd reached a paved circular area from which three avenues radiated outwards. He ignored them all and instead led her on to a smaller, gravelled pathway through a copse. 'I'm sorry if the day has not been to your liking.'

'Of course the day has been to my liking, Mr Alden.' Had she been any younger he would have sworn she would have rolled her eyes at him. 'I found a peacock feather on the drive as soon as we arrived, so I knew it was certain to be a good day.'

He blinked at that, but she did not pause.

'But you are right, I have not been acting myself

and it has taken some of the shine from what might have been a perfect day—and given me a dreadful headache besides.'

'Not acting yourself? Well, then, whose role have you been enacting?'

She cast him an arch look. 'Couldn't you tell? I would have thought you found it a familiar picture.'

They'd intersected the larger walk that would lead them to the gate. Jack stopped abruptly as his feet hit the smooth surface and stared incredulously at her. 'Me? You thought to act like me?'

Was that how he looked to her? Aloof, uninterested, distant? Was that how everyone else viewed him as well? The idea astounded him. He'd thought himself reserved, yes, but not so determinedly remote.

Suddenly he began to laugh. He allowed her hand to drop away from his arm, walked over to lean on a sturdy horse-chestnut tree and proceeded to shake with amusement, long and hard.

'It's not funny, I assure you.' Miss Beecham sniffed. 'I have no idea how you go about like that every day. It's too much work.'

'No, no.' He chuckled. 'You did an admirable imitation of me. I dare say I should have enjoyed it more had I known what to look for.' He straightened away from the massive trunk and grinned at her.

'And, in truth, it was only fair. Now you must return the critique, for I've been doing my damnedest to act more like you!'

'Were you?' She looked diverted. 'Well, without a doubt, you should continue.'

'No! As you say, it's too much work. I've fair exhausted myself.' He wiped his eye and returned to her side. Reaching down, he took both of her hands in his. 'Shall we strike a bargain? Let us just be honest with each other. It's far easier and we got on well enough before.'

She shot him an incredulous look.

'Well, perhaps I should rephrase. I, in any case, quite enjoyed your company. I would like to continue to do so.'

'Honesty?' she asked.

'Honesty,' he vowed solemnly.

'Well, I did enjoy your company before, when you were not being a sanctimonious bore.'

Another burst of laughter escaped him. 'Well, I cannot promise that it won't happen again, but if it does, I beg you to let me know and I will attempt to rein myself in.'

She ran a dubious eye over him. Jack felt the heat of her innocent gaze rush from the top of his head down to the shining tips of his boots. Well, perhaps there were a few things he would have to hold back.

This time when he offered his arm she tucked her hand in the crook of his elbow with a smile. They strolled companionably for a few minutes before he spoke again.

'So tell me, Miss Beecham, how are you feeling about your sojourn into society?'

She wrinkled her brow at him. 'How am I feeling about it? That's an odd question. Most people just ask me if I am enjoying myself.'

Jack carefully kept his tone neutral. 'Excepting today, of course, it is obvious to anyone who lays an eye on you that you are enjoying yourself.'

She watched him closely, and then smiled. 'How do I feel?' she mused. She took a moment to consider the question, her brow furrowed becomingly. 'Well, I am enjoying myself, of course. No one spending any amount of time with your mother could do otherwise. But...' she sighed '...I admit to a little anxiety as well. To be honest, I hadn't expected everything to feel so alien.'

'Alien?' he repeated, surprised. 'How so?'

'I was born to this world...' she gestured about them '...just as surely as you were, Mr Alden. My father was a wealthy gentleman landowner. My mother's family has multiple connections to the nobility.' She shrugged. 'But the last years of my life have been so drastically different from all of this, and I find that those years have altered the way that I view certain things.'

She fascinated him more every second. 'Would you share some specifics?' he asked.

'Well, all this, for example. Chester House.' She glanced back towards the house and at the guests they could glimpse wandering through the vast and varied gardens. 'It's fascinating and beautiful and educational. I'm very grateful that Lord Bradington invited us to experience it all, but I can't help but think of all the people who will never view anything like this. I walk through here and I imagine the pleasure these things would bring, the awe they might inspire, if it were all open to the public—in a museum or a pleasure garden, perhaps.'

'Would not most Evangelicals disagree?' he asked. 'I thought they wish to educate the masses only so far as it will help them do their duty and accept their lot in life?'

'I suppose you are right about that,' Lily admitted. 'But to stimulate the mind, to expose it to the greatness that might be achieved by man and perhaps invite it to travel along the same paths—that can never be a mistake, in my opinion.'

Her words set off a burning deep in his chest. She was lovely and generous. *And you are a fool,* whispered some dark and no doubt perfectly correct part of his soul. He shushed it and struggled to speak in a normal tone. 'You interest me more by the second, Miss Beecham,' he said. 'You also remind me a great deal of a friend of mine.'

'Really?' she asked with a half-smile.

'Truly,' he affirmed. 'Though you could not be more opposite on the outside,' he said with amusement. 'Chione is half-Egyptian. She is newly betrothed to a gentleman who spends his time searching out antiquities. He has always in the past sold them to collectors. Dragons, Chione calls them.'

Her blue eyes lit up in delight. 'That is it exactly! Dragons, sitting atop their hordes, jealously guarding it from all but the most distinguished visitors.'

'I shan't tell Lord Bradington you said that.' Jack laughed. 'Trey, Chione's betrothed, says that dragons pay best, though.'

'And his fiancée says…?'

'Oh, she's convinced him to commit to the British Museum instead. Now everyone will be able to see the treasures he finds in his travels.'

'I think I should quite like your friends,' she said decisively.

Like a bolt from out of the sky, Jack suffered a moment of blinding insight. He recalled the turmoil and frustration he'd endured all day and he knew that he'd felt something similar before. It had crept up on him as Trey and Chione had grown naturally closer. Their intensifying fascination with each other and the mission they were to set out on had left him feeling shut out. Extraneous.

Was that when all this unwanted emotion had begun leaking past the barriers of his internal dams? No, he thought with a twist of gut-wrenching honesty—perhaps it might have begun even earlier, when Charles and Sophie had become so wrapped up in each other and their new family. But no matter when it had begun, there was no doubt that his every encounter with Lily Beecham intensified the problem and left a bigger breach in his internal bulwarks.

Well, he would just have to do some shoring up—and fast. He had a job to do here. He must force himself to forget such nonsense and focus on his objective.

'I am very glad that you are not a dragon, Mr Alden.'

Her words startled him. 'What?'

'You have a vast deal of knowledge. You have obviously spent a great deal of time in research. Yet you don't hide away in a study somewhere, hoarding your knowledge and expertise like artefacts or jewels. You share it. As you did today. As you do with your journal articles and speeches.'

She looked at him with something he hadn't seen in her eyes before: respect. Esteem. Jack's gut clenched in a visceral reaction. He'd seen a beggar child once, standing outside a bake shop, his face a picture of longing and need. God, but he felt just the same way right now. He'd been starving for that look of respect his whole life.

'It is just as I spoke about earlier,' she continued. 'Your passion infects others with the urge to learn, the wish to expand their own horizons. It is a very great gift that you give to the world, and I, for one, am thankful.'

Her words were a surprise and a pleasure. And perhaps a torment. It had been as nothing to take that hungry child inside and gift him with the largest, meatiest pastry the baker had on display. Jack had even left coins in an account so the boy could return. He feared it would be a much more difficult thing to accomplish his aim and still bask in the warm glow of her regard.

A sudden image flashed in his mind's eye—an ugly picture of his father raging, sweeping a day's work from his desk, parchment and paper and ink scattering like dust motes through the air.

He blinked. And he hardened his heart and clenched his fist in resolve.

'We promised honesty, Miss Beecham, did we not?'

'We did.'

'Then I wish to be honest with you. Chione is

actually part of the reason I wanted to walk with you. I hoped to tell you a little more about her.'

Her brow furrowed in question, but she gave an encouraging nod.

'When we spoke of my injury, I told you that my friends and I had foiled a robbery.'

'Yes, I recall.'

'Well, there was more to it. We were lucky to have stopped a kidnapping plot as well.'

Her eyes widened, but she did not speak.

'Chione's grandfather was kidnapped and held for months. The night I was shot, Trey and I and a few others only just prevented the scoundrels from taking her as well.'

She gasped. 'Thank goodness you were there, then, and able to stop them.'

'In fact, we were not able to stop them all. One of the villains got away. A very evil man, I'm afraid. A slaver.'

Her expression grew serious. 'That is unfortunate. I know something of the terrible things such men do to their fellow humans. Mother and I have worked hard to educate our corner of Dorset against the evils of slavery.'

'It is a shame that a woman like you must be familiar with the depths to which these men will sink. But I think you will understand when I tell you how worried I am. This man is obsessed with vengeance. Chione and her family may still be in grave danger from him.'

'How horrible,' she breathed.

They had reached the stone gate. Neither of them paid it a bit of attention. Jack steeled himself and spoke again.

'I believe that you might be in a position to help.'

Shock widened her eyes and hitched her breath. 'Me?'

'Yes. You—and your cousin, Matthew Beecham.'

'Matthew? What can he have to do with any of this? He is in America!'

'Actually, he has gone missing.'

Now suspicion darkened her eyes and clouded her features. 'How could you possibly know such a thing?'

'Miss Beecham—Lily,' Jack said, half-pleading. 'You appear to be well aware that slavery remains a reality in America, just as it does in the British colonies. It is the *trade* in slaves that has been made illegal in our country and the import of new slaves that has been outlawed in theirs. But apparently Captain Batiste, the slaver we spoke of, misses the days of putting his ship into port and selling poor souls like cattle right off his deck.'

'But what has any of that to do with *Matthew*?'

'I'm nearly there. From what I can gather, your cousin got into some kind of trouble with Batiste. A debt of some sort. Batiste demanded repayment—in the form of some adjustments made to a few of his ships. False compartments, secret holds, that sort of thing. All to enable him to resume his illegal trafficking in people, with those slaveholders unscrupulous enough to deal with him.'

Jack walked away from her horrified stare. The old gateway beckoned. If only the legends were true. He could pass through the archway and his problems would be solved. Well, hell, he would take help where he could get it. He tried the iron gateway set into the stone arch. His arm protested the effort, but it was to no avail anyway. The gate was locked. He should have known.

'The American government caught on to Batiste's tricks,' he continued. 'But the man is as slippery as an eel. They next went to speak to your cousin, but found he had fled. They want him for questioning.'

'I don't believe it,' she said flatly.

'I don't care about any of that, Lily. I just want Batiste. And your cousin may be able to tell me where to find him.'

Her expression hardened. 'And that is what all of this has been about, has it not?' Her slate eyes turned to chill, blue ice as she gestured about them, to the park and the house and the carefree revellers grouped in the distance. 'Or has it been only that from nearly the very beginning?'

He shook his head.

'What a lucky coincidence that it was I who you nearly ran down in the street, no?' she whispered.

'No. It's not like that,' Jack protested.

'I think it is. You think that I, in turn, will be able to tell you where Matthew is?' She gave an ugly, bitter laugh. 'Well I am destined to disappoint you once again, Mr Alden, because you know far more about all of this than I! I knew nothing about any of this. Nothing! I did not even know that Matthew had left his home. And I refuse to believe that he could be mixed up in something so foul as slavery.'

She whirled around and walked away from him and the gate. Before Jack could call out, she let out a sudden gasp and turned back. 'Does your mother know all of this as well?'

'No! Of course not,' he said.

Her shoulders slumped in relief.

'She knows nothing about it and she won't unless you choose to tell her. Please, just listen to me,' Jack asked quietly. 'You said you were close with your cousin, that you still correspond. All I ask is that you tell me if you hear from him.'

He'd thought her indifference was painful. The

contempt that shone from her now cut deep and was nearly unbearable.

He winced and sighed. 'I can help Matthew. I want to help him. All I need to do is ask him some questions about likely spots where Batiste would hide away. He's spent a considerable amount of time with the man; he might know something that will enable us to find him.' He took a step towards her, held out a beseeching hand. 'My brother has a great deal of influence. He will use it to help your cousin.'

She turned her back on him once more. 'And if he does not possess the information you want? What will you do then?'

Jack did not even wish to contemplate such a thing. 'Charles and I will still help him, even if he does not. I swear.'

Her head dropped and she began to pace. Jack watched her graceful form and sent out a silent plea to the heavens. He needed her help. God help him, he was beginning to fear he needed *her*.

Avoiding his gaze, she passed him and approached the gate. She ran a hand along the elaborately carved stone until she came to the middle. There she ceased her restless motion and gripped the iron railings of the inset door.

'You don't know what you are asking!' She spoke not to Jack, but to the empty park beyond. In the distance people chatted and laughed, but Jack's world had shrunk alarmingly. Naught mattered save her and him and this gateway to their future.

'I simply cannot believe my cousin would be mixed up in this. Matthew is a good person. He's the only person left alive who knows me. Really, truly, deep down inside, he knows me. When we were young he never cared that I preferred a good gallop to gossip, that I would always choose to climb a tree over embroidering a sampler.' She sent a pleading look over her shoulder. 'Even now, when he writes, he doesn't ask me the same inane, irrelevant questions that the rest of the world seems to focus on. He asks me about the crops, and my tenants, and whether I've convinced my mother that attendance at a local assembly will not taint my soul.' She turned to face him again and he saw that her gaze had grown distant and unfocused. 'He even occasionally remembers to ask if I've seen two blackbirds sitting together on a fence post.'

'Blackbirds?' Jack began to feel as if they were carrying on two separate conversations.

'Blackbirds,' she answered firmly. 'You see—he understands me and all my foibles and still he cares for me. That is the person you think could stoop so low, the one you are asking me to betray.'

'It would not be a betrayal. You can trust me, Lily.'

'Trust you?' Her voice fairly dripped scorn. 'I do not even know you, Jack Alden.'

'Don't be absurd. You know me well enough to trust my word.'

'Not I! In fact, I question whether anyone in your life can claim to truly know you. I thought you hid behind your books, but today I begin to wonder if perhaps it is only in your intellectual pursuits that you are open and accessible. At all other times you've shown yourself to be distant and cold—closed behind walls that you only think are protecting you.' She crossed her arms in front of her. 'I cannot know you or trust you, Mr Alden, until you learn to know and trust yourself.'

With her every word Jack could feel the intelligent, rational man he knew himself to be fading away. She was an innocent, naïve little fool, but he felt wild, frenzied, like a child on the verge of a temper tantrum. She did this to him. Every time he got near her she shone a light on his every flaw, magnified his every emotion until he thought he would go mad with it.

He thought of Batiste, a malevolent threat hovering over Trey and Chione and their family—in just the same way his father had hovered contemptuously, dangerously in the background for most of his life—and he knew he would indeed go mad if Lily Beecham did not co-operate.

'You don't know as much as you think you do, Lily. Of a certainty you don't know what you are asking of me. But perhaps you are right,' he said, moving closer, his heart pounding, his blood surging. 'There are also many things that I do not know—including why you feel such antagonism towards me.'

'I…I don't,' she whispered, suddenly flustered.

'You do.' He was glad to see her unbalanced. It was only fair. She stirred him up until he felt as if he must prove his manhood or die trying. He approached her stealthily, a hunter prowling forwards with soft, light steps. And she, she was his prey. 'You lecture me, but I think you must follow your own advice. Everything I see and hear of you tells me that you are a warm person, giving to others. But you will not consider my request—even though it might benefit your cousin and will help save a family from a dangerous and unscrupulous man. And why not? Because the request comes from me?'

'No.' Her freckles disappeared again in the flush that rose from beneath her gown.

'It's true.' He advanced further, trapping her between him and the iron bars of the gate. 'Look deep, as you've asked me to do. You are allowing your dislike of me to influence your judgement.'

Her breathing quickened. He could see the flutter

of her pulse in her throat, the quick casting about of her gaze as she searched for an escape. 'I don't dislike you.'

Discipline had gone. Reason and judgement had disappeared. The other, darker side of Jack's soul ruled now. It roared to life inside of him, loosing a great whirl of longing and want and more than a bit of anger too. The small bit of sanity he had left knew that anger had no place in this, and urged control. But it was too late for restraint. He held Lily's gaze prisoner with his own and asked the question to which he must have the answer. 'Then what do you feel, Lily, when you look at me?'

'I...'

'Honesty, remember? Tell me the truth.' Their lips were but a whisper apart.

She shook her head, looked away, breaking the hypnotic link between them. 'Not dislike,' she said to the ground.

He knew that she meant to hide the desire in her eyes—the same desire that flowed molten through him even now. Did it burn like fire through her veins—as it did his? He reached out to trace a fiery path, drawing a fingertip over her collarbone, along the smooth and shimmering nape of her neck. He lifted her chin and forced her to confront him, herself and the truth.

'Something else entirely,' was all she said.

The darkness inside of him rejoiced. She was caught—pressed up against the cold iron bars at her back. Jack's erection bulged hot and leaden between them, and he suffered a brief, stabbing need to press it against her, to trap her between hot and cold, hard and harder. Yet he didn't do it. Not yet.

Logic and reason put forth one last try, tossing a fleeting image of Batiste at his mind's eye. Jack ignored it. He'd gone beyond the reach of logic, into a place where pure emotion and hot, liquid lust held sway. Batiste could go to hell. Jack had given himself over to animal need and he revelled in it, sucking in the clean scent of her, gazing with wonder at the flushed expectation on her lovely face.

Then his eye fixed on her mouth. She stared back. That gorgeous, plump lower lip beckoned. As if she knew what it would do to him, she caught it suddenly between her teeth. The startling contrast of soft lush pink and hard white enamel made him want to howl. And then, ever so slowly, her bottom lip slid free, and the tip of her hot tongue traced a soft, wet trail along it.

His heart thumped. His cock surged. He slid his fingers into her curls of red-gold, cradled the back of her head for one long, tender second, and then let go to grasp the bars on either side of her. Pain flashed in his arm, but she made no protest, and only anticipation showed on her face. Jack slipped loose from the last vestige of reason and control, leaned in and branded her with his hot, searing kiss.

Honesty. That's what Jack gave her with his wild, insistent mouth. It was not what he'd set out to do. Lily had seen the calculation in his eye when he took his first step towards her. But she'd seen it disappear, too. Driven further away as he grew physically closer, supplanted by longing, and need and pure, undiluted want.

Almost from the first moment they met, Lily had asked, pestered, demanded that he come out of hiding and show her his true self. Now at last he'd taken the first step and opened a crack in the protective barriers around him. Her arms crept up, across the expanse of his chest and over his shoulders, locking behind his neck and pulling him close. No matter what he said, and despite his unreasonable request, she knew she had an obligation, a responsibility to meet him halfway.

He deepened the kiss, tempting and coaxing with lips and tongue and mouth, while a cascade of voices clamoured an alarm in her head. They threw accusations at her, ugly words like *immoral* and *shame* and *sin*.

She ignored them. This entire trip to London, she realised, had truly been about shutting out other voices and distractions, and learning to hear her own.

So she listened. At first she could only hear the clear and happy note that was born of his kiss. *Jack*, it hummed. *Jack, Jack, Jack.* But she forced herself to concentrate further. And what she heard was music, learning and debate. Camaraderie and intercourse with other people with similar interests. And a great clamouring for *more*. More of all of that, but above all, more of Jack Alden.

Joy erupted within her, stretching and growing until she had to give it voice. She moaned her approval and happiness and relief. And he answered in kind, emanating a low, appreciative rumble that originated in the back of his throat, but somehow ended up pooling hot and deep in her belly. Neither of them could deny the reality and the truth of this moment, just the two of them coming together with nothing else between.

Their kiss changed in the moment when her lips parted and her mouth opened under his. Suddenly he was inside, and the hot, slick slide of his tongue made her wild with need. Passion poured out of him and into her. She took it, honoured by the enormity of his gift, and gave it back to him twice over.

Slowly he coached her, taught her tongue how to play. An eager student, she met him thrust for thrust and pressed herself closer against him. His hands came off the bars and settled into the curve of her neck and shoulder, steadying her while he kissed her with long and languid strokes.

He drew back a fraction and Lily gasped, her breath coming fast and rough. It nearly ceased altogether when he buried his face in the curve of her throat. Her pulse tripped and pounded against him as he made his way down her throat with alternate hard, biting nips and soft, teasing kisses.

But honesty is a rare and fragile thing, and Lily should not have expected Jack's first foray into the light to be a lengthy one. He gradually slowed and stilled, until they stood clasped unmoving in each other's arms, his face still buried in the crook of her neck and her cheek pressed hard against his shoulder.

He was the first to disengage. Their hot breath mingled as their gazes met. His chest heaved as desire and need faded.

Lily knew how difficult this must be for him, and yet she had not expected to see regret loom so quickly, nor so strongly that it almost resembled despair. She shook her head. 'Jack, don't,' she whispered.

But the breach was repaired and he had already retreated behind his walls and into safety. His head was shaking, too, in constant small movements that nevertheless signalled a large degree of denial.

'No,' he said. 'This isn't right. It isn't *me*.'

'Jack...'

'No! I'm sorry—you ask for something I just don't have in me to give.' His brow furrowed, his lips compressed. 'All I want is to speak with your cousin. I'll do everything in my power to help him, I swear. If you hear from him, tell him that.'

He spun on his heel and walked away.

Lily could not bear to watch him go. She turned and gazed through the gate once more. For the first time in a long time, she felt she truly knew what she wanted. And it was not the iron bars in front of her blocking her path to good fortune.

Chapter Seven

Jack did not wait for the gathering to officially end. He took a terse leave of his mother, a more polite one of his host, and then he traded a spot in the landau next to Lily for Keller's mount. Within thirty minutes he was on his way back to London, cursing himself for an uncontrolled idiot and Lily Beecham for a damnably tempting vixen.

Why? He pondered his ridiculous dilemma as the miles passed. Why did the one time he *needed* to maintain his usual calm and rational focus become the one time he found it impossible to do so? The thought of how badly he'd botched nearly every moment with Lily Beecham sickened him.

He needed to think. Traffic entering London forced him to slow his pace and he cursed under his breath. He longed for the peace and serenity of his rooms. He would refocus, forget the taste of her, the incredible feel of her under his hands, and try to figure out what the hell his next move should be.

Fractious fate intervened, however. When Jack finally made his way home, he sprinted up the stairs—and froze at the sight of his door standing partially open. Wariness, confusion, and finally white-hot anger blossomed in his chest. Silent, he crept forwards. Tense, on alert for any sound or movement from within, he eased the door open. Nothing stirred. Amidst a rising, ever-more-familiar rush of rage, he stepped inside.

Whoever the intruders had been, they'd done a thorough job of it. Every drawer, book, stack of papers, even the clothes in his wardrobe had been torn apart and tossed asunder. Speechless, he stood in the midst of the devastation.

What in hell was this all about? He couldn't explain this ransacking of his rooms, any more than he could stem his rising tide of temper.

Already weakened by his encounter with Lily Beecham, surrounded by the wreckage of his life, discipline stood not a chance. Jack reached down to pick up a book, sorely tempted to throw it against the wall himself. A whisper of a sound outside gave him pause.

He waited. It came again. The steady, slow sound resolved itself into a set of footsteps on the stairs and only served to fuel his fury. He sunk into a crouch and let it wash over him. Rational thought ceased and blind, pure instinct took hold.

His brain fought back, trying desperately to send the message that something about the approaching threat rang peculiar. But Jack was in thrall to his jangled nerves. The enemy approached, stood just beyond the still-open doorway, set a cautious step over the threshold.

And at his next rational thought, Jack discovered he held a man pressed to the wall. His uninjured forearm pressed tight and cruel into the man's throat, even as he desperately wished for his knife.

'*Effendi.*' The soft voice in his ear cut through the angry red haze. 'I do not think you wish to be doing this.'

Startled, Jack glanced to his right. That accent, the silent approach, it could only be… 'Aswan?' He looked back, then, to the man he'd pinned. He stepped abruptly away. 'Oh, God. Eli!'

'Aye,' the old sailor-turned-groom grunted, rubbing his throat. 'And I'll thank ye for leaving my head attached. Bad enough that I'll be crossin' to the other side without my leg. I don't think the good Lord'll be so understanding, should I lose my head as well.'

'I'm sorry.' He turned to Aswan. 'But what the hell are you doing here?' Jack had to admit, he'd felt a surge of satisfaction at the sight of them. These two had been as deeply embroiled in Trey and Mervyn's search for the Lost Jewel as he had. Jack knew all too well just what this enigmatic Egyptian and peg-legged former sea captain were capable of.

'There's news.' Eli glanced about at the mess. 'Though I can see we left it a bit too late.'

'What in blazes is going on? Is Trey with you?' Jack had jerked suddenly to attention. 'And who the hell is looking after Chione and Mervyn and the children?'

'Treyford watches over the family. The slave-taker is still abroad,' Aswan said. 'But still he holds sway over many evil men in this country.'

'Aye, Mervyn's offices in Bristol and Portsmouth have both been broken into, and both on the same day, it looks like.' Eli tossed aside a pile of jumbled shirts and settled himself into a chair. 'I been stayin' in Wapping, but when I heard, we went up to Mayfair to find the town house looking just like this. We came straight over to warn ye to be on the lookout for trouble.'

Jack laughed bitterly, but not for long. 'Portsmouth and Bristol both?' he'd asked. 'And a synchronised effort? That's significant manpower.'

'It's clear enough now that Batiste is still after the Lost Jewel. Trey cannot hide the fact that he is preparing for a large expedition. He thinks word has leaked to Batiste and that's why he's searching the offices.' Eli glanced about. 'I s'pose it's why he'd do your rooms. The bastard wants to know jest where Trey's headin'—and he's thinkin' ye might know.'

Aswan spoke up. 'This man has a demon in him. He will not stop until he has what he wants.'

The three of them stared at each other in silence. They all knew what Batiste was after did not really exist—and that he would never be convinced of that truth.

'We've got to get our hands on him,' Jack breathed. 'He'll always be there, otherwise. Hanging in the background, waiting for his chance.'

'Trey's working on it. He says as you're to be careful. He feels bad enough about the trouble he's caused ye.' Eli exchanged glances with the Egyptian and they both headed for the door. 'You concentrate on finding Beecham. We'll uncover what we can about this mess.' He gestured. 'We'll be back to fill ye in before long.'

Dismayed, Jack watched his unlikely allies disappear. He hadn't the heart to call them back and tell them how badly he'd bungled his search for Matthew Beecham. His anger returned as he stared at the chaos of his rooms. But this time his brain remained engaged. Frantically he began to rifle through the mess, searching for older, sturdier clothing.

There was more than one way to skin a cat, his mother had always told him. Surely there must also be more than one way to catch a scoundrel like Batiste.

Thunk. The tankard hit the table hard, sloshing a wave of dark ale over the brim.

'Ye'll need to be drinkin' a mite more, if ye'll be taking up the table for the whole of the night,' the bleary-eyed barman grunted.

'I'll order the whole damned place a round when the man you spoke of shows up,' Jack shot back.

The tapster shrugged and wiped the spill with his stained and dirty apron. 'Told ye—I'm no man's keeper. The sod'll show up, or he won't. Plenty of other pubs to find 'is grog in, ain't there?'

God knew that was the truth, and it felt as if Jack had been in nearly every squalid dockside tavern and low riverside inn in London over the last few nights. 'I'll wait just the same,' he replied and slid a coin across the scarred wood of the table.

The barman eyed the gold, then Jack for a long moment. Finally he scooped up the money, turned and pushed his way back through the low-hung smoke to the tap.

Jack settled in to nurse another pint. The Water Horse might be the seediest, most disreputable pub on the river, but it was the only one that held a promise of a lead to Batiste.

Of all the sailors, dockyard labourers, whores and wharf rats Jack had questioned over the last few days, only the tapster here had flinched at Batiste's name. A very large purse had bought him the information that one of Batiste's former crew sometimes drank here.

It was a long shot at best, a fast route to a watery grave at worst. Yet what was the alternative? Pestering Lily Beecham until she heard from her cousin again? Torturing them both and allowing her to goad him into forgetting himself again? He'd rather spend a thousand nights in this sinkhole.

Jack took a drink of the warm ale and grimaced. He'd need an ocean of the stuff to drown his frustration with that girl. Her image hovered in his head, beautiful and lovely and all too tempting. He fought to ignore it, to forget the mad embrace they had shared in Bradington's gardens. Even the thought of her stirred the emotional turmoil he fought so hard to control.

And perhaps at last he'd come to the real reason he sat at the Horse again tonight. Here he had no attention or emotional energy to spare. Here he had no choice but to focus on his surroundings, on getting the information he sought and on getting himself out alive.

As the hour grew later the likelihood of the latter began to come into doubt. All manner of transactions took place around him, both above board, and by the furtive look of some of the participants, below. The crowd ebbed and flowed like the tide, but through it all someone besides Jack remained constant.

A high-backed booth flanked the door, and two men occupied it most of the night. A massive bull of a man, whose short dingy blond hair peeked from beneath a seaman's cap, sat silent and watchful with a smaller, swarthier man. They were not drinking either, Jack noted, but the tapster didn't stir himself to chide them. Not once did Jack see a word spoken between them, but as the taproom grew emptier, the smaller man began to flick an occasional, tell-tale glance his way.

He rose. Better to take his chances in the open than to risk events coming to a head here, where those two might have allies and Jack certainly did not.

He left the pub and strode quickly out into Flow Alley. The fog hung thick and rife with the stench of the river. It swirled and clung to him, making him feel as if he had to swim through it instead of walk.

A lamp hanging outside a pub cast an eerie pool of wavering light as he passed. From the mist floated an occasional snatch of disembodied conver-sation. It was not drunken revelry or ribald negotiations he strained to hear, but it was not until he reached the wide, empty intersection with Great Hermitage Street that he caught a hint of it—the faint echo of a footstep on cobblestones.

Jack ducked instantly into the doorway of a chandler's shop. If luck was with him, then whoever it was behind him would walk right on by. If it was not, then at least his back was covered.

Much as he'd expected—Lady Luck had abandoned him. First one figure emerged from out of the gloom, then another. The men from the Water Horse.

Jack drew his knife. Nobody spoke. The shorter man hung back, the larger pulled a stout cudgel from his bulky seaman's sweater and advanced with a menacing stride.

'Are you here at Batiste's bidding?' asked Jack.

The smaller man spat on to the rough stones of the street. 'Questions like that is what got ye into this mess.'

'I just meant to ask if you knew what sort of man you were taking orders from,' Jack said, never taking his eyes off of the big lout.

'The sort with gold in his pockets,' snickered the first man. 'And before ye ask, no, I don't care how he come by it—as long as he's forkin' over my share.' He thrust his chin towards Jack. 'Do it, Post.'

The big sailor moved in. Jack braced himself and

waited…waited…until the cudgel swung at him in a potentially devastating blow. Quickly he jumped forwards, thrusting his knife, point up and aiming for the vulnerable juncture under the man's arm.

But the goliath possessed surprisingly swift reflexes. He shifted his aim and blocked the driving thrust of the knife with the cudgel. The point buried itself in the rough wood. With a grin and a sudden, practised jerk, he yanked the blade right from Jack's grip.

His gut twisting, Jack knew he was finished. But he'd be damned if he went down without a fight. He ducked low and aimed a powerful blow right into that massive midsection.

He swore his wrist cracked. His fingers grew numb. But the giant just grinned. He reached for Jack. Those thick fingers closed around his neckcloth—and suddenly the great ham-hand spasmed open.

Jack looked up into the broad face so close to his. He met a pair of bulging eyes and flinched at the sight of a mouth wide open in a wordless grunt of pain. From this vantage point, the reason for his silence was clear. Some time, somewhere in this man's violent past, his tongue had been cut out.

Jack strained, trying to slide out from against the door as the brute turned half-away, reaching behind him. His gaze following, Jack saw the hilt of a knife protruding from the man's meaty thigh.

The giant grasped the knife. With a thick grunt, he pulled it free. Jack acted instantly, kicking the blade out of the oaf's hand. Never too proud to take advantage of an opponent's misfortune, Jack aimed another hard kick at his wounded limb. As the leg began to buckle, he reached up and, yanking hard, pulled his knife free from the cudgel. In a flash, he had it at the man's throat. The point pricked, drawing blood, before his opponent realised his predicament.

The giant froze. Jack looked over at his companion. 'Back away,' he snarled. 'I'll cut his throat if I have to.'

A curious, regular tapping sounded out of the mist. Jack tensed, waiting to see what new threat would emerge. Someone had thrown that knife. But which combatant had it been meant for?

His mouth dropped and a wave of surprise and relief swept over him as the fog gave up another figure, wiry, grizzled and wearing an elaborately carved peg below one knee.

'Eli!' Jack grinned. 'You're like a bad penny, always turning up where you're least expected.'

The diminutive groom brandished another wickedly long knife. 'Fun's over for tonight, mates,' he said.

The swarthy man let out an ugly laugh. 'Says you.' He gestured to his partner. 'Kill 'em bo—' His sentence ended abruptly as his legs flew out from beneath him. He flailed briefly and hit the cobblestones hard. In a second's time, the dark-skinned man in a turban kneeled over him and rested a pistol nonchalantly against his chest.

'Good evening to you, Aswan.' This time a dose of humiliation mixed with Jack's relief. How many times would the Egyptian have to snatch him from the jaws of death?

'The pair of ye got nowhere to go, 'cept to hell,' Eli told the villains with a nod. He gestured for Aswan to release his captive. 'Unless you're in a hurry to get there, get up and off wi' ye both.'

'Aye, and you keep your friend where he belongs,' snarled the small man. 'If we see him again we won't be giving him his chance—it'll be a knife in the back from out of the dark.' He glared at Jack. 'Understand? Keep to your own lot, bookworm.'

The pair faded into the fog.

'Come on.' Eli clapped Jack on the shoulder. 'This damp is makin' me leg ache.'

The three of them walked to Leman Street, where they hailed a hackney and had it convey them to a still-open coffee house in the Strand.

The place was empty. The shopkeeper had thrown the chairs up on the tables to sweep, but he was thrilled to stir up a cheery fire and arrange three of his best seats in front of it. He bustled off to fetch coffee and Eli groaned as he settled in and rubbed his leg. 'Well, which is it, man?' he asked Jack.

'Which is what?' Jack gazed, puzzled, from one of his rescuers to the other.

The groom exchanged a glance with the Egyptian. 'We told ye we'd deal with this lot. And then we hear tell of a Mayfair toff askin' questions all over the riverside.' He shrugged. 'A man don't get hisself into a situation like that unless he's got either a death wish or woman trouble. So which is it?'

Jack groaned and hung his head in his hands.

'Woman trouble.' Eli sighed.

Jack peered up at the pair of them. 'Well, I suppose I should thank you, at any rate.' He grimaced. 'What do you hear from Devonshire?'

'We heard from Trey today. He's got everything well in hand.'

'Well in hand?' Jack scoffed. 'Batiste's got his fingers in every pie from here to there and Trey's got it well in hand?'

'What I want to know,' Eli demanded, 'is why you were at the Horse tonight.'

Jack explained, but Eli just shook his head. 'It's more likely that tapster's in league with Batiste's men. He probably lured you there and tipped them off.'

'Well, I had to take the chance, didn't I?'

The coffee came then, and Eli sighed as he

wrapped his hands around his hot cup. Aswan glanced at his mug with distaste.

'*Effendi*, why do you feel as if you must take this chance?' the Egyptian asked.

Jack stared blankly. 'You just said it, Aswan. Batiste is a dangerous man.' He glanced around at the empty room, but still lowered his voice to a whisper. 'Chione is your family. Trey and the rest will be soon enough. Can you stomach the thought of him out there, hovering, just waiting for his chance to hurt them? They deserve to live their lives free, without fear and without a constant nagging threat in the background.'

'Batiste's more'n dangerous. He's obsessed, I'd say,' Eli replied. 'Treyford wants him taken jest as bad as ye. He's not above throwin' his title around, neither. Aswan says as how they've had the Navy in Devonshire, and the Foreign Office, too. Even had a couple of Americans in.' He took a long swallow and grinned in satisfaction. 'Damned good coffee here.'

'Treyford sends a message. He has a favour to ask of you,' Aswan said abruptly. 'He says you have done well with your cors—corres—?' He looked to Eli for help.

'Correspondence. Damned good idea, that. But he's got someone he'd like you to talk to, as well.'

'Who is it?'

'Broken-down seaman, as used to sail with Batiste.'

'Yes, I've heard that one before.' Jack grinned.

'No, this one should be no threat. Mervyn's had word of him. Name o' Crump. He's poorly and been set up in the new Seamen's Hospital. Mervyn says as it's unlikely he'll be coming out.'

'Why me? Wouldn't he be more likely to speak with you, someone who knows the life he's led?'

'No.' Eli shook his head. 'He'll know of my relationship with Mervyn and there's a risk he won't want anything to do with me. Crump crewed with Batiste when the bastard still worked for Latimer Shipping. He went with Batiste when the pair o' them fought and Batiste struck out on his own. He'll know much about where Batiste hides his head when the chips start to stack against him.'

'But why would he want to share any of it with me?'

Eli looked him over, considering. 'Well, Trey says as how yer brother has a title, too—mayhap he wouldn't mind using it in the name of a good cause?'

'Oh, well, I'm sure he would not mind, if I asked him.'

'That ain't all, though. Trey says ye'll have been mucking about a bit with some Evangelicals?'

Jack started. 'Where the hell does Trey get his information? If I didn't know him better, I'd suspect him to be near as bad as Batiste.'

Eli laughed. 'Treyford does have his ways. And when ye pair him with Mervyn...' he shuddered '...I don't think there's nothing the two o' them couldn't tackle.'

'And just how do they think to use my Evangelical connections?'

'Crump's converted. Mervyn thinks he left Batiste when he saw how bad things get on a slave ship. If you could let on that you were of a like mind...'

'I have friends among the Evangelicals. I'm not one myself,' Jack said.

'Crump don't need to know that, do he?'

Jack sighed. He thought he'd rather take his chances back in the East End, rather than lie to a sickly old sailor. But he'd said he'd do anything that would lead to Batiste's capture, hadn't he? An image flashed in his head—Lily, her lips red and flushed full from his kiss, an unuttered plea in her eyes. Immediately, he pushed it away.

'I suppose not,' he said.

'Would you be needin' anything else, miss?'

Lady Dayle's footman did not look at Lily as he spoke. His gaze was very firmly locked on the pump house at the centre of the garden in

Berkeley Square, where several giggling maids had gathered.

'No, thank you, Thomas, I am fine here,' she said, settling on to a bench situated under a shady plane tree. She'd come seeking solitude, and would not have brought the footman at all, had Lady Dayle not insisted. 'I shall call you when I am ready to return.'

'Very good, miss.' He turned away with an eager step, but then paused a moment, looking back. 'You're sure you're all right, Miss Lily?'

She was touched by the concern in his tone. 'I'm fine, Thomas.' She smiled. 'But thank you for asking.'

He pivoted back to face her again, but kept a respectful distance. 'I don't mean to overstep, miss, but I hope you don't mind if I tell you: I think you've adjusted—to London and the fancy, I mean—right well.'

'Thank you,' she said again.

'It's just that I was new here, too,' he said earnestly, 'a few years back. I think your world, your old one, I mean, it was…different?'

'Oh, yes, vastly different,' she agreed with fervour.

'Mine, too. I was green as grass—and I made mistakes, some real whoppers. But I got used to it, and you will, too, and, like I said, I think you're doing fine.'

'Thank you,' she whispered past the growing

tightness in her throat. Kindness from such an un-expected source cheered her—and made her realise how unskilled she must be at hiding her emotions.

'I shall wait for your summons, then,' he said, but his cheery grin negated the formality of his words.

Lily nodded and watched him join the knot of maidservants at the centre of the square. They welcomed him with enthusiasm and more than one flirtatious smile. Clearly Thomas had made a suc-cessful transition from his old world to his new.

She sighed, fearing her own task would turn out to be more difficult. For she did not seek to leave one sphere for another. She meant to somehow meld two very different worlds into a new one. All she wanted was to carve out a place of her own, a space of comfort and acceptance, where she could thrive and grow. But she had begun to fear that Jack Alden was right, she was asking for more than *anyone* was ready to give.

No. Jack was a spike in her heart and every thought of him ripped her open a little wider. She'd spent the last days in a restless state of anxiety and indecision. Over and over she played in her mind's eye those exciting moments, that soul-searing kiss. At every private moment, she relived the passion and the nearly magical sense of spiralling desire. She'd touched his lips, his body, his heart and mind.

And he had turned on his heel and coldly abandoned her.

Incredibly, Lily had understood. Not only did they come from different worlds, but different perspectives as well. She felt more than a little torn herself, and when she was not reliving the excitement of their embrace, then she was wavering helplessly between agony and joy. Joy because she'd reached him. She'd peeked inside him and seen that this indefinable pull, this attraction between them, was real and it ran deep. Agony because *he* had also asked too much of *her*.

She could never believe that Matthew had gotten mixed up with slavers. It was not possible, as anyone acquainted with him would know. He could not be capable of such cruelty.

Jack was a scholar. His brother did have political ties, and had seen more than a little success. But she knew from Lady Dayle that none of it had come in the area of diplomacy. According to the viscountess, Viscount Dayle's area of interest lay in economics and reform. He'd never, to his mother's knowledge, had dealings with the Foreign Office or contact with anyone in the American government.

Lily did not doubt Jack's wish to help Matthew. But she very much doubted his ability to do so. He wanted to see this Batiste captured so badly that he'd turned a blind eye to the likely consequences to her cousin. Even the suspicion of such a thing could ruin him.

She glanced up, wanting to make certain that Thomas was fully occupied. And sent up a prayer of thanks. Another man in livery had joined the group and Thomas had entered a full-scale war for feminine attention. While every eye locked on to the thrilling sight of a grown man in full livery and powder scaling the mounted statue of George III, Lily slipped away towards a more private corner of the garden.

The paths here, like the garden itself, lay in an elliptical shape. It did not take long to turn a curve and find herself alone. She breathed deep. This morning a parcel of forwarded mail had arrived from home. And in it had been a letter—slanted across with Matthew's familiar bold handwriting.

Lily's hand shook as she reached into her pocket to pull it out. Quickly, furtively, she broke the seal.

Dearest Lily,

In that moment, she knew the tidings could not be good. Every other letter she'd ever had from Matthew had been addressed irreverently to Lilikins, his childhood name for her. Her eyes filled, making it difficult to read on.

*I don't know what you might have heard, if
indeed you would have heard anything at all.
But I want you to know—a good reason lies
behind my actions. I cannot explain now, but all
will be clear when next we meet.*

*I've only just left Le Havre, and I know not just
where we will go. Please don't believe the worst
of me. I will contact you again when I can.*

Yours,

Matthew

Lily raised shaking fingers to her mouth. Jack
could not have been right. She would not believe it.

But wait a moment. His story coloured her interpretation. This told her nothing, really. She braced
herself against a tree, sucking in air. She could not
tell Jack about this letter.

Would he understand? She suffered a pang of
doubt. The intensity with which he spoke of the
danger to his friends suggested otherwise. She
drew away from the tree, folded the note and
stood upright. She would make him understand.
Surely he was not so insulated behind his walls
of intellect and scorn that he could not understand loyalty.

Suddenly a voice rang behind her, calling her

name. 'Thomas?' she answered. 'Here, I'm just here, around the bend!'

It was not Thomas who came hurrying down the path, though.

'Fisher?' What was Lady Dayle's staid butler doing in the garden square?

'Miss? Oh, Miss Beecham, thank goodness. Please, come! You are needed in Bruton Street!'

Lily's heart stopped. She reached out and clutched the man's arm. 'Lady Dayle?' she breathed.

'Is in urgent need of you, miss. No, she's well, in the physical sense,' he rushed to reassure her. 'But more than that I cannot say. Just please, come with me, won't you?'

'Of course!' The situation must be dire indeed, if Fisher had come for her himself. Lily lifted her skirts and hurried after him, her own troubles forgotten. Fortunately, Bruton Street lay just outside the Square. In a matter of minutes they'd reached the town house. She followed the butler across the front hall and into the family parlour.

The viscountess stood inside, bent over her desk, scribbling furiously. Her hair hung in filthy strands; her hands, arms and the front of her gown were covered in thick, black soot.

'Martha, you go up to the attics; Susan, you can take care of the still room.' She clipped out orders like a military sergeant to a cluster of frightened maids. 'Linens, towels, soap, ointments... Oh, lord—' she coughed violently, then sagged suddenly and moaned aloud '—I cannot think!'

'My lady!' gasped Lily. 'What has happened?'

'Oh, Lily!' Lady Dayle looked up. Her face crumpled, and Lily saw a large red scrape across her forehead. 'You can't imagine—the most terrible thing!' Dirty tears began to track down her face. All the maids began to wail and the butler stepped forwards, wringing his hands.

But Lily was a country girl. She knew how to handle herself in a crisis. Her father's training kicked in and she crossed the room with a determined step. 'It's all right, my lady,' she said firmly. 'Out now, the rest of you!' she ordered. 'We will give the viscountess a moment to collect herself. You know what to do.' She paused a moment to gather her thoughts. 'Fisher, I think we'll need a tea tray in here,' she said. 'Send for his lordship, and gather as many of the staff as you can and ready them to send messages.' She waved the gawking footmen away from the door and shooed the maids out. The butler nodded, casting a look of profound thanks in her direction as he closed the door behind him.

As if the closed door were a signal, Lady Dayle sank into a chair and began to cough. The dry, hacking sound quickly deteriorated into heartrending sobs. Without a word, Lily enfolded her in a tight embrace and let her cry. She crooned softly and her mind raced while the viscountess cried herself out. When the storm had passed she took both of the dear lady's hands in her own and said, 'Tell me.'

'I'd been to that linen draper's in Long Acre, the one that had that roll of blocked dimity? I had it in mind to have it made into clothes for baby Maria.' The viscountess's voice was rough and strained as she spoke.

A soft knock on the door signalled the arrival of the tea. Lily took the tray from the butler and quickly poured, encouraging Lady Dayle to drink and go on with her story.

'It was a fire, of course.' The viscountess spoke more easily after she'd finished her first cup of tea. 'It began in an engraver's shop, but quickly spread to the orphanage next door. Traffic stopped. I was stuck in the carriage down the street, but I could see what was happening. The flames, and the heat.' A massive shudder tore through her. 'But the screams! I had to help!'

She looked up as if needing validation and Lily nodded encouragingly. 'You absolutely did! As would any person of feeling.'

'At least ten of the children are dead,' Lady Dayle said. Another sob broke through, but she got herself quickly back under control. 'As many are severely injured. Fifteen or so are frightened out of their wits and suddenly homeless.' A single tear welled up and over, the sight breaking Lily's heart. 'We have to do something, Lily. I can't bear it, otherwise.'

'Of course we will,' affirmed Lily. Her heart began to pound. A vision arose in her mind—a glorious image of two worlds uniting. 'And we won't have to do it alone. Just think!' She smiled at the staring viscountess. 'Between your connections and mine, my lady, we will raise an army to help your orphans.'

Chapter Eight

It was only a few days later that Mrs Bartleigh's carriage splashed round the corner at Devonshire House, though so much had happened that it felt like many more. Rain spattered down from a desolate sky and back up as it was thrown from the rumbling wheels. Lily sat back away from the window and smiled gently at her friend. 'What a dreary day!'

The elder lady nodded her agreement. Lily feared she was too tired for small talk.

'I'm afraid that we've done too much. We're already on Berkeley Street now, though. Soon enough you can drop me off and go home for a nice, long nap.'

'Mmm, that does sound nice,' Mrs Bartleigh said wistfully.

'Mr Bartleigh will be furious if you overdo things.' She reached over and tried to rub some warmth into the older woman's cold hand. 'I do so much appreciate all of your help. We've made a good start. And just think—if Minerva Dawson's ball goes as it should, we may well be able to build the orphans a bigger and better home than they had before.'

Mrs Bartleigh heaved a sigh. 'I pray it will be so.'

Lily pursed her lips and reached for the right words to say. 'Perhaps, ma'am, it would be better if you were to forgo Miss Dawson's ball?' She grinned to take some of the sting from her suggestion. 'It would not do for you to fall ill on my watch, for you know that Mother would never forgive me. She relies so heavily on your support at home.'

The serene smile that had soothed so many of Lily's anxieties over the years failed to do so now. 'I'm already ill, and well you know it, Lily Beecham. I'll ask the same of you that I have of my husband—let me do some good with the time I have remaining.'

Beyond words, Lily squeezed her hand again and merely nodded.

She sighed. So many people had worked so hard the last few days. She and the viscountess had worked nonstop to recruit those acquaintances of Lily's likely to lend a hand in an emergency and those of Lady Dayle's who might be convinced to do so. Together they had indeed raised an army, or at least an entire squadron of kind and generous people willing to help the group of poor children who'd lost their home.

Already they had seen the tragic dead laid to rest with proper ceremony, the severely injured accepted into beds in various foundling hospitals and the rest welcomed into temporary homes. Still, there was much to do—and Lily welcomed the workload. It kept her from dwelling on more disturbing issues, such as Mrs Bartleigh's failing health and the fact that her mother would soon be returning. But, most of all, it gave her precious minutes, sometimes even hours, in which she fixed her mind on something other than Jack Alden.

The carriage pulled up to the Dayle town home. Lily kissed her friend goodbye and allowed the footman to assist her down. She waved, unmindful of the drizzle, as her friend pulled away, but her mind had already gone right back where it did not need to be.

No one had heard from Jack Alden since the expedition to Chester House. She heaved a sigh as she headed in. She couldn't help but wonder if she had driven him into hiding behind his books once more.

Fisher opened the door. 'Good afternoon, miss. I hope your errands went well.'

'They did, thank you,' Lily said with a smile. She

handed him her bonnet and he in turn handed it over to a waiting footman. 'Several dozen lengths of the finest linen and softest flannel are being rolled into bandages as we speak, and eleven little girls have at last learned the lyrics of "The Well of St. Keyne".' She paused at the foot of the stairs. 'Lady Dayle and Miss Dawson went on to discuss arrangements with the musicians for the ball, Fisher. They should be arriving shortly.'

'I'll have Cook prepare a tray.'

'Thank you.' She turned to go, but stopped once more. 'Has his lordship arrived from Sevenoaks yet?'

'He has indeed, miss. The viscount is currently closeted in the library with Mr Alden.'

Lily froze. Here? Jack was here?

'I shall announce you, should you like to join them,' Fisher continued, moving towards the library door, just a few steps into the hall.

'No!' She didn't want to face Jack for the first time since their…encounter…in company with his all-too-observant brother. 'I mean, perhaps not just yet. I really should…' She did not stay to finish the sentence, but started quickly up the stairs.

Too late. The library door opened and Jack came backing into the hall. 'Fisher,' he called softly as he turned towards the foyer, 'my brother has fallen asleep over his brandy. I do believe the rigours of fatherhood are more strenuous than those of government.' He stopped as he reached the entry hall and caught sight of her on the stairs.

'Oh,' he said lamely. 'Hello, Lily.'

'Mr Alden.' His gaze shone far more intent than his tone. She glanced away from it, trying to slow the sudden hitch in her breathing, and hide the skittering beat of her pulse.

Fisher looked from one to the other. 'I shall just fetch a blanket to throw over his lordship.' He retreated to safety behind the green baize door.

Lily followed suit and started again for the safety of her chamber, but she was stalled as Jack awkwardly cleared his throat.

'Er, how have you been, then?' he asked.

'Fine, Jack. And you?' Perversely, much as she wished to speak with him, she was not about to make it easy for him.

He did not answer, just watched her with an uneasy sort of yearning. Or perhaps it was only solemnity in his expression, and she was endowing him with her own mental tumult. She hoped not. She would hate to be the only one in an emotional uproar.

'I heard that Charles was due back, and thought I'd ask him to accompany me...' he paused '...on an errand.'

'I'm sorry that he is too tired to be of use to you, then.' She hated this awkwardness. And the letter hidden away upstairs weighed heavy on her mind. All she wanted was to get away, lock herself in her room before she did something foolish—like blurt out Matthew's last known location or, worse, barrel down the stairs and beg him to stir to life once more the embers of desire he'd left smouldering inside her.

Suddenly his features hardened. 'Charles told me all about the fire and the work you and my mother have been doing,' he said.

'Yes,' she managed to reply with satisfaction. 'We've made a remarkable amount of progress in just a short while.' She paused. 'We've wondered where you've been.'

He shifted on his feet. 'I've had a…special project to attend to. I'm sorry I was not here to help, but I hear that Sophie has sent along a cartload of supplies for you to use with the orphans.'

She looked up at that. 'How kind of her. We shall certainly put them to good use.'

The entryway grew silent again. From the back of the house came the clang of a pan and a muffled shout of laughter. Lily could bear the tension no more. She turned to go.

Jack put his foot on the first step and called up, 'Charles also told me about the scheme you've cooked up for Miss Dawson's engagement ball. Some sort of performance?'

'Yes, we thought we would involve some of the orphans. They would like the chance to thank all of those who have been so generous.'

'Not to mention that seeing the pitiful victims firsthand might stir others to help with their plight?' he said with sarcasm.

Lily shrugged. 'If it does, the help will not go amiss. We've still much work to do. It was Minerva's idea. Apparently she recalled that Lady Ashford and her daughter did something along those lines a few years back.'

'I thought Charles counselled against it?'

'Yes, he did. But I confess, I don't understand his objections.'

'Charles has a great deal of experience in dealing with society's fickleness. If he doesn't feel it will go over well, then you should heed him.'

Lily hardly knew what to say to that. She spread her arms in a helpless gesture. 'It really is not my decision to make.'

'I hope you will at least try to talk some sense into them.' He watched her with half-closed eyes, yet still she could see the trouble glittering there. 'I recall the event you mentioned very well,' he continued. 'Sophie suffered a devastating setback at that charity ball. It was an extremely painful time.' He paused, and then said awkwardly, 'I would not wish the same to happen to you.'

She was touched and more than a little encouraged. 'But from what I understand, what we have planned is a very different matter altogether. Much more subdued and discreet. So you see, there is no need to worry.'

'I can't help but worry.' His voice had gone low and urgent again and he took another step up towards her. Briefly, she considered descending to meet him, but then the import of his words began to sink in.

'I've only just had a rather devastating lesson myself on straying outside my own sphere.' He gave a bitter laugh. 'And then Charles tells me that you have a plan elevating it to an art form. He says that besides performing orphans, you intend to invite moralists and reformers to mix with the *beau monde*?'

'Why do you speak with such scorn?' Lily asked, exasperated. 'Are you dreaming up more obstacles to throw in our path?'

'I don't have to—you insist on creating your own.' Frustration throbbed in his voice as well. 'Have any of you truly thought this out? I don't think you've yet been exposed to the sort of people who will attend this ball. I know the *ton*, Lily. I've been subjected to them for years. Most of the people there will be shallow, vapid, self-absorbed fools. Is this who you want to introduce your friends to?'

She raised her chin. 'Why don't you try for a little optimism, Jack? Perhaps the two groups will have something to teach each other.'

He snorted. 'Do you comfort yourself that it is only your Evangelical friends, then, that you have invited? Lily, you are a lovely, tolerant and open-minded girl, and even you confessed to feeling alienated in society. How will the more conservative—the Mr Cooperages—of your set react? He and others like him view the aristocracy either as a necessary evil or as a corrupt assemblage waiting to be led to the righteous path. In turn the *ton* will look at them as hopeless provincials or utter bores. It's a recipe for disaster.'

Disappointment swamped her. Her spirits, already agitated, slid further down into dark depths. 'Your mother and Minerva and I—and so many other people as well—we have all been working day and night. We have brought people together to help these children and we've been forging new relationships as we've gone. There is nothing wrong with that! And yet you seem determined to wrench it all apart!' She gazed at him in despair. 'Why, Jack? Why must you always believe the worst of people?'

He drew back. 'I don't do any such thing.'

'You do. You create walls. You hold people at a distance. Why?' Tears welled in her eyes. 'You speak of not wanting to see me hurt, but I think there is something more selfish going on here. I think you are afraid that *I* will hurt *you*.' She had to stop a moment. 'I don't want to hurt you, Jack.'

He retreated to the bottom step. 'Don't be ridiculous. I don't know what you are talking about. I've never said anything to make you think so.'

'Yes, you most certainly have,' she said with heated anger. 'You've held me at arm's length and held yourself back as if I were poisonous. Oh, perhaps you have not said it with words. But you've told me so over and over again with your eyes and your body.' She gestured contemptuously to his position of retreat. 'You're doing it now.' She narrowed her eyes. 'But the worst came the other day. You kissed me, Jack, but you only did it to push me away.'

Lily turned her back on him, sending her skirts flaring. She gathered them up, and raced up the stairs and away from Jack's shocked reaction.

'Lily,' he said, and in his tone lived a wealth of sadness and regret.

They both jumped when the door opened and his mother and Minerva Dawson spilled in.

'Oh, my, the wind is picking up! What good is an umbrella when the rain insists on coming in sideways?' Lady Dayle asked no one in particular. 'Minerva, do come in and get dry. We'll have tea and perhaps the rain will have gone by the time we finish.'

Wrestling her soaking bonnet off, the viscountess caught sight of her son. 'Jack! We've been wondering where you've been!' She grasped her son by the shoulders and kissed him wetly on the cheek. 'You look worn to a frazzle. What's been keeping you so busy?'

'This and that, Mother,' he said and returned her embrace. If his answer was falsely jovial, the viscountess did not appear to notice. 'But I must be going. Charles is back, though, and sound asleep in the library.' He walked towards the front door without glancing up at Lily.

'Wait, dear. I haven't seen you in days. Don't rush off!'

'Apologies, but I must. I've got an important errand to run.'

'Will we see you at my engagement ball, Mr Alden?' Minerva asked. 'It's nearly upon us, now.'

This time he did cast a neutral glance at the top of the stairs. 'Miss Beecham was only just telling me about it. I wouldn't miss it, Miss Dawson, and let me take the opportunity now to wish you very happy.'

He bowed over Minerva's hand, kissed his mother once more and walked out.

'Well,' Lady Dayle breathed. 'To be young again.' She looked up at Lily. 'Whatever is Charles doing sleeping in the library?'

'I'm sorry, I have no idea, my lady. I've only just arrived myself.'

The viscountess gestured imperiously. 'Well, do come down and take some tea with us, my dear. I wish to hear all about your afternoon.'

Lily could think of no polite way to refuse. She descended the stairs yet again, tired and feeling foolishly like a child's plaything.

Minerva took her arm as she reached the bottom. 'Come, let's forget our cares for a bit. We've been so busy planning for the ball, we've scarce discussed what we'll wear!' She exchanged a significant glance with Lady Dayle. 'Mother has had my gown planned for ages, but, you know, we need to decide what we are going to do with you.'

With effort, Lily was able to keep her eyes from straying to the door Jack had just walked through. 'I would like to wear something special,' she said slowly. 'But I'm afraid I don't own a ballgown. And I've just been too busy to worry about it. Now, I suppose it's too late.'

Minerva nearly glowed with triumph. 'Not at all,

my dear, for Lady Dayle and I have made time to worry about it. We've been working with the *modiste* who altered your gowns.'

'We have something truly special ready for you, my dear—and I don't want to hear even a peep of protest out of you.' Lady Dayle's smile shone almost feral. 'The gentlemen—*tonnish* and Evangelical alike—are not going to know what's hit them!'

The sky above Jack's head hung heavy and grey as gunmetal. The Thames ran nearby, slate-coloured and sluggish as well. He blinked away the fine drizzle doing its best to diminish his vision and cut him off from the rest of the world. Even the pretty Greenwich gardens were reduced to a mere muddle of drab greens.

He hardly noticed. The weather only reflected his own bleak, inner landscape. The sharp repeat of Lily Beecham's harangue gnawed at him as he strode towards the river.

Hell, yes, he absolutely held people at a distance—and nearly every day he was convinced of the extreme wisdom of such a course. *Distance.* He even liked the sound of the word. A solid, secure word, and a perfectly sound principle on which to base the doctrine of one's life. Certainly it had served him long and well.

Walls, she'd said. And damned if she hadn't got that right, too. In fact, Jack thought it was safe to say that his walls were amongst his most cherished possessions. Right up there with his books and maps, and that rare note of approval from the Oxford don who had encouraged him in his studies of the ancients. Of course, there were a few people allowed into his inner sanctum, his family and even Trey and Chione, to some extent. But the rest of humanity he kept firmly on the outside, where he could observe them with interest and impunity.

Impunity? He stopped short. Damn Lily Beecham and her cursed perception to hell. By God, perhaps he was afraid to let people close. *Afraid?* He never thought of it in those exact terms, but still, admitting that Lily had been at least partly right did not change the prudence of it. The longer he considered the matter, the more convinced he became. Most people were thoughtless and self-absorbed at best, spiteful and malicious at worst. Then there were the truly deranged like Batiste. He was far better off keeping them all at a *distance*.

All of which begged an answer to the real question. Why the hell could he not keep Lily Beecham safely beyond his walls? Every time he turned around, metaphorically speaking, he ran smack up against her. Inside. In his way. On his heels. Always right there.

He stepped lightly down the stairs leading to the river. The marshes of the Isle of Dogs loomed out there, a greenish-brown blur in the mist. His eye fixed on the floating hulk of the HMS *Grampus*, the vessel that housed the newly founded Seamen's Hospital. As he drew near, he read the words painted on to the side: 'For Seamen of All Nations.'

A harried-looking man stepped forwards as Jack stepped across the gangplank. He appeared to relax slightly as he took in Jack's well-tailored appearance. 'Good morning,' he called as he made his way across the scrupulously clean deck. 'Can I help you with something?'

'I hope so,' Jack replied pleasantly. 'My name is Jack Alden,' he said, sketching a polite bow.

'David Arnott. I am the doctor here.'

'Then perhaps you can help me. I'm looking for someone. A former seaman by name of Crump.'

'Ah…' The doctor eyed him with a slightly arched brow. 'Would you be family?'

'No. I've had his name from a mutual friend. I'm just here for a visit—and to ask a few questions.'

Doctor Arnott looked him over carefully and said nothing.

Jack drew a deep breath. 'I've heard that the man is not likely…to set sail again. My visit just might offer him a little comfort.'

Still, the doctor paused. 'All right, then,' he said at last, 'but I don't want him upset.'

'I'll do my best.' He nodded as the man raised a brow in his direction. 'I give you my word.'

They went below deck. Here Jack could see that the normal fittings had been removed to make room for rows of beds. Most of them stood unmade and empty. Their footsteps echoed in off the close wooden walls.

'We are still recruiting staff and laying in supplies. Really, we are not yet ready to take on patients.' He shrugged. 'But we do not mean to turn away anybody if we don't have to, and Crump...' He gestured. 'Well, you'll see for yourself.'

All Jack could see was a small form huddled in the furthest bed, trembling violently. Even as he stared, another man pushed by them, carrying a large leather bladder, long as a man's torso. He took it straight to the shivering man in the bed.

'Here, now. Nice and warm,' he said gently as he pulled the covers back and tucked the bladder in quickly.

Crump, for Jack presumed it was he, curled gratefully around what must be a homemade warmer and gradually his trembling subsided.

'Now, by the time that's gone cold, I'll have the bed-warming pan nice and hot for you,' the caretaker said in a reassuring voice.

'Thank ye,' croaked his patient.

The man nodded at Jack and the doctor as he passed. Arnott waved Jack in, but he shot an all-too-clear warning look as he did.

As Jack approached the bed, the reason for the doctor's caution became clear. The man in the bed was old and emaciated beyond anything Jack had ever seen. Beyond what seemed capable of support-ing life, he would have guessed. But though the man's skin appeared to be as thin as paper over his bones and the tone of it shone a horrifying shade of greenish-yellow, still his eyes burned bright and in-telligent from the wreck of a face.

'Mister Crump?' Jack asked as he drew near.

The small man let loose with a wheeze of laughter. It quickly turned into a cough. 'B'ain't no mister, jest Crump. Who are ye?'

'My name is Jack Alden.'

The seaman shot him a skeletal grin. 'Neptune's eye, but I hope that ain't s'posed to mean anythin' to me. I been comfortin' myself that at least my mind's still shipshape. Be a shame to find out I was wrong now.'

Jack returned the grin. 'I'd say your mind is in good enough working order. We've not met before.'

'Ah.' The old sailor waved towards a chair sitting at the end of the row of beds. Jack pulled it over and sat close to Crump. He watched as the old man settled himself on his side, curled up around the warmer and eyed Jack steadily.

'Tropical fever,' he said conversationally. 'Been stalkin' me for years. Goin' to get me this time.'

'I sincerely hope not.' Jack strove for the same nonchalance.

'Wotch'er here for?' Crump said, suddenly abrupt.

'I'm learning what I can about the Evangelical branch of the Church of England: their accomplishments, their beliefs, their wish to reform society. I understand you are familiar with them?'

'Oh, aye.' His inquisitive gaze had gone shuttered.

Jack asked several innocuous questions until the seaman began to relax. Crump remained curt, however, until Jack began to ask him about the role of Evangelical women.

'Weel, now, I knows as how some folk dinna like to see a woman working for summat like abolition, but they's no denying the good they do. On t'other hand, look at Hannah More—fine, upstanding woman that she be—she's ruined her health working for Evangelical causes.' He shrugged. 'P'raps them as say that a woman b'ain't made for such things is right?'

'Perhaps.'

Crump chuckled, but it rapidly turned into a wheeze. He shook a moment with a hard cough, before he recovered himself. 'They can say all they like, but I don't see them Evangelical women givin' up the fight any time soon. Abolitionists will press on 'til slavery itself is outlawed, and womenfolk are a sight better 'bout confronting the evil in this world than us men.'

Jack sat, distracted by this train of thought, until the sharp edge of the seaman's voice cut into his reverie.

'Ye goin' to tell me wotch'er really here for?'

Jack met his gaze squarely. 'I truly am collecting such information. You've actually been quite helpful.' He paused and watched Crump closely. 'But I would also like to ask you a few questions about one of your former captains.'

'Which one?' The sailor's tone rang with suspicion.

'Batiste.'

Crump sighed and turned slightly away. 'Should ha' known that without asking.' He sat silent a moment. 'Why?'

'Why what?'

'Why do ye want to know anythin' about that devil?'

Jack thought carefully before he answered. 'He means to hurt someone I care about.'

Crump closed his eyes. 'That do sound like 'im.' He shifted position and, with his eyes still closed, said simply, 'Will ye tell me about 'em?'

'Them?' Jack asked.

'Those ye care about, as ye said.'

So Jack did. Sitting there in the chill, empty deck, with the sound of the river in his ears and the ship rocking slightly against the tidal pull, he talked. He told Crump about Trey, his daring friend who'd had adventures all over the world, but found his greatest treasure when he'd been reluctantly forced back home. He spoke of Chione, describing her tenacity and her commitment to keeping her family together against all odds. He spoke of Will and Olivia, the resilient children who never gave up the hope of getting their missing father back. He lost himself in the telling, but at the same time he felt a tightening around his chest at the thought of them all in danger.

Suddenly he realised that Crump's eyes were open and he sat watching him with canny intent.

'Tell me, what does she look like—this girl ye speak of?'

'She is beautiful, of course. What sort of tale would it be if she were not?' Jack answered with a smile. 'Actually, she is as lovely outside as she is inside. Long ebony hair, exotic skin and dark eyes with the most wonderfully thick lashes.'

'I knew it,' Crump whispered. 'Mervyn's girl. Isn't it? 'Tis Mervyn Latimer's granddaughter ye talk of?'

Jack hesitated—but he had to tell the truth. 'Yes,' he said, 'it is.'

''Tis Mervyn's family Batiste is going after?' His gaze was troubled.

'Yes,' answered Jack, and he fervently hoped he had not just ruined his chance of finding anything of use from the man.

'And is Mervyn Latimer still gone missing?'

'No—he is home. It turns out Batiste had him all those months he was lost—locked up in a slave hold of one of his ships.'

'God in his heaven,' breathed Crump. 'Batiste's finally gone stark, ravin' over.' The seaman looked stricken. 'Is he back to takin' up slaves, then?'

'Apparently so. Not in the same volume as before the trade was abolished, of course, but there are still those who wish to cling to the old ways.'

'Aye. So's I've told 'em all. There's still a battle to fight. It won't end 'til slavery is driven from the face o' the earth.'

'I fear you are right. And the battle is far from over for Mervyn's family as well. Batiste's men have only recently broken into the Latimer shipping offices, and Mervyn's home.' Jack paused. 'And my home as well.'

The seaman watched him with a shrewd eye. 'Ye'll be knowin' what he's after, then.'

'I do.' Jack leaned forwards and spoke low. 'And I can tell you unequivocally that he will never find it. The Pharaoh's Lost Jewel doesn't exist—not in the way that he thinks.'

For a moment, Crump's face burned with a bright curiosity. But then he shook his head as if to clear it. 'No, I don't want to know. I'll have answers to the biggest mystery soon enough, lad.' He lay back, looking exhausted.

'I can see you are tiring. I'm sorry.'

'Aye. Fever'll be next. It always comes on the heels o' the tremors.'

'I won't keep you long, Mr Crump, but I need to know where Batiste might be hiding. I thought you might know some of the likely places he would hole up in.' He let all the urgency he felt leak into his voice. 'He has to be stopped.'

'And ye think I'll turn on 'im, do ye?' Crump's voice was bitter.

'I hope you will. The man has caused so much suffering and pain. We must stop him before he can cause even more.'

Crump lay back and closed his eyes once more. He stayed still and quiet for so long that Jack began to wonder if the old sailor had fallen asleep. And then he wondered if the man would still be alive were he forced to come back tomorrow.

Jack nearly jumped out of his skin when Crump suddenly asked, 'Where was he seen last?'

'Gibraltar,' Jack answered, his chest suddenly filled with a fierce hope.

Silence reigned for a time again.

'Tazacorte,' Crump whispered eventually.

'Excuse me?' Jack leaned closer.

The seaman opened one eye. 'Ever been to Islas Canarias, lad?'

Jack shook his head.

'Go, then, do you get the chance. Each one o' them islands is a whole 'nuther world. Each different from t'other, but all beautiful.' He sighed. The other eye opened. 'They's Spanish, ye ken. Safe harbour if Batiste be running from the King's Navy.'

He sighed. 'Tazacorte—on the island of La Palma. Sheerest cliffs, then they suddenly open up to the sweetest little harbour. Not much, just a fishing harbour, with a village and a black sand beach. One long promenade filled with the prettiest girls this side o' the Atlantic.' His words trailed away and his eyes slid closed again, this time in remembrance, rather than exhaustion, Jack thought.

He shifted over from the chair to sit on the side of the man's bed and grasped his arm gently. 'Thank you, Mr Crump,' he said quietly.

The old man nodded. 'Oh, aye. Done a lot of things in this life I wisht I hadn't. Goin' to meet my maker soon enough—be as well to have a little more credit with 'im.'

Suddenly his arm lifted and his bony fingers gripped Jack with surprising strength. 'I give ye what ye needed, lad, and now I'll be givin' ye something ye didn't ask for—some advice.' He breathed deep and looked earnestly into Jack's face.

'Greed is the devil's friend, man—don't let it be your'n. It'll blacken yer heart and sour yer soul 'til ye don't even know the monster ye've become.' Tears welled in his eyes.

Stricken, Jack nodded.

'And don't let fear into yer heart neither. Life is short, lad. So short.' He managed a trembling grin. 'Find yerself a girl like yer friend did, spend yer life makin' her happy. Then p'raps when yer lyin' on yer deathbed, ye won't feel the weight of so many regrets.'

Jack said nothing at first, just squeezed his hand. Slowly the skeletal hand relaxed its grip.

'Thank you,' Jack whispered again.

Crump didn't answer. After a moment, Jack realised the old sailor was asleep.

He didn't leave right away. He sat there, watching the slight rise and fall of the seaman's chest, absorbing the impact of the old man's words. All of his words. Finally, when the dim light from the passage beyond had faded away, Jack rose. He'd head to

Whitehall and the Admiralty House tonight. Someone there would hear him, if he had to wait all night.

He gazed one last time at the frail form in the bed. Crump's words echoed in his head.

There were still battles to fight.

Chapter Nine

Lily pressed close behind Lady Dayle as they made their way through the crowd to the receiving line. It would seem that Mrs Dawson had achieved her heart's desire. Minerva's engagement ball could only be deemed that most coveted of appellations: a sad crush.

But it was not the crowd that had Lily's heart pounding and her knees shaking. Nor was the sense of anticipation in the air the reason behind her smile. No, that was partly the result of nerves—and part pure, wicked satisfaction at the chance to live out one of her own girlish fancies.

She felt as if she had stepped out of reality and straight into one of the stories her father had used to spin for her. A sigh of anticipation escaped her. Now if she could only craft a happy ending as easily as her father had.

Lady Dayle and Minerva Dawson had done their bit. They'd primped and pinched and powdered until Lily had cried out in protest. Their answer had been to drag her over to the full-length mirror, where her complaint had died a quick death.

She had not recognised the creature staring back at her. Never had she dreamed she could look like this. The evening gown flattered her with shades of creamy ivory and the softest, shimmering green. Embroidery of darker green and a pale rose colour trimmed the round neckline and the low-cut bodice. The same colours echoed in short, slashed sleeves. A broad ribbon tied round the mid-level waist, and the ends trailed down behind her. They fluttered in her wake now as she moved forwards to embrace her friend.

'Is it not the most exciting thing?' Minerva asked with a smile. She looked exquisite and very mature in a magnificent, rust-coloured frock.

'So many people!' Lily whispered in awe.

'I know. Mama is over the moon!' She pulled Lily in close again. 'Word has spread that we have something special planned for tonight—everyone has been asking about it.'

'Where are the girls?'

'Upstairs. My Aunt Lucinda is, as usual, all doom and gloom, but you are not to mind her,' she admonished. 'My niece Claudette is simply smitten with the children. She's up there dressing and coiffing them as if they were dolls come to life purely for her amusement.'

Lily smiled. 'How are the children feeling about it?'

'Well, they were nervous as cats, but I think they are enjoying the attention.' She grinned and gripped Lily's hand. 'How are you?'

'Nervous as a cat.'

Minerva laughed. 'Don't be! I want you to enjoy yourself tonight.' Next in line, Lord Lindley smiled at Lily and tried to pull her away, but Minerva would not let go of Lily's hand. 'This is your night as much as ours, Lily dear,' she whispered. 'I'm so glad we are able to share this.' She released her over to Lord Lindley. 'Now, go and make this a night to remember.'

Lily smiled back at her as Lord Lindley swept her off her feet and into an embrace. 'You look nearly as ravishing as Minerva,' he said into her ear before passing her along to Mrs Dawson. And within moments she was through the line and on the other side. Lady Dayle stood just a few steps ahead. She had stopped to greet Mrs Montague and it sounded as if their conversation had quickly turned to the hospitalised orphans and all the supplies the foundling hospitals found themselves in need of.

Lily nodded and smiled a greeting and moved

past. Ahead lay the ballroom, and she faced it with both anticipation and anxiety. So much was at stake tonight. Over that threshold lay her first step into a new world—neither her father's or her mother's, but one of her own making. *Please*, she sent out a silent plea with all the yearning in her heart. *Please let this work—for all our sakes.*

And then she stood there on the brink, transfixed by the beauty of it all. Mrs Dawson had truly outdone herself. Lush potted plants lined the dance floor and graced every flat surface while garlands of fresh blooms draped the walls and twined gracefully up the pillars. Hundreds of glittering candles shone in three stunning crystal chandeliers. They cast their glow over a vast number of people—and they were all in motion. Even the air seemed to flow with the swell of the music and in time with the diaphanous drift of the ladies' gowns.

It looked a faerie world, unreal, like a glimpse into a shining, shimmering bubble. Such a fragile and delicate thing, to hold all her hopes and dreams.

'It is beautiful, isn't it?' Lady Dayle's tone was all admiration.

'Unbelievably so.' Lily met her gaze and tried to convey all the warmth and gratitude in her heart. 'Thank you so much, my lady,' she said fervently. 'I can't tell you what this has all meant to me…your

friendship, all that I've experienced, the opportunity…' she made a helpless gesture '…everything.'

Lady Dayle smiled and took her arm. 'No, my
dear, it is I who must thank you. I've thoroughly
enjoyed our time together and you've shared something infinitely precious with me—yourself.
Spending time with you, watching your uninhibited
joy, learning the generosity of your spirit, it has
been all my pleasure.' Her smile wavered a little, but
she pressed on. 'You've reminded me of the great
capacity for good that lies in all of us.' She waved
at the throng of people ahead. 'Just take a look at
the company assembled here. We've taken a tragedy
and salvaged something good from it. We've
worked hard and done well.'

And it appeared that they had indeed. As Lily
moved through the ballroom she greeted many
familiar faces—and they were all wreathed in
smiles. Around every corner she found a new and
gratifying scene. Dignified men of the church stood
in casual conversation with society's leading ladies.
Moralist matrons giggled at the bucks of the *beau
monde*. She found Mrs Bartleigh at one end of the
ballroom, exchanging stillroom receipts with a mar-
chioness. Her husband stood nearby, eagerly absorbing horrifying stories from a half-pay naval
officer. Even Mr Wilberforce had come. He sat en-

throned in a comfortable chair in a corner and radiated good will on the crowd of admirers ebbing and flowing about him.

Taking it all in, Lily's heart overflowed. Hope flared high and lit her from within. Perhaps it had not been just a foolish dream. Her eye wandered, searching for Jack. She longed for him to see the success of their venture.

Suddenly the music ceased. Every eye turned to the dance floor where a proud Lord Lindley led a flushed Minerva to the centre. He nodded at the musicians and they struck up a waltz with a flourish as the betrothed pair opened the dancing. For the first set they danced in solitary, happy splendour, but when the second began there was flurry of movement as people paired off and joined them. Lily ducked behind a pillar. All she wanted was a moment alone to absorb the grandeur and fix it firmly in her mind.

She was not to get it. A spark of awareness sizzled down her spine. Her pulse ratcheted up a little faster. Slowly she turned her head—and found Jack Alden watching her intently from just a few feet away.

Her breath caught. For once he looked as neat as a pin. His hair tamed into a smooth and shining crop of curls, in spotless linen and a dark coat that moulded splendidly to his athletic build, he looked the very picture of dark, masculine elegance. But it was his expression that sent a dark heat spiralling inside of her.

He looked shocked. Not the most flattering of reactions, she realised, but there was something else there, too, something primal and hot. There could be no mistaking the heat in his stunned gaze as it travelled up and down the length of her. She straightened her shoulders. The thrill of turning a man's head with her beauty might be a new one, but this bone-deep recognition of her own power must be as old as womankind.

She lifted her chin. Now she would discover just how solid Jack Alden's walls really were.

It had taken Jack a long time to find Lily in the congested ballroom. Tonight, pockets of sober-hued, conservative dress punctuated the usual gaily-coloured throng and he instinctively sought her there. She was not to be found. He did bump into his mother and ask her if she could tell him where to find Lily, but she only shot him an enigmatic smile and informed him he would have to search her out himself.

He wandered through the crowd, feeling foolish and impatient, but also unexpectedly carefree. He had indeed had to camp out at Admiralty House after he spoke with Crump. In fact, he'd been kept waiting in a sterile antechamber all night and into a day, and been asked to return the next. He'd returned all right, but not until he'd gone to the Foreign Office and the American Embassy and dragged a delegation back with him. This time, they'd only had to wait an hour before they spoke with the First Lord of the Admiralty himself. Jack had shared the information that he'd had from Crump, and the orders had gone out. The Royal Navy had a ship in Porto Santo and it could be at La Palma in a matter of days. A matter of days, Jack had breathed, and Batiste might be in custody. It had left him feeling lightweight and free.

Free of any real reason to attend tonight. And yet here he stood. Tonight he could concentrate on Lily Beecham without any ulterior motive or need to worry about her cousin. He was surprised—and a little uneasy—at how much he looked forward to it.

Finally, just as he was wondering if the tiresome girl had not come tonight at all, a gleam of red-gold in the candlelight caught his eye. He stepped forwards eagerly. But disappointment soon had him stumbling to a halt. Merely another débutante, although this one had the good sense to stay half-hidden behind a pillar rather than put her empty-headed charms on full and painful display. Impatient, he turned away to continue his search.

He had not got far before the information picked up by his senses finally connected into a startling conclusion in his brain. Very slowly he spun on his heel. He examined the girl again, in surprise, disbelief and, finally, wonder.

He had not expected this. Jack had come with an apology ready. Now it simply…disappeared, slid away, forgotten, as he stared at Lily Beecham, his jaw slack. When would he learn? Every time they came together she found a new and inventive way to knock him off kilter.

This…this vision before him must be the most shocking one yet. Gone was his conservative, young idealist dressed in necklines up to here and sleeves down to there. In her place stood a flame-haired siren.

No, not a siren, not in this lush, green environment. She must be a dryad—a spirit of the forest, dressed in the colours of spring.

Every such nymph represented in art and architecture put on a generous exhibition of flesh. Lily was not nude, of course, but her low-cut bodice clung tight to her curves and she most definitively had a glorious expanse of creamy skin on display.

Lord, and her hair! He gazed, spellbound, at her glorious tresses, dressed elaborately and with tiny, cream rosebuds anchored throughout. It shocked him that those delicate flowers were not incinerated amidst those fiery curls—for Jack certainly felt inclined to burst into flame.

His palms itched. He clenched his fists and slowly approached her. She'd caught sight of him, too, and she stood straight and proud. He stopped, inches away. She held out a hand, encased in long, ivory kid. He took it and bent low. As he straightened he lost himself in the endless blue of her eyes, unable to look away, forgetting even to speak.

A nearby giggle recalled him to his senses. He dropped her hand. 'Good evening.'

She inclined her head. 'Mr Alden.'

'I'd thought we'd got past the need for formality, Lily.'

'Given everything that has occurred, I think perhaps it best if we retreat back into it,' she said firmly.

'I'm sorry, but I'm afraid it's too late. You are fixed firmly in my head as Lily now.' He made a sweeping gesture that took her in from head to toe. 'And I'm sorry, but you look so formidably splendid tonight, that if I cannot call you Lily I might not muster up the courage to speak at all.'

She rolled her eyes. 'Someone is full of nonsense tonight.'

'Didn't you know? That's what all these events are about—nonsense.'

She watched him closely. Never would he let her

know how that look unnerved him. 'Your mother warned me,' she said ruefully.

'Warned you? Now, just a minute, she's *my* mother—surely she should be on my side?'

She lifted her chin. 'Your mother is too great a woman to take sides,' she said loftily. 'And if she did, she'd take mine.'

Her playfulness enchanted him. 'Unfair,' he returned. 'You've had undue influence over her. You'd best cease, or I'll be forced to tell your mother—' he grew suddenly serious '—how incredible you look tonight.'

She grew flushed. 'I hope I haven't said anything to lower your estimation of my mother,' she said, her tone serious. 'Truly, she's a good person, and she's had to bear more than her share of hardship.' She shot him a wry grin. 'Not the least of which is a wilful and boisterous daughter.'

'I wouldn't dream of thinking ill of her,' Jack said. 'Unless she fails to value the treasure she has in you.'

'Of course she values me,' Lily declared. She stilled a moment. 'She just misses what she's never had.'

'What is that?' Jack asked quietly.

'A son.'

Silence fell between them. She rushed to fill it. 'You see, my mother was always the more serious of my parents and over the years, as she endured one failed pregnancy after another, she grew even more unhappy. It was very hard on her, not being able to give my father a son. I think she felt unwomanly, unworthy.'

'That's ridiculous,' Jack stated.

'You and I might not agree, but you cannot tell another how to feel.' Lily sighed. 'When I was ten years old, though, she did give birth to a son. My baby brother,' she said tenderly. 'My parents were ecstatic. But that winter the influenza swept through the countryside. He died when he was only months old.' She sighed again. 'It was nearly more than she could handle. She grew even more reserved and withdrawn. Then, when my father died…' Her voice trailed off. 'I know how lucky I am to have her at all.'

'As she is lucky to have you,' Jack said bracingly. 'And I know my mother feels lucky to have you, even for a short time. Now, are you going to tell me why she felt the need to warn you about me?'

She took a deep breath and glanced at him with a smile. 'Well, I admit that I found it difficult to believe, but she said you hate these sort of events. You really didn't want to be here tonight?'

'Not until now,' he said, and the truly frightful thing was that he meant it. 'Will you dance with me?'

Her air of queenly confidence abruptly dissipated. Her face fell and she visibly withdrew. 'I'm sorry. I cannot.'

Jack wanted to kick himself. Of course, she'd likely been forbidden to dance, if ever she was even taught. Even after the story she'd just told him, he'd forgotten her upbringing. The sight of her—so beautiful and proud of it—had stirred his blood and scrambled his senses. He spoke quickly to allow them both to recover. 'Forgive me. I should have realised. It's just that you've fair taken my breath away and knocked every sensible thought out of my head.'

She blushed and, encouraged, he pressed on. 'Would you take a stroll with me instead?' He couldn't seem to keep the tone of low urgency from his voice. 'Mr Dawson is a learned man and he keeps a very fine library. I would be happy to show it to you.'

She hesitated.

'If you don't intend to dance, no one will think it amiss if you sit out a set with me.'

'I know that, Mr Alden.' Her ire was obvious.

'Jack, please,' he reminded her.

She squared her shoulders. Her puffed sleeves were so tiny that they were nearly bare. 'This may be my first ball, *Jack*, but I do know how to conduct myself.'

He tried to look contrite. 'You must forgive me—and since I already owe you a rather large apology, you must consider this one a practice run.' He grinned. 'If you'll come along to the library, I will offer it up in proper fashion, on my knees and in sackcloth and ashes.'

She laughed. 'I don't think we have to go that far.'

She allowed him to take her arm and they made their way into the hall. A few people still mingled here and Jack nodded to those he knew. A stout dowager in brilliant yellow curtsied low as they passed and her companion leaned in to whisper something to her.

'Her?' the dowager answered, *sotto voce*. 'She's only another one of these endless Evangelicals here tonight.' She gave a nasty laugh. 'You've heard of mutton dressed as lamb? Well, now you've seen a reformer dressed as a débutante.'

Jack stiffened. They'd been intended to hear the insult, and he was greatly tempted to return the favour, but Lily gently shook her head and tugged him along. He raised his brow at her.

'Oh, don't look at me that way,' she said, her voice low.

'Which way?'

'The one that says loud and clear that you told me so and I didn't listen. The one that says I left myself open to such an insult.'

Though it was difficult, he kept quiet and smiled at a passing acquaintance.

'Well, I know you are right. There are others, too, that are not happy about what we've planned for tonight—Minerva's aunt and uncle have been quite vocal about their discontent. But I don't care, Jack. I've hidden myself away from life for too long. I can't go back. I'd rather tolerate an honest snub. At least with that lady, and the others, I know where I stand.'

They reached the library. The doors stood open and Jack bowed her inside with a flourish and then followed her in. He'd been in the large and comfortable room several times before. In fact, he'd dare say that he'd been in most of the libraries and book rooms in Mayfair. Invariably, he ended up there whenever he was convinced to attend a society event.

This, he had to admit, was one of the best. It was obviously in frequent use. Hundreds of books lined the walls and most of them had indeed been cut and read. A massive mahogany desk dominated the centre of the room, but scattered about were also a large, standing globe, a capped telescope and even a large embroidery frame pulled next to a comfortable chair.

Lily, however, went straight to the large glass doors leading outside to the back garden.

'I'm afraid there is not much to see out there. I don't believe Mrs Dawson is much of a gardener. Her tastes run to embroidery and fashion—and marrying off her daughters, of course.' He watched her peer outside and up towards the darkened sky.

'I know,' she said, 'but this evening is one of those

rare London nights when you can actually glimpse the stars overhead.'

'Ah, a country girl at heart?' he asked, caught by the sight of her long, slender neck.

'More than even I knew,' she answered with a smile. 'I find I do miss my long walks in open spaces and most especially I miss the green of the fields and forests.' She left the doors and walked further away, trailing her fingers along the spines of the books in their cases. 'I suppose I owe you an apology as well. Neither of us behaved well at our last encounter. But since our two apologies will cancel each other out, let's just call it even, shall we?'

'A fine idea, but I have an even better one,' Jack said. Curiosity had been eating at him. 'I propose a substitution. Instead of an apology, I will accept an answer to a question that has been plaguing me.'

She looked puzzled, and a little wary. 'I'm inclined to agree, as long as I get a question as a substitute as well.'

He shrugged. 'It's only fair, I suppose.' He crossed to a grouping of low, leather chairs in the opposite corner of the library and took one. The long table between them held a large selection of periodicals. He picked one up and idly flipped the pages without looking at it. Instead he watched her, half-hidden in shadows across the room.

'What is your question?' she asked across the expanse of the room.

He cleared his throat. 'Yes, well…'

His hesitation clearly intrigued her. She came closer and perched herself on the edge of the big desk. She was so small that her feet did not touch the floor. Captivated, he watched her legs swinging. She looked like a goddess, but acted as unconcerned as a girl. The incongruity of it had him starting to sweat.

'Yes?' She cocked her head at him, her brows raised in question. A heavy curl fell forwards and draped the extended curve of her neck.

He strategically placed the periodical over his lap.

'What in hell,' he enunciated clearly, 'do two blackbirds on a fence post have to do with *anything*?'

'Oh.' She gave an involuntary laugh and hopped down off the desk. 'Promise you won't laugh,' she ordered.

'I promise I'll try not to.'

'I suppose that will have to do.' She leaned back against the desk and grinned at him. 'It begins with my nurse. She was Cornish, and she had the greatest respect and fear for all things supernatural.'

Jack lifted a brow in disbelief. 'Such as?'

'Oh, all of it. She knew hundreds of ghostly tales and something about every sort of other-worldly being.'

'How many could there be?' he asked.

'Hundreds,' she said with conviction. 'And Nurse knew them all—marsh spirits, banshees, hags, trolls, all of them. She left tiny bits of food and milk on the windowsill every night—for the pixies. But her real speciality was at reading signs.'

'Signs?' Jack's logical mind was becoming more muddled by the minute.

'Yes, you know the sort of thing? Portents of good fortune or ill luck?'

'I swear, I've never heard of such a thing outside of a text book,' he said with a shake of his head. 'The Etruscan priests, you know, were famous for scrying the future in animal livers, but I thought we left oracles behind with the ancients.'

'Indeed not. Signs are all about if you know what to look for.' She smiled at him. 'For example, I'm sure you did not know that finding nine peas in a pea pod means good luck, but three butterflies together means bad?'

He stared at her, aghast. 'Surely you don't mean to say that you believe in such things?'

She hitched one shoulder up in answer.

'But…those superstitions are hardly in line with the teachings of the Church. Your mother must be appalled to think you would pay attention to such nonsense.'

She crossed her arms defensively in front of her.

'"There are more things in heaven and earth, Horatio…"' She let the quote trail off. 'Perhaps Shakespeare had it right and there are things we just aren't meant to understand? Then maybe those logical thinkers like you are correct and most mysteries can be explained away by coincidence? But I've often wondered…' She abruptly stood straight and walked away to the other side of the desk. 'And in any case, that's only one of many things about me that appal my mother.'

'Come now, it can't be that bad.'

She shrugged again. The large piece of furniture between them appeared to bolster her courage. 'There. I've given a thorough explanation. Now, I believe it is my turn to ask a question?'

Jack was still shaken by her admission of belief in such rubbish. 'I suppose so,' he replied absently. 'What do you wish to know?'

'I want you to tell me about your childhood.'

The statement jolted him suddenly to awareness. 'That's not a question.'

'Come now, no semantics,' she chided. 'You must play fair.' She breathed deep. 'It's just that I've so enjoyed my time with your mother. She is so cheerful and generous and giving—'

'And you were wondering how she could have raised a curmudgeon like me?' he interrupted.

She laughed helplessly. 'Something like that.'

Her request unnerved him. It had never been a conscious decision, but he didn't talk about his childhood. He did his damnedest to never think about it. But he doubted she would give up easily on this, and he had no wish to raise further questions in her mind.

He sighed. 'What do you expect me to say, Lily? I am the son of a viscount. I had a privileged up-bringing. I lived in a large house, and had plenty of food to eat. I had my family, lots of servants, a pony and a fine education. If you are thinking to find a reason for my character deficiencies in my past, you are barking up the wrong tree. The blame for any defects must lay squarely with me.' He blinked. 'Maybe I was just born this way.'

'What way?' she asked, looking intrigued.

Damn. He shot her a sharp look.

'I answered your question thoroughly. You must do the same,' she insisted.

'You did, but now I almost wish I hadn't asked. Perhaps you will feel the same.'

'Jack—'

'Very well.' He glared at her. 'What way, you want to know—but I think you already answered that question yourself. What was your word? Distant? It's a damned good word. I find I quite like it. It fits.'

'I'm sorry, Jack.' Her expression had gone sober. 'I did not mean to make you angry.'

'I'm not angry. You asked. I'm answering. It does fit—and it fit even as a child. My brothers were older, you see. They were closer in age to each other than they were to me.'

She had come out from behind the desk, though she still lingered near it. 'But I'm sure they still cared for you, no matter the age difference. You were their brother.'

He laughed at her, and it came out sounding bitter. 'Words of wisdom from an only child.'

She cringed.

Jack immediately pulled on the reins of his temper. *Control*, he reminded himself. 'I'm sorry. Yes, you are right. Of course, they loved me, as I did them. They just cared for each other more.' He shifted a little on the chair. 'I was occasionally jealous, especially when they were gambolling about the countryside on their mounts or romping in the forest. Sometimes I trailed after them and they would usually let me in on their games.' He hesitated before continuing. 'But most of the time I remember being relieved.'

She blinked in surprise. 'Relieved? I find that hard to believe.'

'You should not. What did their closeness get

them, really, except a heartache?' He could see that she did not understand. 'My father, you see, had high expectations for his first son. He required much of Phillip and none of it had anything to do with running about with his unruly younger brother. Charles was hurt terribly when Phillip was forced to spend more and more time training to take over the estate and the title. Phillip was, too, though he did not show it in the same way.'

She'd crept closer now and he forced himself to breathe. 'The whole notion of love has always seemed completely arbitrary to me. Father loved Phillip, and he nearly suffocated him because of it. He didn't love Charles and that nearly destroyed him, too.'

He had no wish to reveal how all of that mis-placed emotion between father and sons had twisted itself into something ugly and tragic. Or how he had congratulated himself on avoiding the pain, and realised how much better it was to stick with his books and regard such sentiment as just another subject to study. How he far preferred never to be touched by such feelings at all.

'I think I see,' she said and he was afraid that she did. She stood right next to his chair now, her eyes huge and her face troubled and all of her concern centred on him. He reached up and took her hand. Her mouth trembled at the corners. Lord, her mouth.

He could feel her pulse racing at her wrist. It echoed the pounding of his heart and the sudden throbbing of his shaft. He was far beyond rational thought, had been since he'd first glimpsed her in the ballroom. So he listened to his instincts instead. He pulled, gently but inexorably, on her arm and dragged her on to his lap.

She landed on the periodical. Harsh and impatient, he ripped it out from under her and settled her more comfortably across his legs and the yearning bulge at his crotch. He grasped her head with one hand and rubbed a thumb over her open, gasping mouth.

'You do see, don't you?' he asked in a rough whisper. 'Now you know where and why it all began—why I started the laborious process of building my walls. I built them tall and strong, and they've served me well and kept me safe— except from you.'

He moved in to kiss her, but she drew back and ran a finger gently down the side of his face. 'Why me?' she asked.

He groaned. 'I wish I knew.' He kissed her gently on the mouth, and then moved to her nose. He nipped her there, then brushed a fluttery kiss across her forehead and on her lovely, stubborn little chin. 'Because you are open and warm and kind?' His hands gripped her tight. 'And yet an infuriating, irresistibly wicked minx at the same time. It's a heady combination.' He pressed another soft kiss on her mouth, capturing her lush lower lip between his. 'Or perhaps it is just that I am a fool.'

He took her then, in a fierce, hard kiss. Desire surged in him and through him, burst past his restraints as he strained towards her. And she answered, opening at the urging of his lips and tongue and pressing herself closer against him. Her hands roamed over his chest, then curled round his shoulders and buried themselves in his hair. The softness of her breasts pushed against his chest, their hard little peaks teasing him right through the heavy fabric of his waistcoat.

Music swelled from the ballroom, and the echo of laughter drifted in from the open door to the hall, but Jack couldn't give a damn. Lily was in his arms, and they were alone, tucked away into the dim corner of the room and it might as well have been a continent away from the rest of the party.

He tightened his hold on her, drifted his hand down to her bottom and settled her firmly against his arousal. She stilled, but for just a moment. Then, with a moan, she deepened their kiss, touched his tongue with hers, arched her back and rode down, hot and eager, against him.

With nearly an audible crack, something broke

inside of him. How did she do it? She was like a beacon, illuminating all the dark and shadowy corners of his soul—and incredibly, she did not cringe from what she found there. Instead she acknowledged and accepted all the parts of him—even those hidden in his deepest, unplumbed depths.

He was vulnerable, helpless against her power. Up and out of him she drew a great, terrifying mixture of lust and longing and dreadful need. She pulled at him and it washed over him, his every defence swept away before it.

He had to catch his breath. Yet stopping was out of the question. He dragged his mouth from hers while his hands busied themselves at the neck of her gown. In a moment her bodice was loosened, her stays pushed aside and his hand was inside, cupping the glorious weight of her breast, lifting it high.

She gasped.

'God, but you are beautiful,' he moaned. He kissed her in soft reassurance, while he smoothed soft caresses over the eager peak of her nipple. She began to move, writhing eagerly in time with his touch, setting him on fire with the motion.

He was lost, and oh, God, but she was sweet. He needed more. He ran questing fingers down her leg, but as he reached the embroidered hem of her gown, an unwelcome sound penetrated the thick haze of his lust.

'Lily?' The voice sounded heavy with annoyance in the darkness. Whoever it was, they must be at the library door.

Pleasure and longing and lust disappeared. Lily pulled away and sucked in a fearful breath, but he placed a finger on her lips and quickly eased her back inside her bodice. He lifted her up and clambered to his feet beside her. He would have to trust to the low light to hide the massive bulge in his breeches.

'Lily—are you in here?' the voice came again.

'Minerva,' Lily whispered in relief. She shot him a questioning look and he nodded.

She stepped away, towards the centre of the library. 'Minerva? I'm here.' Her words emerged thick with residual desire. She looked dazed and thoroughly mussed—and utterly irresistible.

'What are you doing in here?' came the exasperated reply. 'It's nearly time for the performance! Claudette wants her turn at dolling you up, too.' Her words faded as Lily drew near the door. 'Well, I can see her services will be needed.' She pursed her lips. Then she reached behind her and shut the door.

'Jack Alden, you can come out from skulking in the corner,' Minerva called. 'For if it was any other gentleman in here, you can be sure I'd have a bone to pick with him.'

Horrified and embarrassed, Jack stepped into the light. He winced as Minerva marched forwards and pulled Lily protectively to her side.

'Minerva…' Lily began, in a clear warning tone.

'Yes, I know, dear.' But the young woman was not looking at her friend. She glared at Jack, admonition clear on her face.

'I'd like to strangle the both of you! Could you have picked a worse time and place for this?' She rubbed a hand across her brow. 'We have a very delicate balance to maintain tonight.' She stood straight and made a sweeping gesture towards the door. 'The entire world is outside there—*my aunt* is outside there, looking for any reason to pronounce this evening a disaster and the two of you…' She shook her head. 'I'm not going to say anything about what's been going on in here. But I want you to *think*, Jack Alden. That is what you do best, isn't it?'

'Usually,' Jack answered. He glanced at Lily, but her worried gaze was focused on Miss Dawson.

'Well, start thinking. Clearly. Here and now. Lily's situation is not ideal. I will not have you making things more difficult for her, Jack.'

Jack nodded. He had no words. No excuse, either.

'Let's go,' Minerva said. She took Lily by the hand, opened the door and led her out.

Jack watched them go. It took every ounce of will power he could muster not to follow. God, but he wanted to. They could all go to hell; every one of them out there with a viable reason why he should not. He wanted to run those two down, snatch Lily up and lay claim to her in the most primitive and basic way.

He could not. He stood rooted instead, the barrenness of the room a pale reflection of the inescapable emptiness of his soul.

Chapter Ten

Lily sat silent in front of the mirror while Minerva's niece fussed with her hair and dress. Her gaze was fixed on her mussed reflection, but she felt strangely calm. Absently, she examined herself. By rights she should look drastically different than she had just a short time ago. She did not. She supposed it was only her outlook that had been so radically altered, not her outward appearance.

She had to stifle a laugh at that thought. Surely she was becoming unhinged. The orphaned girls chattered in excitement all around her. She had to hold herself together for their sake. And really, what did she expect? That a scarlet W—for wanton—would appear on her forehead to make known her sins?

Except that it had not felt like sin. Instead, it had only felt…right. So perhaps wanton was the

wrong word. What, then, was the correct termi-
nology for someone who had just indulged in…
what she had?

Lily very much feared the correct words were *in
love*.

No. She was not ready to commit herself to such
an extent, not even in her own thoughts. It had been
wonderful beyond her expectations, and it was true
that Jack had shared something of himself, but
whatever was happening in his head right now
would tell the tale. Would he discover that he had
lightened his burden by sharing it with her? Would
he understand that exposing himself a little would
only make him stronger? Or would he react in fear?
Would he shut down and shut her out?

There was no way for her to know.

So Lily did what she must. She ignored the hollow
place inside of her and fought to keep fear and anxiety
from rushing in to fill it. She summoned words of reassurance and praise for the young performers and
tried hard to believe they applied to her as well.

When it was time, she and Minerva took the girls
down to the music room. A raised dais had been
placed at the front of the room and a partition taken
out at the back to enlarge it. They arranged the girls
on the little stage and Lily gazed over them with affection and pride.

'You look lovely,' she told them. 'Like a group of angels come down from the heavens.'

Guests began to enter the room. Minerva went to direct them in and help them find their seats. A couple of the girls shifted nervously and Lily smiled. 'Do not worry about a thing. I've performed in front of others many times and people are always kind, even if you hit a sour note.'

A couple of the girls giggled. Another one called out, 'But, Miss Beecham, you said you mostly played in church.'

'This ain't church,' someone whispered.

Lily laughed. 'No, it is not. But everyone here is curious and happy to see you perform. They want to see you do well as much as you wish to.' She looked over her shoulder. The seats were beginning to fill. 'It is a little nerve-racking to watch them all shuffle in, isn't it? But as soon as the music begins, you will all know just what to do.'

She chatted with them quietly a few minutes longer, hoping to distract them from their nerves. When Minerva came and took the stage, Lily went and sat quietly at the pianoforte.

Minerva began to speak. 'Thank you all so much for coming to my engagement ball.' She smiled at the quieting audience. 'My mother urges you all to drink freely of the champagne, as I am the last of my sisters to marry and she swears she will never, ever undertake an event of this size again.'

Good-natured laughter swept through the crowd. Minerva's face grew more sober. 'I would also like to thank you all for allowing me to share something more unusual and undoubtedly special.' She gestured to the girls standing behind her.

In a quiet, unassuming tone, Minerva spoke of the fire at the orphanage. With reverence she read the names and ages of the children who had died. Lily could see tears gathered in more than one lady's eye as she went down the list.

'Now you understand how fortunate indeed we are to have these girls with us here today.' She introduced each girl and if a pair of singed eyebrows here and a bandage there elicited a little more sympathy, then so much the better, Lily thought.

Minerva explained all that had already been done to help the remaining orphans. 'Still there is much work to be done, but these girls would like to take the chance tonight to thank those who have already worked so hard on their behalf. In that spirit we have prepared a short programme to sing for you.'

Minerva stepped down and Lily stood for a moment. 'My father had a great passion for music of all kinds. He kept a large collection of broadside ballads. The girls have chosen a few to share with you tonight.'

She sat and began to play. The girls did a marvellous job. Before long they had established a rapport with their responsive audience. Several listeners were visibly moved; one or two openly wept. After each of their songs, the girls were treated to a rousing round of applause and when they were finished and the audience called for an encore, Lily had reason to be glad she'd included 'The True Lover's Farewell' in their instruction.

The river never will run dry,
Nor the rocks melt with the sun;
And I'll never prove false to the girl that I love
Till all these things be done, my dear,
Till all these things be done.

The last notes died away to a moment of silence, and then another long, heart-warming roll of applause. Lily stood with the girls, flushed with relief at their warm reception. They had done it. People approached the stage, offering congratulations, well wishes and their help.

Lady Dayle was there, and Minerva and Mrs Dawson and Mrs Bartleigh as well. They all exchanged glances of triumph and success. Lily's heart swelled with happiness for all that they had achieved, and her gaze swept the crowd, hoping against hope that Jack was here to see.

Jack stayed in the library for a very long time. Pacing back and forth, he tried to adjust to feeling raw, vulnerable and exposed.

What had he done? He'd spoken to Lily of things he'd never shared with anyone. He'd hinted at things he never wanted to even consider himself. He'd ignored all the tenets of good behaviour, cast aside any thought of consequence and run his hands and his mouth all over her. He was so far beyond his normal boundaries that he might never get back. He'd lowered his fortifications and let emotion run havoc. Now he was paying the price.

He could not think. It was as if he'd so long neglected reason and rational thought that now they had abandoned him in turn. Desperately, he tried to organise his thoughts, gather himself into some semblance of normalcy. A futile effort.

He made his way back to the party and sought out a footman for a drink. Then he sought out another. But the alcohol did not help. The small, cold knot of anger at his centre was missing. Oddly, he did not feel better without it. He felt adrift, unrestrained. He felt dangerous, as if he were capable of anything.

Charles found him eventually. His brother clapped him on the back, spoke to him at length and with enthusiasm about…something. Jack couldn't rouse himself enough to discover what it was. He stared unseeing at his drink.

Others joined them. He didn't care who. His breath started to come in ragged gasps. Did most people go about in this way, continually feeling so unprotected? It was insupportable. He felt at the mercy of whatever punishing wind might blow through. He had no defences. He'd let them all go.

He needed an anchor. Lily. He looked up and realised that a stream of guests was moving out of the ballroom. Oh, yes. The performance. She would be there. He followed, wandering away from his brother and the others without a word.

A huge sigh of relief whooshed out of him when he caught sight of her up on the dais, behind the girls who were to perform tonight. She looked beautiful and serene at the pianoforte. He needed her help, or perhaps he just needed her. She'd destroyed his barriers and then she'd left. He didn't know how to deal with the loss. Tucking himself into the shadows near the back of the room, he decided to bide his time. When the performance had finished, he would whisk her away again, beg her to shore up the crumbling remnants of his soul.

The little concert they put on surprised him. The girls were quite good and obviously well rehearsed. The innocent picture they presented contrasted dramatically with the tragic tale of their plight and genuinely touched the audience. Lily played well and when she joined the girls in the chorus of their songs, her rich soprano soothed Jack's frayed nerves.

The only sour note of the presentation came not from the performers, but from a member of the audience. Seated to the side of the dais, but close to the front, a heavy-set man encased in clothes too tight for his well-padded frame watched in avid fascination. The hunger in his eyes disturbed Jack, but as the man sat quietly and applauded enthusiastically, there seemed little he could do.

Jack relaxed as the set ended to accolades. In front of him the audience rose to their feet and milled about, waiting their turn to reach the performers and convey their enthusiasm. Triumph and relief shone on Lily's face and were echoed in the girls' expressions and in those of his mother and Minerva Dawson, too. The warm reception and the rush of well-wishers had Minerva's mother practically glowing in ecstasy. More than just empty praise came their way as well. Many enthusiastic listeners were offering their help along with their congratulations.

Jack recalled the passion with which Lily had

defended this idea, and her belief in their ability to both forge new relationships and stir sympathy for their cause. And she had been right. She had believed in the best of people while he had expected the worst.

Chagrin engulfed him, but he also recognised the rise of other sentiments: pride and perhaps even fledgling hope. It would seem, he thought wryly, that having given way to lust, he would now be forced to endure the whole spectrum of emotion.

He suffered a healthy dose of annoyance in the next moment as Lucinda Whitcomb, Minerva's disapproving aunt, rushed into the room, dragging their beleaguered host behind her. She made her way to the dais, pushing aside guests and children alike in her hurry.

'There now, brother,' she said, hauling Mr Dawson along like a disgraced urchin. 'Tell them. Tell them I've been right all along!'

Mrs Dawson retrieved her husband from his overwrought sister. 'Whatever are you about now, Lucinda dear?'

'I told you this would happen, but would you listen? I knew you would not be happy until you dipped our family name into the scandal broth!'

Mrs Dawson obviously had experience dealing with her sister-in-law's histrionics. She turned her back on the woman. 'Is everything all right, dear?' she asked her husband earnestly.

Mister Dawson scrubbed a nervous hand through his hair and glanced about at their keen audience. 'Er, perhaps you'd better come.' He shot a glance at his daughter, too. 'You, too, Minerva. Shouldn't leave your betrothed to handle this sort of thing alone.'

'What sort of thing?' Minerva asked, suddenly concerned.

'The sort of thing more suited to Sadler's Wells than a betrothal ball, you reckless girl!' Mrs Whitcomb's strident tones grated even at the back of the crowd. 'Your ridiculous insistence on ruining this evening is likely to ruin our family right along with it.'

Jack's heart jumped into his throat. He didn't like the sound of this. He began to quietly push his way through the crowd.

'Do be quiet, Lucinda,' Mrs Dawson begged. 'Dearest,' she said, already starting for the door and bringing her husband along with her, albeit more gently than his sister had, 'do tell me what's happening?' They were out the door and on their way before her husband could respond.

'What is it?' Minerva asked her aunt.

'It's a disaster, that is what it is.' Jack could hear the satisfaction in the harridan's voice. 'There is a crone in the card room lecturing on the evils of gambling! Your betrothed is even now trying to disengage Lord Danley's second son from a bout of fisticuffs. He's out there, sparring with a man who refused to concede the necessity of slave labour on his West Indian plantation! Of course, it was difficult to hear the cause of their quarrel over the vulgar sea ditties being sung by the two drunken men at the punch table.'

'Oh, no,' moaned Minerva. She shot an apologetic look at Lily. 'Can you handle the girls? I'll go see what I can do.'

'Of course,' Lily responded to her friend's fleeing back. 'Come, girls! You did marvellously!' There was a chorus of agreement from those in the still sizeable crowd who had not rushed off after the Dawsons. 'Let us go upstairs. We promised you all an ice, did we not? We will have them sent up.'

'Hold there, young lady!' Mrs Whitcomb had not spent all of her venom yet, it would seem. 'This fiasco will be in every paper tomorrow. We will be laughing stocks—and I know where to lay the blame!'

She shook her finger in Lily's shocked, white face. Jack let out a bark of protest. He tried to move faster through the densely packed mass ahead of him.

'You! You have been pushing yourself and your agenda forwards all this time! This night was supposed to be about the joining of two respectable families, not your ragged urchins and radical notions.'

The crowd had a bird's eye view on the most fascinating incident of the Season. None of them wished to give way willingly. Frantic, Jack began to indiscriminately thrust people aside. Then he saw that he was not the only one trying to break through. The jowly man with the troubling look in his eye suddenly broke through the cluster of gentlemen he'd been skulking behind.

'There you are, my dear,' he said to Lucinda Whitcomb. His wife didn't turn from her target to greet him. 'Is this the impertinent little baggage you told me about?' The words were malicious, but the look he raked over Lily held more than a hint of foul craving.

'Will you *move*? Let me through!' Jack demanded of the portly lady ahead of him. Frantic and frustrated, he nearly picked the woman up and set her aside in his effort to get to Lily's side. He shouldn't have worried, though. His mother had no intention of tolerating such an attack on one of her own.

'Lucinda Whitcomb!' Lady Dayle scolded. 'You are the only one stirring the scandal broth tonight. I should think you've done enough damage for one evening. Take yourself off and leave this girl alone.'

'You have no say here, Elenor,' Mrs Whitcomb retorted.

'Everyone wants to know, Lady Dayle, why you've picked up another stray?' The heavy man—

Mr Whitcomb, one assumed—cast a contemptuous glance on Jack's mother. 'Cannot your sons manage to get themselves wives on their own?'

A collective gasp went up.

'*Enough!*' Jack shouted. He broke his way through the last ranks of spectators. 'That is enough!'

'You are right! I've had enough. I don't care that this social-climbing chit has got her clutches into your family—just keep her away from mine!' screeched Mrs Whitcomb.

Jack drew a furious breath, but never got the chance to retort. Into the breach stepped a new defender.

'That will be all!' Jack recognised the thin woman as Lily's elderly friend, Mrs Bartleigh. Her face shone bright red and she was trembling from head to foot with the force of her anger. 'You will not enact such a scene in front of these children!'

'Perhaps the old woman is right, dear,' Mr Whitcomb said with a lascivious glance at the group of rapt young faces. 'These innocents should not be left in the care of such an obvious opportunist.'

'Don't you take one step near those children, Whitcomb.' Jack tensed with fury. Anger and disgust suffused him, until he thought they must be leaking from his very pores.

'Mr Alden is right,' Mrs Bartleigh said, still in her quiet but forceful tone. 'These children will go with the girl who has laboured so hard for them. I don't know you,' she said with a flick of her eyes over the Whitcombs. 'But I've known Miss Beecham from the cradle and I couldn't be prouder of her, were she my own. She is a good girl, one who puts others before herself. Instead of haranguing her, you would do better to strive to be more like her.'

'Thank you all the same, but I haven't the dramatic skill to cover such a greedy, grasping nature behind a cloak of virtue,' Mrs Whitcomb said nastily.

'No, Lucinda,' Lady Dayle shot back, 'your ugly nature is all right here in the open.'

Jack strained for control. Hatred for these petty, spiteful people ran hot in his veins, urging him to action. They'd taken something beautiful that Lily had created and tainted it. The need to defend and revenge her nearly overwhelmed him. But that would make him no better than they. He longed for the return of his walls, the security of his old emotional ramparts even as he struggled against the tide of emotion that threatened to swamp him.

'Mrs Bartleigh,' Lily suddenly gasped.

Briefly startled out of his anger, Jack saw that the elderly woman did indeed seem to be in distress. All of her bright colour had drained away, leaving her pale and breathless. Suddenly her knees seemed to give way. Lily caught her and called her name frantically once more.

'Mrs Bartleigh!'

'Come, my dear,' said Mr Whitcomb with an unsympathetic glance at the poor woman's plight. 'Let us go back to the party. It seems as if there will be one less irritating reformer for you to worry about soon enough.'

Rage exploded out of the top of Jack's head. There were not enough walls in all of Christendom to restrain him at that moment. He grabbed Whitcomb by one fleshy arm and spun him around. The despoiler of innocent goodwill whimpered in fright. His sudden pitiful fear was no deterrent to Jack. He hauled back an arm and, pouring every drop of hatred into his swing, smashed his fist into the man's face.

'No!' someone cried. 'No, Jack! Stop!'

He ignored the voice, would have shouted his defiance, had he not needed his breath for another vicious hit. Anger sang in his veins, altered his very being, until he was not himself any more, but someone else entirely, someone with a lust for blood and a bitter satisfaction at the solid thud of his fist into flesh.

'Jack, stop! Control yourself!'

The desperation in the voice finally penetrated.

He unclenched his fist, dropped the scoundrel and turned slowly around.

It was Lily. She sat on the ground with her friend cradled in her lap. 'Her husband,' she whispered. 'Go, please, fetch her husband.'

Ignoring the blubbering, bleeding idiot at his feet, Jack stepped over him and went to do her bidding.

Chapter Eleven

A hard, uncomfortable chair sat outside Mrs Bartleigh's sickroom. As she had so often over the last few days, Lily perched on it, waiting for the doctor inside to finish his examination. The gruff physician had not expected the lady to live through the night after her collapse, but somehow she had rallied, and had even appeared to have grown a little stronger since.

A fact for which Lily was profoundly grateful. All of her hopes and her grand plans for forging a new place for herself might have disintegrated along with the success of Minerva's betrothal ball, but her old and dear friend lived still, and that was a trade Lily would gladly make again.

Minerva had escaped the disastrous ball un-scathed, thank goodness. The whole affair had been caricaturised in every London paper and on multiple broadsheets, but Minerva had only laughed. Her engagement would go down in history, she said, and the new orphanage already being planned would stand testament for years to come. For although Mrs Whitcomb had been busy blackening both Lily's and Jack's names all over town, the notoriety only served to bring the orphans' quandary to even broader attention.

A scandal? A fire? Penniless children in need? The tale touched the heart of everyone in London. It became the perfect cause to distract the bored *ton* from their end-of-Season *ennui*, and the perfect chance for cits and mushrooms to involve themselves with noble interests. Bank drafts, volunteers and pledges had poured in. The Duchess of Charmouth granted a lease on a large parcel of land in Kensington, a charter was in the process of being drawn up and Lady Dayle was assembling a board of directors.

Lily had gaped at how swiftly things had begun to move and then quietly stepped into the background. Thank goodness, their plan had been a triumph overall, but the personal price had been very high indeed. Lily had nearly lost a friend, and she had lost her chance at a future with Jack. He had fetched Mr Bartleigh as she had asked, that fateful night, then he had disappeared into the crowd and not been seen in public since. His brother, Lord Dayle, reported that he was shut up in his rooms once more. Lily knew what that meant. He meant to withdraw again, from the world and from her. His walls would go back up and he would live behind them in splendid isolation and safety.

His reversion to his old way of living had come as a blow. It had also acted as the jolt she needed to force herself to step back and look at the situation without the heady filter of desire. What she had seen had shocked her. It was the same old pattern that she had been endlessly repeating with her mother. Once more she found herself striving to please someone emotionally incapable of returning her affection.

She'd wished to come to London specifically for a chance to escape such a fate, and she'd let the intensity of her response to Jack blind her to the fact that he only represented more of the same.

The door opened beside her, preventing another futile round of regret. Lily stood as Mr Bartleigh escorted the doctor out.

'Oh, Lily, I'm glad you are still here.' Mr Bartleigh breathed his relief. 'Doctor Olmer says that she is strong enough to travel, if we go slowly and by private coach.'

'I also said I do not recommend such a course of

action,' the sour physician said. 'Your wife has made more progress than I would have thought possible, but a trip would likely negate it.'

Mr Bartleigh's features set in determination. 'You told us when we first came to London and sought you out, sir, that my wife had not long left among us.'

'And less time does she have now,' grumped the doctor.

'I believe you, sir, but if my Anna says she wants to breathe fresh Dorset air again before she breathes her last, then I'm going to make sure that happens.'

'You'll do as you will, and I can't stop you, but just be sure to take it slow and in short stages.' The doctor reached out and gripped Mr Bartleigh's arm. 'Her spirit is strong, but her body is frail— remember to take that into consideration.'

Tears blurred Lily's vision, but not before she glimpsed the pain in Mr Bartleigh's face.

'Lily, would you be a good girl and stay with my Anna while I go and find us a well-sprung carriage?' he asked. 'We'll want to set off as soon as possible, and she does find you a comfort, dear child.'

'Of course. When will you leave, sir?'

'In the morning, if possible.' Mr Bartleigh waved a hand for the doctor to precede him and the pair departed. Lily wiped her tears and stood for a moment, gathering calm and summoning a smile before she opened the door.

There was no chance to do the same later as she arrived back at Lady Dayle's home. Fisher opened the door to greet her the minute she stepped down from the carriage.

Lily thanked the butler. She'd been trying to decide, on the way over, if she should have asked to accompany the Bartleighs back home to Weymouth. Lady Dayle had plenty to keep her busy with the orphanage now; she would hardly miss her. Minerva had a wedding to plan. Mr Bartleigh could likely use the help and there was nothing else keeping her here. She fought back tears; she'd done enough crying in the last days.

No, her mother would be arriving back in London shortly. Lily would do best to wait for her. She sighed. Never would she have thought to find herself wishing to go back home.

'I hope the good lady is recovering,' the butler said as he took her pelisse.

'As well as can be expected, thank you, Fisher.'

'A message has come for you, miss,' he said. 'The bearer said it was urgent.'

'Oh? Perhaps it is from Mother. She said she would write with the day we could expect her.' Lily took the letter, glanced casually at it, then stopped.

It was thin, probably only one sheet, and she recognised the bold hand.

'Thank you, Fisher,' she said again, and rushed upstairs. She closed the door behind her and broke the seal. There was no date and no signature, and it was composed of only two short sentences.

I need your help. I'm coming home.

Lily clutched the parchment to her breast. The decision had been taken out of her hands. One might even call it a sign, she thought wryly. She threw the letter down on the vanity, crossed to the wardrobe and pulled out a portmanteau.

For the first time in his life, Jack had grown weary of hiding away. Over the last days he had slowly restored order to the neglected mess of his rooms, all the while attempting to do the same for his disordered mind.

An agony of guilt and shame and indecision racked him. Not that he was ashamed of hitting Whitcomb. The beating he'd given that worm might be the only good that had come out of this fiasco. No, the man had deserved it. Jack was more than a little tempted to do it again, in fact, because the lecherous mushroom kept coming around demanding satisfaction, insisting that Jack duel with him, or at least pay his medical bills. He was persistent, irritating and generally making a nuisance of himself.

Jack ignored him. Eventually the man had gone away, but only to begin harassing Jack's family instead of him. Charles had shown up to complain, but Jack had only shrugged. He'd told his brother what he'd observed of the man.

'Oho,' Charles had said. 'I know just how to handle that.' He'd left, but the next day he returned, a satisfied smirk on his face as he dropped into a chair.

'Well, Whitcomb's taken care of,' he said.

'Oh?' All of Jack's attention was focused inwards. He forced himself to look at his brother and concentrate on his words.

'I introduced him to Mills.'

'Mills?' Jack vaguely knew the name. 'Wait—the newspaper editor? At *The Augur*?'

'The very one. I took Mills to Whitcomb's house and we had a very interesting afternoon.'

'What did you do? Threaten to have Mills write an editorial about lecherous asses?'

'No, there was no mention of any of lechery, at least out loud. I merely told the bastard all about the new feature Mills is working on.'

'And what feature is that?'

'Oh, just a piece about the poor souls in service,

the harshness of their life and the mistreatment they suffer at the hands of their wealthy masters.'

Jack raised a brow.

'Whitcomb did pale a little, but he tried to bluff through. But I told him that unless he wanted to be featured on the front page of *The Augur*, he'd best leave our family alone. All of our family,' Charles said with emphasis, 'and our friends and acquaintances, too.'

Jack did not respond. He knew what Charles wanted to hear. He just wasn't ready to talk about it yet.

But Charles wasn't done yet. 'Then I asked Whitcomb to assemble all of his staff, just so Mills could do a little research. He didn't want to. Turns out they have an unusually large contingent of very young maidservants. I promptly hired them all away.'

Jack laughed.

'And I told Mrs Whitcomb to replace them all with strapping footmen if she hopes to have any sort of social standing left in this town. The bounder's too cowardly to try anything with someone who can hit back.'

'Well, you wrapped him up nice and tight, didn't you?' Jack felt vaguely ashamed. 'All I could think to do was pummel the worm. What good does it do a man to possess an intellect if it is so easily overcome by temper?'

'Sometimes a man's passion is greater than his intellect, Jack,' said his brother. 'And that is no bad thing.'

Jack snorted. He watched as his brother stood. Charles went to the bookshelves and spent a few moments examining the titles there. When at last he spoke, he kept his face turned towards the well-worn tomes.

'It wasn't so long ago that I was in the same state as you, little brother—although it does feel like an eon has passed since then.' He sighed and it sounded more reminiscent than troubled. 'We stood in this same room and you gave me some remarkably good advice. Do you recall what it was?'

Jack grimaced. 'Lord, no.'

'You told me to stop, to take the time to look around and decide what it was that I wanted.' He left the bookshelf then and crossed the room, gripping Jack's shoulder in camaraderie. 'Now it's time you followed your own advice, Jack. Decide what it is you want. And I'll make the same offer you made me—whatever it is, I'll help you to get it.'

It was too much. Jack could not meet his brother's gaze. Silent, he nodded and dropped his head. But he reached up and grasped the hand on his shoulder, trying to convey with the pressure of his grip, everything that was in his heart.

'Thank you, Charles.' There was nothing more to say. How could he tell his brother that he'd been too preoccupied with his own ugliness to deal with Whitcomb's? That weightier than the question of what he wanted was the question of what he had the ability to cope with?

'You know where to find me, should you need me.'

Jack nodded again, and his brother turned and left.

He turned his gaze to the fire once more. Getting shot had somehow affected his head as much as his arm. It had cracked his defences. Anger and lust and myriad other unsightly emotions had been leaking out of him regularly since then.

But Lily Beecham had finished the job. She'd opened the locked door inside of him. Jack suspected that it had best been left closed. But now it was far too late. The portal had been thrown open, his barriers knocked down. For so long Jack had thought that those walls had only protected him from what lay outside. Now he discovered that they had also been keeping something locked in. Something not meant to see the light of day.

The idea haunted him, as did relentless images of his father. The man's negligent disdain had poisoned Jack's childhood. He had been able to draw blood with only a casual barb. The rare occasions when he had been moved to use his fist, a crop or a belt had counted as the worst days of Jack's life. But the thing that had always unnerved him the most had been the ugly satisfaction in his father's eyes—the same despicable feeling that had flooded through Jack as he pummelled that vile Whitcomb.

Was this, then, the true reason for his walls? Had he known all along—deep down and unacknowledged—that such a monster lurked inside of him? Had he been as eager to keep himself in as he had been to keep the world out?

He didn't know. He wasn't sure that he wanted to know.

Everyone eventually came to a crossroads in their life. Jack knew that he'd arrived at a defining moment in his. Lily had knocked him off his established path. He'd been forced to look at himself with new eyes and the sight was not pretty.

He had a choice to make now. Should he step back on where he'd left off? He could rebuild his ramparts, lock himself away again. He—and everyone else in his vicinity—would likely be the safer for it.

Or should he summon his courage and blaze a new trail? Could he learn to open himself to the people around him? Life seemed to exist part and parcel with a tidal surge of emotion. Everyone else appeared able to handle it. Could he do it, too, and without inadvertently following in his father's footsteps?

A month ago logic would have supplied the answers to such questions. No doubt it would have urged him towards the former. It seemed the easier and safer decision all around. But logic had deserted him. He was on his own. He looked around, but his rooms, finally in order again, were sterile and empty. He felt miserable and lonely.

It appeared, then, that the choice had been made for him. After days of indecision he was forced to acknowledge it. He could not go back.

Somewhat irritably, Jack readied himself to go out. By God, Lily had got him into this mess. He might have to forge a new path, but he was not going to begin until he had her as his guide. Finally presentable, he yanked open the door and stepped out.

Straight into a uniformed messenger, standing poised to knock.

'Message from the Admiralty, sir,' the man said smartly.

Eagerly, Jack took it. Surely this was the news of Batiste's capture? He laughed as he tore it open. Lily would say this was a sign that he'd made the right decision.

He read the words quickly. Shocked, he read it again, fighting not to drop the vellum from suddenly nerveless fingers.

The *Lady Vengeance* had indeed been holed up in

Tazacorte, but the Navy had failed to take her. Batiste had slipped away again.

Jack burst into the drawing room unexpected and unannounced.

'Good heavens, Jack!' Minerva Dawson exclaimed, dropping the pen she was using. 'You scared the wits out of me!' She sounded distinctly annoyed. 'Now I'll have to begin on this invitation again.'

'Where is she, Minerva?' Jack demanded. 'Fisher says that my mother is spending all of her time in Kensington working on the orphanage, but that Lily has left?' He came to a halt in front of Minerva's writing desk. 'Left my mother's house? Left town? Where is she?'

She set down the pen. 'You took your own sweet time deciding you needed to know,' she grumbled.

'Minerva!'

She sighed. 'She's left London.'

'When?'

'Yesterday. Really, Jack, are you going to break out the thumbscrews? I feel like I'm being subjected to the Inquisition.'

He ignored her attempt at humour. 'Has her mother returned? Have they gone back to Dorset?'

'No—although her mother is expected back any day now. Lily left with the Bartleighs. They were travelling back home to Weymouth and she decided to accompany them.'

'Why?' Jack was pacing through the parlour now. 'Has something happened? Has Whitcomb or someone else bothered her?'

Minerva stared at him, and disgust coloured her expression. 'You have to ask why she left?' She shook her head. 'I suppose she felt she had no reason to stay.' She bit her lip. 'Mrs Bartleigh, it seems, has been ill for a while now. It pains me to think...' She paused. 'The excitement of the ball overset her. She's very unwell, Jack.'

Jack bowed his head. Here was yet another burden he was not sure he could handle. 'I'm sorry,' he rasped.

He paced up and down Minerva's parlour for a moment. Abruptly he stopped. 'But Fisher said Lily received a disturbing message.'

'Yes, I badgered the same information out of him, except that I thought the message had come from you.' He met her gaze and she tapped her fingers together thoughtfully. 'I can see now that it did not.'

Suddenly she shrugged and got to her feet. 'I suppose it must have been from her cousin. I did notice before that she appeared to be a little subdued after she heard from him, but she never said why.'

But Jack had frozen at her first sentence. An instantaneous, icy sweat broke over him. 'What did you say?' he asked and his tone echoed the cold.

She stared. 'I don't know, what did I say?'

'A letter from her cousin?'

'Well, I'm only surmising, after all, but based on how she's acted in the past—'

'She's had others?' he interrupted. 'Other letters from her cousin in America?'

'Yes. Is there something wrong with that?'

But Jack was already heading for the door.

'Jack, where are you going?'

He didn't turn back.

'To Weymouth!'

Chapter Twelve

Reason might have deserted Jack, but necessity could not be got around. Arrangements had to be made, and therefore he was obliged to wait until the next morning to start out after Lily. Two days' lead time that gave her and the Bartleighs. They could easily be in Weymouth already, but Minerva had sent around a note saying that they had meant to travel slowly and at an easy pace, in deference to Mrs Bartleigh's condition. Jack thought that he would begin to watch for them as he neared Dorset.

He didn't yet know just what he was going to do when he caught the infuriating girl. The scenarios in his head were continually alternating. One moment he imagined himself grabbing her up and kissing her senseless, the next all he wanted to do was shake her hard and demand she share the information she'd been withholding.

Either way, he ached for her. He'd agonised over his decision and now that it was made, he found himself burning for her with a desperation that had him driving himself hard and his mounts to the edge of their endurance.

He broke off to change horses often and asked after Lily and her friends at each stop. Yet he could find no word of them. As the day wore on it began to worry and frustrate him. There was a very real chance that he could unknowingly overtake them, and then what would he do? He sighed. Continue on to Weymouth, he supposed, and wait for them there. Lord, but he hoped it didn't come to that. He'd waited too long already.

He made it all the way to Basingstoke, in Hampshire, before he uncovered a hint of them. Evening was coming on as Jack spoke to the ostlers at the Brown Bear. They recognised his description and said Lily and the Bartleighs had stopped here for a leisurely lunch.

'Aye, that'd be them,' the head groom said, rubbing his jaw with dirt-stained fingers. 'They rested here a long spell. One o' the ladies looked to be in a right bad way. The lads were taking bets that they'd end up stayin', but they left and I heard the coachman say they'd only be going as far as Winchester today.'

Overwhelmed with relief, Jack clapped the man on the back. 'Give me your fastest horse, man,' Jack told him. 'And I'll make it worth your while.'

'Yes, sir!'

Moments later, the groom led out a spirited chestnut, easily handling the hack as he pranced and tossed his head. 'This here's a good 'un and he's eager to be away, sir,' the man said. 'Just let him go flat out at first. He knows the way to Winchester in his sleep and he'll settle right out, soon as he's had a good run.'

'My thanks,' Jack said, swinging up and tossing down a purse that had the man's eyes bulging.

'Well, I'm gormed,' the man said in wonder.

Jack laughed and nodded for him to open the yard gate and, with a clatter of hooves, they were off.

Darkness had fallen before he reached the outskirts of Winchester, and rolling mist rose from the fields, spooking his mount. But Jack had pushed them both and the animal couldn't summon the spirit to do more than snort uneasily.

His hopes rising, Jack spoke soothingly and reached down to give the gelding a reassuring thump. He knew Winchester well. It had been King Alfred's capital city and Jack had spent a good deal of time here, researching one of his favourite subjects. He had several colleagues who lived here, in fact, and he'd visited often. He made his way easily to a livery in the centre of town, left the chestnut to be bedded down, and began to search the inns and taverns.

They were not to be found at the first two he visited. Disappointed, Jack stepped out of the Old Vine and stood a moment, gazing at the Cathedral silhouetted against the night sky. He forced himself to breathe deep. He had to stop rushing around and *think*.

What was it that Minerva's note had said? He cursed himself now for not bringing it along. Something about fresh country air? His heart began to pound a little faster. Could it be? He knew just the place he'd go if he were here and in search of a little serenity. Hesitant, he glanced back in the direction of the livery. No, it would take as long to rouse someone and hire another horse as to walk. Praying his instincts were right, Jack set out purposefully for the far edge of the town.

The Wood Grove Inn was aptly named, sprawled as it was in a lovely copse just outside of the bustle of the town. Timbered, thatched and rustic, the buildings and the beautiful gardens behind were well maintained and wonderfully enhanced by the nearby winding stream and the low, ancient granite wall that ran beside it. Jack had stayed here several times when he was here on extended research trips. There was a lovely private cottage at the back of the gardens that he liked to take when he was here. It was quiet and wonderfully conducive to work.

Tense and hopeful, Jack stepped into the familiar old building. Warm kitchen smells welcomed him and mixed with the yeasty tang of home brew. The door to the taproom swung open and the innkeeper stepped out.

'Good evening, sir,' the broad, comfortably padded woman spoke with formality. Then she stopped short and a great smile wreathed her red cheeks. 'Why, and it is Mr Alden, is it not? Bless me, but it's been an age since we saw you last! Come in, come in!'

'Good evening, Mrs Babbit.' Jack returned her smile. 'It is good to be back. I'm hoping most desperately that you can help me.'

'But of course I can! Are you here to consult with the deacon again?' She arched a coy look at him and did not wait for an answer. 'Would you be wishing to take the cottage again? We've had no bridal couples or anyone else, for that matter, in the longest time to take it. The place might be a tiny bit musty, but I swear, I shall have it aired out before the cat can lick its ear.'

'Thank you, no, I don't wish to be any trouble.

Truly, I'm not here to do research this time, ma'am. I'm looking for someone, and hoped they had the good sense to stay here.'

She chuckled. 'And I'm havin' the same hope. Who is it you're looking for, sir?'

'An older couple by the name of Bartleigh. They are travelling also with a young woman, Miss Beecham.'

Mrs Babbit's good-natured smile faded. 'Ah, yes. They are here, indeed, Mr Alden.'

Jack's fist clenched as elation pounded through his veins, yet he struggled to keep his expression sober, to match the innkeeper's. She glanced towards the taproom door, then reached out to pull him towards the hallway nook where she kept the guest log.

'You've likely made it just in time, lad,' she said in a low voice. 'The lady appears to be in a bad way.'

'Yes, I'm aware.' He realised she was trying to tell him something with her lowered brow and pursed lips. 'Do you mean…?'

'Aye, I do. But I'll be asking you to keep it quiet, if you please.' She nodded towards the taproom. 'A death in the house is never good for business.'

'Death?' The sense of urgency inside of him surged. 'Where are they, Mrs Babbit?'

'Upstairs, in the garden wing. I'll make you up a room there as well, if you won't want the cottage.' For the first time she looked at his empty hands and then behind him. 'Have you any bags, then, sir? Or shall I send a boy out to fetch them?'

'I've only a couple of saddlebags I left at the livery in town; if you could send a man there to fetch them, I'd appreciate it. I'd really like to go up,' he said, edging towards the stairs.

'Go on with you, then, and let me know if they're needing anything, will you, please?'

Jack was already halfway up the narrow staircase before she finished.

'You'll find them in the last door on the right,' she called.

Mrs Babbit's news set Jack on edge and thwarted the urgency with which he had rushed to find Lily. He could neither embrace her with relief nor question her about her cousin in this situation. Frustration ate at him, and then shame.

The air up here lay close and silent, and together with the sad tidings, formed a forcible reminder of the tense atmosphere in his home when his father lay dying. Those dark days had seemed nothing but a jumble of grief and scurrying feet, sobbing and bitter recriminations. Suddenly Jack found his feet dragging a little over the squeaking floorboards. How difficult this must be for her. In his mind Jack knew that this situation bore little similarity, yet his reluctance grew.

He reached the door at last and stood a moment, gathering strength. The soft murmur of voices reached his ears. Perhaps this was not a good time? He wavered, and then decided not to knock, but turned the knob slowly and edged open the door a bit.

He saw Lily first and his heart jumped. She sat facing slightly away from him, in a chair at the edge of a bed centred on the left-hand wall. As he watched, she leaned in towards the frail figure lying there and laid a gentle hand upon her brow. Mrs Bartleigh murmured something, but Jack did not hear the words. His gaze remained fixed on Lily.

Even from here he could see that she wore one of her shapeless gowns again. Her sleeves were rolled up and damp spots trailed down the front of her. Several heavy locks of her hair had slipped loose on one side and he could see her fingers tremble a little as she wrung out a cloth and pressed it to the dying woman's forehead.

Jack thought he'd never seen her look more beautiful. The tender light in her eyes moved him, and she exuded such a calm strength that it touched him from here. Her caring and warmth were not even directed at him and yet he felt their soothing effect.

The sick woman spoke again in a whisper and Jack realised that she was asking for something. Her thin hand reached out and grasped Lily's, but she only had the strength for a moment's grip. Her hand fell away again and Lily stroked it where it lay.

'Do sing it, please.' Another voice emanated from a dark corner of the room. Jack looked and saw the lady's husband lying on a cot, an arm draped over his eyes. The window above him was thrown open to the night air. 'You've a lovely voice, dear girl. It will do us both good to hear it.' The man's voice quivered with emotion and fatigue.

Lily nodded. She grasped Mrs Bartleigh's hand, gave her a tremulous smile and began to sing.

Jack stood rooted, listening. The song was vaguely hymn-like, but he had never heard it. Not a song of lament, it spoke instead of peace and joy and homecoming. Mrs Bartleigh's eyes closed, but her face was turned towards Lily and there was a small smile of contentment on her thin face. Her husband did not stir, but Jack saw the wet track of tears slipping from beneath his arm. Jack knew a sudden, fervent hope that the song could bring the man a measure of peace.

Lily's voice, sweet and clear, trailed through the room, weaving a spell of acceptance, of love unending and unbroken. Almost palpable, her sweet spirit touched them all, washed over Jack and through him, bringing him comfort, and in some mysterious way, transferring some of the peace in her soul into his.

He swallowed. This scene could not be more different than he had expected. He could not bring himself to interrupt the tableau. Very slowly he backed up and eased the door closed again.

For a long time he stood alone in the hallway, staring at the portal before him. This, then, was what he had missed out on, shutting himself away from the world. This girl had stirred and shaken him from the first moment they met. Now, without a word, she shattered some of his most entrenched beliefs. All of the standards on which he had built his life and moulded his character lay shattered at his feet.

Lily had burst into his life like a comet, a shining example of a strong woman and a truly giving spirit. His polar opposite. She lent out pieces of herself endlessly, sharing her joy and enthusiasm and her will to make things better. He hid away among his books, hoarding himself and his feelings as if they were gold. She gave of herself freely and emerged ever stronger. He secreted himself away and only dwindled, growing colder and more distant.

The shock of self-awareness left him feeling deeply weary and on the verge of breaking. He stumbled away from the door, turned blindly towards the stairs, seeking solitude and peace.

Mrs Babbit lay in wait. She took one look at his face and, nodding her understanding, she pulled open the front door. Grateful, Jack stepped out into the darkness.

He headed for the gardens at the back of the inn. The sky was clear tonight and the moon rode high and half-full, casting just enough light to illuminate the path ahead. He strolled slowly, breathing deep and allowing the peace of the night to soothe him. An occasional rustle sounded as his passage disturbed a sleeping bird or roving night creature, but he didn't stop. The gurgling stream at the back was calling him. He scooped up a handful of pebbles and perched beside it on the low granite wall.

Surprisingly, perhaps, his brother loomed at the forefront of his thoughts. He'd lied to Charles when his brother had asked if he remembered giving him advice. He did recall the occasion, vividly. Charles had been beleaguered then, and in a state of turmoil—just the state Jack sat in now. *Decide what it is that you want.* It was excellent advice, but Jack had thought that it did not apply. He already knew what he wanted, had known almost since the first moment that he saw Lily Beecham. The question was: did he have the ability—the courage, really— to seize it?

He'd thought he'd finally found the courage. Yet now he found himself hesitating, and for a totally different reason. He realised that the entirety of his focus had been on himself and his own conflicted needs and desires. Lily spent so much of her time thinking of others. It was past time he took a page from her book and thought about what was good for her. The stunning, terrifying truth was that that might not be him.

Open, generous, loving—Lily represented everything good in this benighted world. She could find someone so much better than a surly, stunted scholar. He'd already hurt her, would undoubtedly do so again. Would she think him even worth the pain and effort?

Jack took a pebble and tossed it into the stream. It hit with a satisfying plop and sent out a wave of ripples to catch the scant light. He needed answers to his questions.

A faint step sounded on the path behind him. He turned and she was there, a gorgeous figure lined in softest moonlight. He sighed. Now would be the perfect time to get them.

'Jack!' Lily stared in stunned disbelief. 'It is you. When Mrs Babbit said you'd come, I did not quite believe it.' She took a step closer. 'What are you doing here?'

He rose and beckoned her closer. 'Come and sit.'

Her heart pounded, but she did not heed him. She

could never keep her head when she was too close to him, and she needed to know. 'Why, Jack?'

He stared at her. The darkness made it difficult to see where he directed his gaze, but she could feel its caress, could follow its path by the heating of her blood.

'I came to find you,' he said simply. 'But instead, I think I've lost myself.'

Lily snorted. 'That is exactly the sort of answer I should have expected from you,' she said, piqued.

'You don't sound happy to see me,' he said. She could tell he was trying to sound meek.

He failed miserably.

She gave up. She chuckled and stepped towards the ancient wall where he'd been sitting. 'I am glad to see you, I'm just…I'm feeling too many things to sort out right now.' She sighed.

He swept a hand towards the stream. 'There's a nice selection of rocks here. Perhaps you'd like to throw one at me? It might make you feel better and there's a slim chance that it will knock some sense into me.'

She tsked at him and allowed him to help her over the wall so she could sit. 'Whatever it is that you are lacking, it isn't sense. In fact, I've come to think that you set entirely too great a store by it.'

'Do you?' He opened his hand. She had to look close to see that he held a handful of tiny smooth stones. 'Have some,' he said. He demonstrated by plunking one into the water. 'It helps you think.'

They sat pitching rocks in companionable silence for a while. He was right. It did help restore her balance after a long and heartbreakingly difficult day. The night lay quiet about them and the peace gradually helped calm her frayed nerves. But he sat too close for her to feel truly settled. She could feel the heat rising from him and smell the comfortably masculine mix of soap, smoke and horse.

The silence stretched out between them until, suddenly, Lily felt it had gone on too long. 'The truth, Jack,' she demanded. 'Why are you here?'

At the exact same moment he spoke into the silence. 'How is Mrs Bartleigh?' he asked.

They laughed together. A dangerous moment—she did not want to get too comfortable with him—yet.

'Your friend, how is she?' he asked again, gently.

'Asleep now, but not as strong as we'd hoped. Mr Bartleigh is resting as well. I left a maid to sit in with them.' She threw her last stone and dusted her hands together. 'It will be no more than a day or two, the local doctor said, when we asked him for advice.' She drew a deep breath. 'The worst part is not being able to make it home. But this inn is lovely and the air is sweet. I think it helps.'

'I'm very sorry.'

She looked up into his eyes. 'Tell me, Jack. Why are you here? I need to know.'

He dumped his remaining pebbles and wiped his hand on his thigh. Then he reached for her hand and entwined his fingers tenderly with hers. 'Come, will you walk with me a little? I can express myself a little better if I am moving, I think.'

She nodded and they set off. The gardens were extensive, reaching from the stream, past the main building of the inn and on nearly to the stables on the other side. Plenty of room for pacing and explanations.

'When I left that ball, Lily, I was appalled at myself,' he began. 'The intensity and violence of my feelings—it was unnerving. All of my feelings,' he emphasised. 'Not just the anger I felt towards that bounder Whitcomb, but everything I felt about what…we had done, too. I don't think you can imagine how unsettling it was for me.'

'Then tell me,' she said.

'For so long I've dampened my emotions, ignored them or tucked them away, and suddenly so much was exploding out of me.' He shrugged. 'I don't know how to control the intensity of what I feel. Because I've never really let myself feel much of anything at all.'

She smiled. 'All you need is practice.'

'I need you, too, Lily,' he said, his voice lowering.

'I meant at first to go back, to suppress everything you'd set free and return to the safety of my isolation. But for the first time solitude felt all wrong. I was miserable. It's too late to turn back. I want to learn. I'll do what it takes, but I'll need help.'

'You have it,' she whispered, stepping close.

'Lily,' he said abruptly. 'I watched you tonight. With the Bartleighs. In there.' He jerked his head towards the inn.

'You did?' She felt puzzled and slightly alarmed at the strange vehemence of his tone. 'What did you see?'

He laughed, but there was no humour in it—only pain. 'What did I see?' He drew to a halt and dropped her hand. 'I saw an angel come to earth.' He walked a few steps away, but then spun on his heel and stalked slowly back towards her. 'An angel with eyes the colour of the sky and red-gold hair like the setting sun.' His voice lowered to a rasp. 'An angel with a devil's mouth, continuously tempting me to sin.'

She started as he reached for her, cupped her face in both of his powerful hands. 'I saw exactly what I've been lacking all my life, everything I want to lay claim to—and everything I should not.'

Tears welled in her eyes. She lifted her own hands up to grasp his wrists. The frantic beat of his pulse singed her fingertips. 'Why shouldn't you?'

Abruptly he let go. The absence of his touch was worse than pain. 'Because you give all that you have and I give nothing. You are a tower of strength and I…' He stepped away into the shadow of a tree's spreading branches. 'I am broken.'

Lily dashed away the tears in her eyes. 'Stop it,' she said fiercely. 'First, stop making me out to be so perfect. I am not. I'm human just like everyone else, with all the same faults and foibles. And if you need a reminder, then I will tell you that when I came out here I heard an owl calling twice, and I've been anxiously listening, because if he calls a third time it will mean bad luck!'

He made a dismissive noise and she followed him into the darker shelter of the tree. 'Second, you are not broken.' Sure of herself now, she stepped between his legs and pressed against him, forcing him to lean back into the tree to support them both. Arching into him, she reached up and stroked lightly along his jaw.

'And third, there is only one thing that you lack—and that is a tiny piece of information. It's not a secret, but it's something that few enough ever truly understand.'

She stood on her toes and brushed a light kiss across his lips. 'Whatever you give in this life—that is what you get back. You are right—I do lend my help, my strength, where I see a need for it. But it all comes back to me and makes me stronger.' He started to speak, but she pressed a finger to his mouth to stop him. 'Listen well, for I hope you will take this to heart. If you give nothing to the world, how can you expect to get anything back?'

She removed her hand and pressed closer still. Softly she kissed him again, then ran a line of tender kisses along the strong line of his jaw and into the vulnerable spot beneath his ear. 'One last thing I mean to tell you,' she whispered. 'There is no need for you to lay claim to me. For I am giving myself to you.' She drew back and looked him full in the eye, allowed him to see all the longing in her soul. 'I would appreciate it if you would follow my advice and return the favour.'

He responded at last with a low moan, then he dipped his head and returned her kiss, taking possession of her with lips and mouth and tongue and lifting her hard against him.

Joyfully, Lily gave herself over to him and to the flare of passion sweeping through her. She twined her arms about his neck and her fingers into his dark, unruly hair. He made a sound of approval into her mouth and she felt the reverberation of it slide down into her, settling deep and hot in the pit of her belly.

Boldly he stroked her with his tongue, while his hands moved lightly over her body. The juxtaposition of his hot, possessive mouth and the slow, tantalising dance of his fingers down her back and over the curves of her bottom forced her hunger higher, until she wanted to laugh with the delight of it. Yes, she thought, this is what she'd been waiting for.

We were not put on earth to enjoy life.

The words echoing in her head were Mr Cooperage's, but the ringing tones sounded suspiciously like her mother's. Or perhaps it was just the outraged voice of some deeply buried part of her conscience. She ignored them all.

They were wrong. All of them were so sadly mistaken. Lily knew without a doubt that people were meant to enjoy life. We were all meant to *live* life, and how could one survive without joy? Lily could not. She'd tried. Oh, how hard she'd tried, for her mother's sake, but duty and virtue turned dry as dust when it was not leavened with love and happiness.

Jack was her chance for both. Perhaps some would call her unwise—gambling on Jack Alden could not be called a sure bet. But she had set out to find just who Lily Beecham was, and now she'd discovered a large part of the answer. Neither her mother's daughter nor her father's, but a person in her own right, with her own moral sense of right and wrong. The sort of person who knew the right thing to do was to take a chance on love.

Chapter Thirteen

Jack tore his mouth away from Lily's, but only long enough to press a burning kiss to her sweet nape. She hummed her approval and let her head tilt back, granting him access to the slender column of her neck. He paused to let his appreciative gaze wander over her flushed cheeks and closed eyes. He drank in the enchanting sight, and then buried his face in the lush curve of her neck and shoulder and breathed deep. If only he could inhale some of her strength along with the clean and heady scent of her.

Greedily he covered her mouth once more, rejoicing when she echoed the urgency of his kiss. He pulled her closer, marvelling that she should feel so small, when the force of her personality and the beauty of her soul loomed so large.

He pulled away, suddenly impatient that he could not see the excitement in her eyes. Stepping back, he lifted her hand, kissed it soundly and began to lead her down the path.

'Where are we going?' she asked, breathless.

'I know the perfect place.'

He kept her tucked close as they moved through the gardens, relishing all the points of contact with her from shoulder to thigh and craving a hundred more intimate touches. Even in the moonlight, the gardens loomed luxurious and fragrant, but Jack had more important things on his mind. He led Lily ever further back, until they passed through a marching line of tall yews and she halted suddenly, caught up in the beautiful scene before them.

Jack could understand her awe. The little cottage nestled in the last stand of the wooded grove. Beyond it lay another low granite wall and a pasture awash in moonlight. The moon hung just above, in fact, as if placed there for the sole purpose of illuminating this secret hideaway.

'What is it?' she breathed.

'It used to be a dairy, I believe, but Mrs Babbit transformed it into a cottage. She lets it to those who are staying longer than a night or two.' He pulled her in close for a lingering kiss. 'Or occasionally a bridal couple takes it.'

She heaved a sigh of wonder. 'You're right. It is perfect.'

It was hard to tell, but he thought she was blushing. Jack had to kiss her again, then, because she was so adorable. He pressed his lips to hers once, twice, and then he picked her up and swung her around. He ignored the sudden protest of his arm. Buoyant with happiness, he swept her off her feet and carried her to the door.

Once there Jack grew suddenly sober. He set her down on her feet and pulled her close. 'There is no reason we have to…' He paused. Feebly, he gestured back towards the inn. 'We could just…'

She smiled, though he failed to see the humour here. Grabbing his hand, she repeated his earlier gesture and kissed it, but softly. Then she held it close to her bosom. He could feel her heart pounding with excitement and need.

'Don't be absurd, Jack. What we've found, what we feel for each other—it is a gift. How many people are so fortunate?' Slowly she opened his hand, spread his fingers, and kissed each one. Then she took his hand, slid it down and across until she placed it squarely on her bottom once more.

Jack let out an incoherent moan. No man had ever been this fortunate, he was sure. She was such an intoxicating mix of innocence, wisdom and desire. 'Not nearly enough,' he answered.

'Exactly. And that is why we shall not squander

this honour. We will accept it,' she whispered. 'Celebrate it. With all of our hearts.'

'And our bodies,' he said huskily.

'Yes. Our only shame would be in refusing such a gift.'

Her words set his heart to pounding. He bent to her again. A whispered sigh escaped her and she melted against him, all the tension draining from her body. She opened her mouth beneath his, inviting him in once more, tempting him, setting fire to his blood. He strove mightily to pull back. 'This is an irrevocable step, Lily. I made my choice back in London. I chose you. Your decision comes here and now.'

She shook her head. Her eyes remained half-lidded. 'Yes. No. Of course.' Her lips brushed gently along his jaw. 'All I want is you.'

'No, I mean it, Lily. God knows, I'm a bad bargain at best, and I want you to be sure of what you are getting. If we do this, we will be bound.'

She stood on tiptoe and pressed herself tight against him. 'I can think of nothing I would like more.'

His heart in his mouth, Jack reached behind her and tried the door. It swung wide and he silently blessed Mrs Babbit. Just as he remembered, a lamp lay on a table close to the door. He lit it quickly, and then moved further into the room to ignite a pair of candles on the mantel.

The cottage was all one room, with a handsome, stone fireplace on one end, flanked by a pair of chairs and an all-purpose table. On the other side of the room loomed a wide, four-posted bed, done up in faded, once-rich silk. Lily trailed across the room, examining everything, but Jack noticed that her eye shied repeatedly away from the bed.

'Have you stayed here before?' she asked faintly.

'Yes.' He wanted to put her at ease. Ignoring the existence of the bed, he sat in one of the wide, well-cushioned chairs by the fireplace. 'Come here,' he said, low and urgent.

Relief showing in her face, she came. She obviously recalled their embrace in the Dawson's library as vividly as he did. She turned to sit sideways on his lap as she had then.

'Wait,' Jack commanded. He positioned her so that they were knee to knee, and then with a wicked smile he leaned down to grasp the ends of her skirts. She began to breathe heavily as he allowed his fingers to trail a circuitous route up the length of her legs.

'Like this,' he whispered once her skirts had reached her knees. He urged her forwards until she straddled him in the chair.

'Oh, my.' She sank down and Jack swallowed hard as her moist heat settled right over the growing bulge in his breeches.

'I do so enjoy your way with words.' He grinned up at her, fighting for control. His head settled on the back of the chair. 'But don't you want to kiss me?'

She smiled back, a look full of mischief and longing. 'I want to kiss you…' she leaned down and her breath was a hot caress under his ear '…more than you can possibly imagine.' She hovered enticingly over his lips.

'I beg to differ,' he said breathlessly. 'I have quite an active imagination.' God, it was killing him, but he held still, kept his hands at his sides and allowed her the lead.

A wise move on his part, for Lily made it entirely worth the wait. She spread her legs further apart and settled herself more firmly over his erection. Her bosom pressed close against him, tempting him with the promise of more and then she leaned in and kissed him, sweet and deep. Her tongue stroked his with slow and languid strokes and her soft, yielding lips drove him wild.

Jack could take no more. He was at her mercy and in the grip of a vortex of lust. It surged through him, urging him on as he reached for her and buried his hands in her hair, tearing pins away and loosing a glorious fall of red-gold hair. It spilled down and over them both, teasing Jack's jaw and neck. He suffered a sudden vision of her curls spread across his bare chest as she kissed her way down towards his ramrod-stiff shaft.

Almost fierce with impatience, he tore his mouth from hers and submerged his face in her sweetly scented mass of curls. All the while, he kept his hands busy at her back, searching out the fastenings of her gown. At long last the final button on her bodice popped free and the last tie of her stays came undone. He pushed it all down to her waist.

Only her shift was left, a simple cotton garment that exposed more than it covered and rose and fell with her rapid breath. The magnificent outline of her high, full breasts showed clear. Enthralled, Jack encircled them with his hands, tested their weight, and thumbed her searching, straining nipples until she gasped with pleasure.

He had to see her. A thousand tiny buttons marched down the front of her shift and Jack had to fight the urge to tear them all open. He took his time instead, popping them off one by one and revelling in the sensation of her shifting restlessly over his straining body.

At last it was done. Jack spread her shift apart and pulled it down her arms. Then he lay his head back and let the sight of her drive the breath from his lungs.

She looked unreal, otherworldly with the dim candlelight sparking in her hair and lining her curving figure with gold. Round, high and tipped with rose, her breasts called to him. He answered with lips, fingers and fervent caresses. A sound emerged from deep inside her and her back arched, inarticulately asking for more. He answered again, setting his mouth to one breast, teasing it with his lips and tongue while he gently pinched the nipple of the other.

For long moments he pleasured her, licking one nipple with slow thoroughness and then moving to the other. Lily's breathing grew ragged and she began to rock her hips against him in quick, untutored motions. He could feel the hot, wet heat growing at her centre.

With a growl, Jack came off the chair. She whooped in surprise and locked her legs around him. Laughing, he carried her to the bed and set her square in the centre.

'I think we're both wearing entirely too many clothes,' he said with a smile.

She nodded and he worked the rest of her clothes up and over, down and off. Standing back, he gazed at her perfect form with reverence. Elation filled him. Tonight, for the first time, he would be free to let go, to loose all holds and let his emotions roam free—because for the first time he did not have to fear their heavy weight. Lily was strong. Beautiful, yes, and so amazingly formed that he itched to run his hands over her again. But it was her tenacious hardiness that made her so perfect for him. She knew her own mind and somehow she managed to bolster his own strength with her own.

Impatient, wanting to touch her again, he began peeling his clothes off. Propping herself up on her elbows, she watched him with unabashed curiosity. As the layers fell away, a sensual smile lurked on her face, igniting another erotic vision, a picture of those full, luscious lips locked around him. When at last he sprang free he was as hard as stone. Her eyes widened. The look of utter fascination she wore had him swelling impossibly huge.

He crawled up next to her on the bed. 'You are so incredibly beautiful,' he breathed in her ear.

'As are you,' she whispered back.

Jack laid a hand on her breast, stroking it with idle caresses as he gazed seriously into her eyes. 'You were right all along, you know. I had built walls around myself. And then you came along and reduced them all to rubble.' He kissed her softly. 'But now I find I am tempted to build them up again, just to keep you inside.'

She lifted a hand to his face. 'You don't need walls to keep me close,' she said. 'I'm not going anywhere.'

He kissed her then, in gratitude and something more. He might have worked out what that more was, but she trailed a hand over his shoulder, down his chest and poised it over him. She pulled back and there was a question in her eyes.

'Yes,' he moaned. 'Touch me.'

She touched her index finger to the tip of him and Jack fought hard to keep from thrusting further into her hand. He held back and let her explore. It was the most exquisite torture. Lightly caressing fingers ran all over him, from crown to sac, until at last he could not wait. He took her hand and wrapped her fingers firmly around him.

'Ah,' she said. 'Like this?' She gave an experimental stroke.

'Yes, just like that,' he begged. 'More.'

She grinned her triumph, but only until his hand left her breast, trailed down her body and burrowed into her nest of copper curls. Beneath them she was hot, slick and wetter than he could have dreamed.

'Ohh,' she said, loudly. The sound echoed through the small room.

'Lie back.'

She complied and he spread her wide, and bent to suckle her breast again as his fingers stroked, teased and circled her into a frenzy.

'Like this?' he asked, his voice heavy with humour and lust.

'More,' she demanded.

He laughed low and kissed her hard. 'As my lady pleases.'

He rolled above her and nudged her legs apart. She hissed long and low as he reached down and parted her. Gritting his teeth to hold on to the shreds of his control, he fondled her again, letting his fingers roam in her slick heat until she squirmed beneath him once more.

Now. He had to have her now. He sucked in his breath when he encountered the wet evidence of her desire. Slowly, carefully, he pushed in, easing his way into the hot, tight core of her.

Good God. He could feel her body stretching, giving way, but still surrounding him with a snug embrace. He'd had bed partners aplenty, but never had he experienced this blinding sense of intimacy. Never had he felt so close, so connected with another person, body and soul. It was exhilarating, and a little frightening.

Lily wiggled beneath him, a frown of concentration on her lovely face.

'Are you all right?' he asked. He eased further and held his breath, sure he would die if he had to stop now.

'Yes. No. Just a moment.' She shifted again and suddenly opened wider. 'Yes. That's it.' She sighed. She threw her head back and gripped him tight.

He needed no further encouragement. He rocked

his hips and began to move, slow and sure. Gradually, she caught on, caught his rhythm and began to move with him. Incredibly, his shaft flexed and stretched again.

'Oh, Lord.' Jack gripped her bottom and braced her for a series of long, hard strokes. She met him thrust for thrust. Her hands roamed, restless, until they finally settled on his buttocks and urged him on. Together in breath, body and rising hunger, they climbed. Jack could feel the mounting tension in her body. He swore as her passage tightened again.

'It's coming for us, Lily,' he murmured. 'Let it take you.'

'I don't know how,' she cried, desperation in her voice.

Jack could not wait much longer. She was too perfect in every way. He slid his hand between them and found the aching centre of her pleasure. She keened her response and the reaction of her sex was instantaneous as it began to flutter around his surging shaft. Lightly he stroked her, coaxed her along, until suddenly, without warning she broke apart, pulling him in even deeper.

It was too sweet, too much. A great swell of emotion grew inside him, a rushing tangle of affection, gratitude and, God help him, it was true—love. It swamped him so he thought he would drown in it. Harder and faster he thrust, mounting ever higher. With a roar, he went over, abandoning himself to the flood, letting it drag him through shattering need and gusts of pleasure. For endless moments he arched into her and no longer was he a lonely, flawed being, but one part of a glorious whole. He crested, riding high, reaching new heights never possible without Lily's support. He shuddered, poised in tight ecstasy above her until gradually the emotional tide receded, and he drifted home, wrapped in the contentment of Lily's arms.

Afterwards they sat together in the chair once more. The hour grew late and the little cottage filled with caring words, affectionate banter and soft laughter. It was perfect, just as Lily had always dreamed. She rejoiced in the simple pleasure of acceptance, the immense thrill of just being herself and finding that he neither expected nor wished for anything else.

But gradually Jack's mood grew sombre, his hesitation more obvious. With a sigh, Lily snuggled against him and prayed he wouldn't end their idyll so soon.

He shifted in the chair beneath her and cleared his throat. A smile tugged at the corner of her mouth and she gazed up at him. 'What is it, Jack?' She traced a tender line across his brow and down the strong plane of his face to his jaw and tried to lighten his mood again. 'You're not regretting the loss of your virtue, are you?'

His chest heaved as he choked with surprised laughter. 'No, you saucy chit.' A frown creased his brow and he looked down at her with concern. 'I hope you are not, either.'

'Not in the least,' she said, planting a kiss on his lips.

But he was not to be distracted. He took her hand and spoke earnestly. 'I want you to understand, I consider tonight the greatest gift, the highest honour of my life.'

'As you should,' she said with a smile.

'I'm perfectly serious.' His brow furrowed even further. 'We've both been through so much lately and death can act as a powerful influence. I would hate to think that your grief has led to something that you would regret later.'

She sat up straighter in his lap and gripped his hand tight. 'You need to understand as well, I will never regret spending this night with you.' She imbued her voice with all the earnestness and fervour in her heart. 'Everything we feel tonight is true and beautiful. You are right, my friend is dying, but her passing will be easy. Do you know why?'

He shook his head.

'Because she's lived a good and full life. None of us is perfect, but she's done her best. She's done what good she may and she has no regrets to weigh her down or mar the peacefulness of her last moments.' She breathed deep and softened her tone. 'If we had *not* done this, I would have regretted it for the rest of my life, and I would have carried that disappointment with me to *my* death bed.' She gave him a gentle smile. 'We will take the future as it comes, but rest easy knowing that tonight was meant to be.'

She thought his eyes filled, but he only nodded and gathered her close. She sighed and enjoyed his embrace for a moment, but something of what he'd just said nagged at her.

'You know, you were right about death being a powerful influence on the living,' she said. 'I've learned that lesson in hard school.'

'Your father?'

'Yes, his death was so hard for me and it certainly changed the path of my life.' She looked up at him. 'As I'm sure your father's death did for you.'

She saw his jaw clench, and the hated, empty look stole back into his eyes. And right then she knew. 'What is it, Jack? Is there something about your father I don't know?'

Jack let out a bitter laugh. 'Undoubtedly there is— nearly as many things about him that I never knew.'

He stood abruptly, carrying her off his lap and setting her on her feet. 'I'm sorry, it's just that he was a hard man. We were not close. He wasn't close to anyone, really, not even my mother.' He began to putter about the room, straightening the already made bed and other things that had not been disturbed.

'How sad, for all of you.' Lily sighed.

'I think he tried with Phillip, my eldest brother, but in the end he only pushed him away. And then Phillip died and my father followed, not long after.' He glanced over at her. 'They both had a heavy load of regrets, I would imagine.'

Pieces of the puzzle were rapidly joining in Lily's head. He never mentioned his father. He had not been close with him. Their relationship had been distant, one might say.

'I truly am sorry, Jack. At least while I had him, my father was loving, open and warm. I still miss him so much.'

He didn't respond. Lily watched as he went to the door and opened it a crack. 'It will be dawn soon,' he said. 'We should get back.'

'I never told you how my father died.'

That got his attention. He came back and gathered her in his arms. 'It's not necessary, Lily. I'm fine.'

'I've never talked about it with anyone,' she whispered. 'But I'd like to tell you.' She tried to ease his discomfort with a smile. 'And as you are fond of saying, it's only fair.'

'Let's go outside, then, into the garden.'

She nodded and they closed up the little cottage and found a bench near a bank of sweet-smelling roses.

'I told you how I bewildered my mother as a child,' she said, snuggling up close to him. 'She didn't know quite what to do with me. But that changed when I turned fifteen. She took a sudden interest in me and decided to rectify the lack of ladylike refinements in my education.'

He chuckled. 'Was it horrid?'

'No, not really.' She smiled. 'I was just so happy to find a way to please her. I applied myself to learning about fashion and decorum and whom to sit where at the dinner table.' She shot him a grin. 'Of course, I did not give up my horses or my rounds about the estate with my father, but still, she was thrilled. I think she had got it in her head that even if she couldn't have a son, she was going to make sure I made the finest marriage in the county.'

'What happened?'

'There was an assembly being held in Weymouth. It was to be my first. Mother was determined I should go, get my feet wet, so to speak, and begin to polish my manners locally before she took me to London to bring me out.'

She sat silent a moment, preparing herself to speak aloud things that she had never spoken of to anyone before. Jack did not push her; he just held her close and drifted his fingers through her hair.

'It began to cloud up, but Mother was adamant. Nurse muttered and moaned about weather signs, but Father just laughed and said he could wait no longer to dance with me.' She sighed. 'The storm broke while we were on the road, nearly halfway there. It was a terrible thing to see, with the trees bent nearly sideways and the rain coming down so hard you could not see from one end of the carriage to the next.'

'You must have been frightened half to death.'

'We all were, I think. The road turned into a quagmire in an instant. The horses were in a panic. The coachman climbed down to try to calm them, and promptly slipped in the mud and broke his leg. Papa said there was no help for it. He bundled the coachman into the carriage with Mother and me, cut the horses loose and set out on foot to find help.'

'What happened to him?' Jack's voice was heavy with empathy.

'Oh, it took hours, and by then the storm had passed, but he made it back with a farmer's dray heavy enough to navigate the mud. It wasn't until the next day that he started to feel ill. He caught a putrid sore throat and died a few weeks later.'

'Oh, my dear, I am so sorry,' he said. He wrapped her in a comforting embrace.

'It was bad,' she said quietly. 'Grief was a heavy burden, but the guilt and the fear were worse.'

'You had nothing to feel guilty about!' he protested.

'I know that now. But I was fifteen and I thought the world began and ended with me,' she said with a sad smile. 'Nurse rumbled that we had ignored her and all the signs. I worried that if I had not wished to go to the assembly, we wouldn't have been caught in the storm. My self-recriminations were endless—and then my mother…'

'I cannot begin to imagine her pain,' Jack murmured.

'I told you she was reserved before, but after my father died— Well, you've seen what she has become. She is so dour, and refuses to take any pleasure in life. I worried that her transformation was my fault, too.'

He kissed her temple. 'My poor girl.'

'It was Mrs Bartleigh who saved me. We got to know her as Mother became more involved with the Evangelicals and their charitable efforts. She and Mother grew close and she saw how terribly hurt we both were. Eventually she helped me to see that none of it had been my fault. She showed me that my job was to grieve and move on. Never to forget—but not to let it ruin me either.'

'She sounds a wise woman.'

'She is, and a very dear friend. I wish, though, that she had been able to help my mother. It was a long time before I realised that Mother is frantically trying to do good to somehow balance out what she thinks of as her fault. I wonder when, if ever, she will realise that her guilt exists only in her own mind.'

Lily pulled away and looked into Jack's eyes, so hard to read in the dwindling moonlight. 'I've watched you, Jack, and thought I would never begin to understand what drives you. But now I wonder if you might not share some of my mother's burdens.'

He looked as if he'd been kicked in the gut. 'What?' he asked in shock.

'No one in your family speaks of your father much. You, on the other hand, have never mentioned him at all. When I do, or someone else does, then you look exceedingly uncomfortable and you invariably change the subject.'

'That does not mean I have anything to feel guilty about.' He was beginning to sound outraged.

'No, of course not. And if I am wrong, then I am sorry. I just wanted you to know that it's possible that I once felt similarly. If ever you wish to talk about…anything, then I am always ready to listen.'

He shook his head and smiled down at her, but she

could tell it was forced. 'I told you I was broken—now you are trying to fix me?'

'I'm just trying to help,' she said, worried that she had perhaps spoken before he was ready to hear her.

He rose and pulled her to her feet. 'Thank you. It isn't necessary, but it makes me feel good just to hear it.'

It was a lie. Her questions had clearly disturbed him, set his nerves on edge.

He pressed a soft kiss to her mouth. 'Come, it's time we went in. If we go in the servants' entrance, we can get upstairs without anyone knowing.'

Her heart falling, she nodded her agreement. The sense of contentment and peace imbuing the night had flown. What else could she do to win his trust? He claimed his walls were down, but still he would not open his heart and mind to her.

Chiding herself, she tried to rally. She'd had tonight, and they had a chance at tomorrow. She could move at as slow a pace as he needed. Clasping his hand tight, she followed him in.

Chapter Fourteen

Jack spent a few restless hours trying to sleep, but his mind was awhirl and what little sleep he managed was racked with disturbing images. He tossed and turned until he had his bedclothes as muddled as his head. When he finally got his foot so entangled that he nearly cut off the circulation, he put a period to the attempt.

His saddlebags had been delivered. He rose, exchanged one rumpled set of clothes for another and went in search of breakfast.

'There's precious little to be had, I'm afraid,' Mrs Babbit said in answer to his enquiry. She huffed as she carried linens up the stairs. 'There's a fair in Winchester today. Half the servants have the day off, the other half are sulking because they don't. Even the cook's gone in search of some fancy spice or other, much good it'll do in a place like this where folks expect good, plain English fare,' she grumbled. 'There's bread and cheese and cold meat in the larder, Mr Alden. Help yourself. Your friends are occupied now, in any case, as the young lady is helping me to change the linen on Mrs Bartleigh's bed.'

'Thank you, Mrs Babbit.' Jack watched her climb the rest of the stairs. Lily's talk of her father—and his—had set him on edge. It had also reminded him forcibly of his other reason for searching her out. But it did not look as if he'd be able to question her about her contact with her cousin any time soon.

'Oh, ma'am, just a minute,' he called after the innkeeper. 'Do you have room for my mount in your stables?'

'Aye, should be plenty of room,' she called back. 'Just check with one of the grooms.'

The single groom left behind confirmed that there was an empty stall. 'And plenty o' good feed, too,' he assured Jack. 'Not like the half-rotten stuff the livery in town'll be givin' your mount.' He looked almost hopeful. 'Do you want me to go in and fetch him for you, sir?'

'Thank you, no,' replied Jack. 'I think I'll go myself.' He could get a hot breakfast while he waited, as long as Lily was busy in any case.

The long night had taken its toll and Jack's pace slowed as he entered the town proper. A savoury meat pie from a cart vendor revived him a bit. Feeling better, he began to make his way through the crowds, in the direction of the livery.

A coldly familiar sound brought him up short. Definitely that was the echo of leather slapping against flesh. He cast about until he discovered the sound bouncing eerily from the high walls of a nearby lane.

A poorly dressed man, a farmer by the looks of his work-stained hands and the contents of his cart, stood at the mouth of the small space, smacking his thin belt against his palm. A young boy cowered in front of him.

'What good do ye think ye'll do me, boy, if ye land yer arse in gaol for thievin'?'

The boy bowed his head and didn't answer.

'Ye've whacked him once,' a feminine voice said. Jack saw a woman in worn but clean clothes at the back of the cart. 'He's learned his lesson. Haven't ye, Tommy?'

The boy nodded vigorously and wiped his nose.

'Aye, and he'll be spendin' his fair day workin' for the man he thought to steal from,' the farmer growled.

Dismay bloomed in the boy's face and Jack moved on. But the image of the man's anger conspired with his fatigue and the unease brought on by last night's conversations. Together they called forth an uncomfortable vision from his own childhood.

'What good is he?' his angry father had demanded. Perhaps ten years old he'd been that time? He vividly remembered emerging from the library to hear his father's shout echoing through the hall. 'Your indulgence has ruined him! He's soft and weak.'

'He's got a brilliant mind.' He'd heard his mother defending him. 'And a devastating wit, as you'd discover if you spent any time with him.'

'And so I would if the boy would begin to show an interest in worthwhile pursuits. As it is, I've got no time to waste on babes and books!'

The words echoed painfully even through so many years. And stirred up the same roiling sense of resentment and determination. Jack shook his head and set off purposefully for the livery. He had not let his father's disdain sway him from his course then. In the same vein, he could not let either Lily's misguided loyalty or his own feelings for her deter him now.

The livery was as crowded as the streets and they were glad to see him free up an empty stall.

'I'll have your mount saddled right up, sir,' the owner said. He started to say something further, but the precipitous arrival of an obviously blown team ahead of a carriage full of merrymakers had him striding out into the yard, shouting orders as he went.

Jack waiting impatiently, ignoring the noise and bustle until a youngster brought his rented hack. He tossed the fees to the boy and mounted with resolve. It was time he got back to the inn and back on the trail of both Matthew Beecham and Gustavo Batiste.

'Oy!' the livery owner came back on a run, shouting as Jack left the yard in a flurry of hooves. 'Hold a moment, sir!'

His bellow blended into the racket in the yard.

'Did ye tell him about the men who come by lookin' for him?' the owner demanded of the boy.

The young groom shook his head.

'Ah, well, then.' The owner turned back to his business with a sigh. 'They'll find each other, if 'tis important enough.'

Mrs Babbit thrust a tray into his hands as soon as he burst in the door. 'Thank God, you're back,' she said urgently. 'Take this up with you, please? The poor lady's time is nigh and the two of them won't leave her side for a minute.'

'Oh, no.' A host of conflicting reactions hit Jack at this sad news. Ruthlessly he suppressed the impatience that surged to the forefront.

'Go on, then! Hurry on up.'

'Oh, yes, of course.' For the second time in two days he trod with high-running emotion and reluctant feet to the dying woman's chamber. This time he knocked before swinging the door gently open.

It was a wasted effort. Neither occupant of the room heard him. Lily sat in the same spot as she had yesterday, but now she cried quietly into a handkerchief. Mr Bartleigh was leaning over his wife. Gently he closed her eyes and kissed her lips. 'Goodbye, my love,' he whispered.

For a long moment Lily's soft weeping was the only sound in the room. No one moved. Then the gentleman stood straight.

'I'll take her home,' Mr Bartleigh said in a rough voice. 'We are near enough to make it in a day's journey.' He looked over at Lily. 'I'll see to a cart and a bo—' He stopped and swallowed. 'A co—'

And right before Jack's horrified gaze, the man crumpled. Harsh, broken sobs tore their way out of him. He sank to his knees beside the bed. Jack's chest burned just hearing the horrible evidence of this man's grief and his eyes welled alarmingly.

'I can't do it,' Mr Bartleigh sobbed wretchedly. 'How am I supposed to face each day without her?'

Tears streaming down her face, Lily dropped down beside him. Crooning wordless sounds of comfort, she enfolded him in her arms.

'You know, Lily,' the older man rasped. He gazed at her with stricken eyes. 'You know—she's my light, the greatest joy in my life.' His voice broke.

'She was my heart,' he said on a thin, piteous cry. 'How am I supposed to survive without my heart?'

He went limp, his body curled around his pain. His entire form shook with the force of his sobs.

Jack ached with crippling compassion and grief. His hands trembled, setting the tea service on the tray he still carried to clattering. The sound caught Lily's attention and she looked up. Her face was flushed, her nose red. Relief flashed briefly in her eyes as she caught sight of him. She raised her arm and beckoned.

In that moment, Jack could not have moved if his life depended on it. Terror reached down his throat and choked him. All thoughts of Batiste, of his father, disappeared. With sudden, terrible certainty, he knew. He'd made a mistake.

Almost against his will, he had fallen in love with Lily Beecham—and he had wondered if he was strong enough to bear the emotional burden of it. Last night he'd told himself that he could do it. He no longer had to be impenetrable or impervious to emotion. He could allow himself to be vulnerable for her sake and the rewards would be more than worth the risk.

But he had never considered this. Watching that wretched old man bent double with grief, Jack felt his own heart crack open. Sheer, utter panic gripped him hard and shook him to his core. If he opened himself to her love, then he would be equally susceptible to pain as well. And pain such as this he had never witnessed, did not even know existed. It was more than he could handle, more than he could even contemplate. He would never survive such a loss.

He shook his head. He stared at a future that he could not face and he knew. This moment would remain with him for ever, imprinted indelibly in his mind. It would fester there, and grow. It would taint their life, their love. It would ruin their chance at happiness.

He needed to go. Needed to think. He cast a last, imploring look at Lily, begging silently for her forgiveness, and then he set down the tray with trembling hands and walked out.

Chapter Fifteen

A good deal of time passed before Lily could leave Mr Bartleigh and go in search of Jack. Evening was falling again as she searched fruitlessly through the inn and the gardens. Her anxiety growing, she even peeked into the cottage, but he was not there. Finally, she found him in the stables. A pair of saddlebags lay propped against the wall and he was lugging a saddle from the tack room.

'Jack?' she said sharply. 'What are you doing?'

Sadness etched in his face, he stared at her. 'I'm sorry, Lily. I'm leaving.'

'Leaving? But—' She stopped herself. Her burden of grief grew heavier as a sudden flood of anger added to it. 'Where are you going?'

'Back to London.'

All of her pain and disappointment must have shown, for he turned away. She struggled to find calm. 'It's too late to shut me out, Jack. You're going to have to talk to me.'

'I'm sorry,' he repeated. 'I know that after last night you must have expected me to stay, and that we have not had a chance to talk.'

'No, we have not. I've been preoccupied,' she said with bitter irony.

He did not meet her gaze. 'While I have had plenty of time to think,' he said as he tightened his cinch. 'You spoke so eloquently last night of regrets and it was timelier than you knew.' He crossed back to retrieve a bridle. 'I haven't been able to get it out of my head.'

He regretted last night? Lily drew a deep, shuddering breath. This was what she had feared when she glimpsed the icy, carefully blank expression on his face earlier.

But he had seen her flash of emotion and at least partially interpreted it. 'No, I don't regret last night,' he said in a rush. He left the stall and crossed to take her hand. 'We were so…absorbed with each other and then today…' His voice trailed off. 'I did not get the chance to mention it to you, but we nearly caught Batiste. We had a good lead and he only just slipped away. Today I realised that for me—he is unfinished business. If I don't see this through, see him caught and punished and prevented from harming more people, then that would be my greatest regret.' He stopped and pulled her close. 'I'm sorry, but I can't—I won't feel free to pursue my own happiness until this job is done.'

Her anger was growing, solidifying into a solid, steadying mass. She glared and watched him hasten to throw up a wall of words between them.

'I know about your letters from Matthew, Lily.'

She stepped back, out of his arms. 'How?' she asked. She felt quiet, calm and quite deadly.

'Minerva let it slip. Don't hold it against her—she did not mean to do it. But I want you to know, I'm not going to ask you to betray your cousin. I'll find another way. I'll comb through every ship's log in the Latimer Shipping offices, I'll camp out in front of the First Lord of the Admiralty's doorstep, by God I'll beg a ship off of Mervyn, if I have to, and track him down and bring him in myself.' He heaved a sigh. 'And then I'll be back.'

Disappointment rose up from the deepest pits of Lily's soul. Wrath came close behind. He was doing it again. Jack was creating barriers, telling lies. Except this time, she could not tell if he lied only to himself or to her too. 'You've got it all worked out, don't you?' she asked quietly. 'All wrapped up tight and neat in a logical little package.'

'Lily?'

'I don't believe you, Jack.' Her voice rang out, harsh sounding. She hardly recognised it as her own.

'You don't believe me?' He sounded as if he could hardly believe her.

'You *are* just like my mother—just as I suspected. You are using the world's ills to keep from confronting your own.'

'Lily, I—'

But she stopped him with an abrupt gesture. Eyeing him coldly, she said, 'Do you know? I think I am going to give you just what you deserve, Jack Alden. I'm going to give you exactly what you think you want.'

He took a step back. 'What do you mean?'

'I'm going to take you to my cousin, Matthew.'

Suddenly his entire demeanour shifted. 'You know where he is?' he asked eagerly. 'He's told you?'

'I do. But you must promise to keep him safe.' She waited a moment, and then huffed impatiently. 'Promise me, Jack!'

'I do promise. I will do my best to protect him.' He was all earnestness and anticipation now. 'They only wish to question him, you know. He should be fine.'

'Then I will take you to him,' she said with disdain. 'With any luck he will know where your Batiste is.'

'Thank you, Lily,' he breathed. His eyes were alight.

'I want you to find Batiste, Jack. Take him in, watch him hang. Do what you think is so very important to you. And when he is gone and you find that your demons still haunt you—I hope that then you will finally remember all that I've told you.' She spun on her heel and marched away. Without stopping she spat over her shoulder, 'Just know that by the time you finally reach that point, it may be too late.'

Against Jack's will and Mrs Babbit's protestations, Lily arranged to have one of the inn's mounts ready for her as well. 'If I don't go, you don't go,' she said stubbornly.

'But what of Mr Bartleigh?' Jack asked.

The exhausted, grief-stricken man had folded in the face of her vehemence. 'He does not need me to travel with him. His arrangements will be complete tomorrow and he can head home. I'll be back there in plenty of time for the services.'

Jack sighed and shot her a look of resignation. 'Where are we going?'

'I'll tell you when it is too late to turn back,' Lily said grimly.

She swung up, refusing to give way to her own weariness, allowing her anger and her determination to be done with this once and for all to keep her straight in her saddle.

Jack must have suspected when she took the road heading south and west, but they rode in dismal silence for several hours before he spoke.

'He's at your home, then?'

Lily merely nodded. 'If he's not there now, then he soon will be.'

'How long before we reach it?'

'We'll get there by daybreak.'

'You mean to ride all night?' He looked at her with disbelief.

She shot him a scornful glance. Her brow raised as she ran a disparaging look down the length of him. 'If you cannot keep up, then I'll welcome you when you get there.'

There it was again—that smile. *Her* smile. The one that played around the edges of his mouth when she did something to amuse him. It made her want to weep.

'Let's go then,' he said. 'Totton is just ahead. We'll change horses there.'

It was a long and miserable ride, though Lily would have died before admitting it. Grief and sorrow made for dreadful travelling companions. Her dear friend was gone and Jack was running scared. He'd become spooked and closed himself off again and Lily wanted to scream her frustration to the universe.

Only her righteous sense of anger kept her on her horse and moving. Anger, and a heartfelt determination that she was done trying to please the unappeasable, convince the unconvincible. She'd determined to break that pattern with her mother and she did not plan to begin it with Jack. He would come to her with an open heart, ready to share all that life had to offer—both good and bad—or she would not have him.

Dawn had arrived, the sun heralded by a riotous sky, when they finally reached Weymouth. Any pleasure she might have felt at her homecoming had been muted. Instead she only felt empty and resentful. Jack, on the other hand, looked the picture of anticipation; he'd perked up further with every mile they'd ridden.

At last they reached her home—a sprawling, two-storeyed farmhouse constructed of ancient, weathered stone. Without waiting, Lily jumped down from her horse, leaving him for Jack to attend to, and hurried inside. The housekeeper met her in the wide entryway, her steps echoing on the flagstone floor, her keys jangling at her side as always.

'Miss Lily,' the woman exclaimed with surprise. 'I can scarce believe it is you! We had no idea of your coming.' She bobbed a quick curtsy and, smiling, looked beyond Lily towards the door. 'Is your dear mother with you?'

'No, Mrs Tilbury,' Lily said wearily. 'Mother is still on her tour. She—' Before she could get any further she was tackled bodily from the side.

'Lilikins!' a shout rang out.

'Ohh,' she gasped. 'Matthew!' Her cousin lifted her up and began to spin her around, whirling her until her feet flew out behind her, just as her father used to do. 'Have you gone mad?' she croaked. 'Let me down!'

The housekeeper smiled at their antics. 'I'll just go on back to…' She paused and directed a look at Matthew. 'To the kitchen. I'll send one of the men out to fetch your things, Miss Lily. You just go and catch up with your cousin.'

'Thank you, Mrs Tilbury,' Matthew said. He turned to Lily with a huge smile on his face. 'I'm so glad you came. I was so afraid you would not make it before we had to…' His smile faded away and he let her slide to the floor. Lily followed his gaze and saw Jack framed in the front door. 'Who is this?' Matthew asked. She could feel the sudden tension in his arms.

'Matthew, this is my…friend, Mr Alden.'

Her cousin sketched a quick bow in Jack's direction. 'Forgive me,' he said. 'I didn't expect anyone other than my aunt to arrive with Lily.'

'Mother is still travelling, but she is due back in London any day now.' She laid a gentle hand upon her cousin's arm. 'I brought Jack because he knows about Batiste, Matthew.'

Her cousin recoiled in shock, before casting a look of resentment and betrayal on her. 'They got to you already? I'd hoped you'd keep my secret, if only for the sake of our old fondness for one another.'

'He wants to help you,' she responded quietly. 'I would not have brought him, otherwise.'

'I am not with the ministry, nor with the American government either.' Jack stepped in. 'I'm after Batiste. I want to see the bastard hang.'

Matthew sucked in a deep breath. 'Well, then, that's a different kettle of fish.' He grasped Lily's hand. 'I'm sorry, cousin, it's just that—well, can we sit somewhere and talk? I've a long story to tell.' He shot a curious look at Jack. 'And I think I'd like to hear yours.'

The three of them trooped to her front parlour, which Lily was glad to see sparkled and shone just as it always did. They each chose a seat somewhat equidistant from the others. Lily glanced uncomfortably from one of the men to the other.

Matthew leaned forwards and addressed Jack. 'Will you tell me how you got mixed up with that devil?' he asked. He raised a brow at Lily. 'Then I'll make my own explanations. A confession of my sins is the least I owe you.'

So Jack began by explaining his connection with Lord Treyford, his betrothed, Chione Latimer, and the rest of her family. Lily saw an immediate reaction from her cousin as he spoke.

'Latimer, you say?' He squirmed a little in his seat. 'I know the name. I heard Batiste ranting over a Mervyn Latimer more than once in my dealings with him. He's got a powerful grudge against the man.'

'Powerful indeed,' Jack agreed. 'He kidnapped Mervyn and held the old man captive for nearly a year and a half.'

Matthew scrubbed a hand over his mouth. 'Kept him locked up on his ship, did he?'

'Yes.' Jack stared at her cousin. 'How could you possibly know that?'

'Did he kill the man?'

'No,' Jack answered. 'But it was a near thing.'

With a sigh of relief, Matthew rose. He paced to the window and back again, one hand at his temple, the other braced on his hip. 'Oh, Lord,' was all he said.

'What is it?' Lily asked, fearing the answer.

Her cousin turned decisively. 'I built the prison cell the man was kept in.'

'Matthew!' Lily exclaimed in horror.

Jack, however, remained calm. 'Just how did that come about?'

Matthew sat again and hung his head in his hands. 'I was a damned fool, that's how.' He looked up at Jack. 'The bastard crimped me!'

'Ahh,' Jack said knowingly.

'What?' Lily asked. 'Crimped? What is it?' She looked at Jack in confusion.

'It used to be a common enough practice—back when slave-ship captains had difficulty finding a full crew for their ships. They would make an arrangement with a certain tavern, then they would lure in boys and men, get them roaring drunk, and then either cheat them at cards or in some other way convince them to sign an article of debt. To pay off the debt, the men would be forced to serve as crew on the slave ship.'

'How horrible!'

Jack looked thoughtfully at her cousin. 'I gather they did not want you as crew, though.'

'No.' Matthew sighed. 'Batiste wanted me to make alterations to his ships.'

'Prison cells? Did you not wonder at such a thing?'

'That was not what he asked for at first. The first job was on one of his merchant ships. He had me alter the cargo hold—disguise a section of it that he could use as a slave deck. I had to build it small, and be sure it could be easily disguised and quickly hidden with supply casks.'

'But the slave trade has been abolished,' Lily said, bewildered.

'Yes, the trade of slaves has, in England and her empire,' Matthew said. 'The fine for slaves found on board is as high as one hundred pound per head. He was tired of risking his profits or losing any chance of them by tipping the poor people overboard.'

'What?' Lily suffered a childish urge to cover her ears, to block out the picture of such evil. 'He's a monster,' she breathed.

'The Americans have banned the import of new slaves. All that has done is raised their value. Plenty of them are still bought and sold in the slave markets over there,' Matthew explained. 'Men are getting rich growing cotton in the southern states. Batiste said there were plenty of planters willing to circumvent the law and pay a large price for able bodies.'

'And the prison cell?' urged Jack.

'That was a later job. On his own *Lady Vengeance*. A cell, he wanted, small, for one person. Well ventilated, as it might be used for some time, and watertight and secure. By that time, I knew what sort of man Batiste was and realised the trouble I'd got myself into. I knew I had to run. The villain was never going to forgive my debt. He'd wait until he was done with me and then I had no doubt he'd have one of his men slit my throat.'

Lily raised a shaking hand to her mouth.

'I bided my time and made my plans. I knew I was going to have to give up my business, start over somewhere with a new name, but it was my only hope. By this time, I had free run of the ship, coming and going as I needed to get tools and supplies.'

'The American government has already pieced together much of your story,' Jack said. 'But they said you did something to anger him greatly. He apparently ranted and raved about getting vengeance on you, but they could not discover what it was you had done. In fact, at first they thought you were dead. Later they heard different—someone let it spill that you had run.' He looked thoughtfully over at her cousin. 'What did you do, to anger him? It wasn't just that you skipped out on your debt, was it?'

'No.' Matthew glanced towards the door. 'Will you wait here? I have something to show you.' He left the room in a hurry.

Lily stood and began to pace the room. She could not believe that she'd been wrong, that Matthew truly had done the things Jack had inadvertently accused him of. She wanted to weep, to hide away from both of the men who had stripped her of her illusions. Finally stopping at the window seat where she'd loved to read as a child, she sank down and gazed out over the drive and the circular patch of garden in the middle. She stiffened a little as Jack approached her from behind.

'If it makes you feel any better,' he said, 'I think the Americans have sympathy with his plight. If he tells them his story and answers their questions, then I believe they will release him right away.'

Lily nodded her head and fought back tears. So much sadness. And temptation, too. Jack stood close behind her. She could almost feel his heat. She turned to drink in the sight of him. So beautiful, with his dark, earnest eyes and his unruly mop that begged for her taming fingers. All she wanted to do was hurl herself in his arms and beg him to stay with her. But she knew he would not.

She stood as the door opened behind them. Looking over his shoulder, she saw Matthew come just a step into the room. His face shone full of anticipation.

'You asked how I angered him?' he asked Jack. 'The answer is simple. I took something that belonged to him.' He opened the door and nodded encouragingly. A very lovely, obviously pregnant Negro lady stepped into view, her gaze darting nervously around the room.

'I'd like to present my wife.'

Lily's legs trembled. She sat down hard again on the window seat.

Chapter Sixteen

'This is Anele,' Matthew said after both Lily and her new cousin had been seated comfortably in the middle of the room again. Lily smiled at the girl and she shyly returned the gesture.

'Anele and her sister were captured by a rival tribe and sold as slaves. One of Batiste's captains bought them and brought them to Charleston. I'll spare you the more horrific details of the voyage,' Matthew said with a glance at Lily. 'But though the women were allowed to roam the decks free during the day, they were at the mercy of the crew. They had little food and no hope. Anele's sister did not fare well. She was weak when they arrived in the Carolinas and Batiste decided to keep them both for a while—for his own personal use.'

Lily shuddered. Jack sat beside her and took her hand.

'I found her one day, lying sobbing in a passage on

the *Lady Vengeance*. She was chained, wrist and ankle, to her sister. Her dead sister. Batiste had been called away and had not bothered locking her up, because where was she going to go chained to a corpse?'

Tears started to flow and Lily was helpless to stop them. She gestured for Matthew to continue and accepted the handkerchief that Jack offered.

'What could I do?' asked Matthew. 'You would not have wanted to see her then, Lily. She was wasted away, bruised. She could hardly stand, let alone walk. I was running anyway, I decided to get her away, too. I used my tools to break her shackles and I sneaked her off the ship.'

Jack nodded his approval. 'It could not have been easy.'

'No. It upset all my plans. But I went to a friend and he hid us in his warehouse for a few weeks, until Anele was stronger and able to travel. We've been in hiding and on the run ever since.'

'I'm so glad you saved her,' Lily said.

'I hired myself on as ship's carpenter to get us passage to France. I thought we could make a life there, where Anele would be more accepted. We were happy and settled in Le Havre for a while, but not long ago we spotted one of Batiste's men and I panicked. I didn't know where else to go, so we came here.'

'Just as you should have,' Lily told him. 'You will be safe here.'

'But Matthew should come with me,' Jack interrupted. 'It's more important than ever that we find Batiste. You two face the same sort of danger from his twisted outlook that Trey and Chione do. The man is sick. If he can harm you, he will.'

Matthew looked uncertain. 'What do you want me to do?'

'Talk to the Admiralty and the Americans. Tell them everything you can remember about Batiste and his men. Everything they ever said, every place they ever mentioned. I will speak for you. If you co-operate, I'm sure they will let you go in peace.'

Matthew shared a long glance with his wife. 'I suppose I'll have to do it,' he said slowly. He squeezed her hand. 'It's our only chance to live without fear.'

It was soon arranged. Lily lent them her father's travelling carriage and the two men were loading and preparing to leave the next morning. Lily hauled out a large basket of food that Mrs Tilbury had packed. Jack caught her as she set it in place. He locked her in a tight embrace and they stood, silent for several long moments.

'I will be back, Lily.'

She closed her eyes and did not answer.

'I hope you do not doubt me.'

She sighed. 'I'm not doubting your intentions, Jack. But I am wondering what will happen once Batiste is caught. Perhaps you will come straight back here. Or perhaps you will discover some other mission, something urgent and requiring all of your energy and focus. Something to enable you to avoid that with which you are not entirely comfortable.'

He winced. 'I suppose I deserved that.'

'You know I want you to return, more than I can say. But I am not willing to settle.' She looked up at him. 'These weeks since we met, they have been the best of my life, and the worst as well.'

He ran his hands up her back and pulled her a little closer. 'I understand.'

'I wanted a journey, and truly, I've had one. Though it has taken place in my head and my heart rather than on roads and highways, it has been the most important one of my life. And you helped set me on the path. Do you remember?'

His eyes narrowed, he shook his head.

'The day we met, you asked me what sort of woman I was. I didn't know the answer, and it frightened me more than I can say. But I've been thinking and learning and discovering that answer. What has been amazing and so wonderful is that each time I found a new piece of myself, I shared it with you. Sometimes you laughed with delight, sometimes you frowned with concern, but each time you met it with acceptance and value. You've accepted and valued me. It's meant so much. You've been a catalyst and a help and the prize at the end, and for that I thank you.'

He laughed. 'You're the first to consider me a prize, Lily, but I'm glad to hear it.'

She did not return his smile. Indeed, she hoped that he could see the gravity and seriousness that had led her to take this step. 'You told me once that I did not know what it was that I asked of you, and I've discovered that you were right. One of the things I've discovered is that I need to share my life with someone whose heart is open, as well as his mind—I just had no idea what a rare commodity that is.'

His smile had faded. 'I'm trying, Lily.'

'I know you are, and I love you for it.' She snaked her arms around him and held him close, hoping he could feel all the love and longing in her heart. 'I've already spent too many years living with avoidance and silence, grief and guilt. I'm ready to leave all of that behind. I want to live my life with hope and joy and optimism. I want to share myself and I want someone who will share themselves as well.'

Her hands gripped his arms hard, and she swallowed against the most difficult words she'd ever had to speak. 'With all my heart and soul, I want that person to be you, Jack. But if you are not, then perhaps it is best that you don't come back.'

His face hardened. 'I think you are forgetting the pact we made several nights ago, Lily. You gave yourself to me, and in more than just the physical sense.'

'Yes, and you walked away. And now here you are, distancing yourself even farther. And I don't mean distance in miles. This trip is about more than Batiste and we both know it.'

'There might be consequences. If there are—'

'There will not be. It became certain this morning.' She sighed. She'd almost been disappointed, but it was better this way. 'It is for you to decide,' she whispered. 'You know I want you, I wish I could show you just how much. But I want all of you.'

He nodded. Something large and important loomed in his expression, but he didn't speak. Matthew approached from the house and they stepped away from each other. Lily ached as he walked away from her and climbed aboard. His face set, he sat silent, waiting as Lily said goodbye to her cousin.

'I explained it again to Anele, but she is emotional, as you can expect. Are you sure you will not mind her staying, Lily?' her cousin asked anxiously.

'Not at all. She is family, is she not?' Lily took Matthew's hand. 'You've chosen a difficult path. It won't be easy for Anele. Or for you.'

'I know,' he said, his voice hoarse. 'But I had no choice.'

'I'll do all I can to smooth the way for you both. I think Mother will, too. If naught else, you'll always have us.'

'Thank you.' He bowed his head.

'Now,' she said briskly. 'You go on. Mrs Tilbury and I will take care of your wife. The whole staff is already looking forward to the next addition to the family.'

Matthew kissed her cheek. 'Thank you. I'm sorry I involved you in all of this.'

'Don't be. It will all work out as it was meant to. You followed your heart and saved Anele's life. Now Jack will help you—and he is a paragon of logic and rationality. If the two of you combine your heart and head, then I believe that there is nothing that you cannot accomplish.'

Matthew climbed aboard and, without looking at her, Jack gave the signal for the driver to go.

A draining sense of fatigue crept over Lily as she watched them drive off, stealing the breath from her lungs, the strength from her limbs. The thought that she might never see Jack Alden again paralysed her. She wanted to sink to the ground and cry out her despair and fear and loneliness. But she could not. She'd done the right thing, though it was no comfort to know it. She gathered the tattered shreds of her confidence and squared her shoulders. Then she slowly made her way inside and went to comfort her new cousin.

Chapter Seventeen

Sodden, Jack stood in the courtyard of the White Horse, trying to ignore the lowering notion that each drop of the pouring rain pounded him ever further into defeat. Before him, Matthew Beecham scrambled over the wet cobblestones, handing over his portmanteau to be loaded on to the Portsmouth-bound coach.

'I can't believe it, Jack,' Matthew called over the sound of the deluge. His manner was anything but defeated. 'Still, I just cannot believe my good luck.'

Jack forced a smile, trying to raise some enthusiasm. There were a few things he had difficulty believing, too, foremost being the fact that he was up and out at this ungodly early hour. Not far behind lay the sad fact that they'd been in London for nearly a fortnight and there had been no further news of Batiste.

Matthew had endured several days of close questioning in Whitehall. He'd been informed that he would be required to return to give testimony at Batiste's trial, but his name had been cleared. Mervyn Latimer had also come to town and talked at length. The Foreign Office now had quite a case built against Batiste; they just had no idea where he'd gone.

Matthew had manfully apologised for the part he had played in the old man's kidnapping.

'Ah, but I would consider you a victim of Batiste's greed as much as any of the rest of us,' Mervyn had said on hearing his story. 'And you more than made up for any mischief when you rescued your wife from his clutches.' The old adventurer had chuckled. 'I have to admit, you do good work. I tried to break out of there any number of times.'

Mervyn had been so impressed with Matthew, in fact, that he'd offered the man a job working for his shipping company. 'If you can outfit an entire ship as watertight and sound as that hellhole, then you'll save me hundreds of pounds per year,' he'd said, grinning.

Mervyn had left to return to Devonshire, taking Eli and Aswan with him. Matthew was heading to Portsmouth, happy to begin his new employment and planning to find a little house before fetching Anele to their new home.

'I can't believe my luck,' he said again.

Up on the top of the coach, the driver blew a blaring note on his horn, calling the passengers to embark.

'Time to load up,' Jack said.

Matthew held out his hand. 'Thank you, Jack. For everything.'

'It is I who should thank you, for having the courage to come forwards,' Jack said, shaking his hand. 'When you get to Weymouth, tell Lily I'll be there soon.'

'I will.'

Jack bid Matthew goodbye, then stood, staring after the coach long after it had gone, wondering if he'd spoken true. God in heaven, but he hoped so. His longing for Lily was a constant ache.

Around him men shouted and horses splashed through puddles. Dogs barked and women hurried through the rain, calling out in shrill, nervous tones. But jealous as he felt at the idea of Matthew returning to the woman he loved, still Jack did not move. Once he did, once he took a step away from this spot, he would be forced to face the awful truth; he would have to acknowledge the idea that Batiste might never be found.

He sighed and glanced towards the taproom. Perhaps a dram or two or ten would make that reality more palatable. He shook his head, knowing it would not even as he turned towards the door. Ah well, maybe a drink would warm his innards and ease the biting cut of frustration.

He noticed a gentleman standing to the side, under the inn's extended eaves. The man's gaze remained fixed on Jack as he approached and then he made a sweeping bow and moved to hold the door for him. Jack thanked him and noted the tall figure, the well-cut clothes and the fancy waistcoat with an elaborate fob. The man was older than he, his face brown and lined, his hair held back in an old-fashioned queue.

The gentleman fell in behind him and entered the taproom on his heels. As Jack headed for the scratched and scarred bar, the man stepped in close.

'Pardon the intrusion,' the stranger spoke with a slightly accented flair. 'But you have the appearance of a man who could do with a drink. I hope you will allow me?'

Jack shrugged and took a seat. His shadow perched beside him and called out for service. When the tapster shuffled from the back and slapped down two pints of ale, Jack raised his in thanks and drank deep of the bitter brew.

No one else occupied the room at this early hour. The pair of them sat in silence for several minutes.

'Was that the coach to Portsmouth that lately left?' the man asked companionably.

'It was. Did you mean to be aboard?'

'Not I. I do wish I had gotten here just a little earlier, though.'

'It's a daily run,' Jack said absently. 'You can have another go at it tomorrow.'

The gentleman smiled into his ale. 'I rather thought you were the one who meant to be on it. Forgive me for saying so, but you were staring after it as if it held your heart's most enduring desire.'

Jack flinched. The man hit uncomfortably close. He drank deep and tried to laugh the suggestion off. 'No, I merely stood there trying to decide if such a thing exists.'

'Oh, but of course it does.' The stranger's eyes glittered as he glanced over at Jack. 'Every man knows the thing his soul yearns for—even if he does not care to admit it.'

Jack set down his glass and stared at him. 'Do you truly believe that?'

'Without a doubt.'

'And do you have a secret yearning?'

The gentleman chuckled. 'Oh, I have many, and not one of them a secret.' He sighed. 'For a very long time I have known my greatest desire.' A hint of frustration crept into his tone. 'The difficulty is that I am not sure how to go about finding it.'

Jack brooded silently for several long moments. He could not imagine a more ridiculous conversation to be having with a complete stranger. And yet it fit so appropriately with the junction he'd reached in his life.

'Ahh,' the man breathed. He leaned in, oddly intent. 'I see that you have indeed discovered your greatest desire. But my question is—do you know where to find it?'

Jack stood. He tossed a coin on the counter and met the stranger's gaze. 'Weymouth,' he said simply. Shock blazed on the other man's face, and a bright flash of triumph, but Jack's eye was focused inwards. 'Yes,' he said, 'I rather think it is in Weymouth.'

He turned to go. The stranger reached out a restraining hand. He stared at Jack intently, his expression alight with an intensity as odd as the conversation they'd been having. His fingers dug into Jack's arm, and then abruptly, he let go. He nodded. Jack turned and walked out.

Jack stalked out of the courtyard and on to Piccadilly, heedless of both the steady rain and the relentless human traffic out in it. He'd reached new depths, sharing drinks and sentimental foolishness with strangers. And yet he had told the man nothing but the truth. His heart lay in Weymouth with Lily.

Then why the hell wasn't he there with her? That was the question, wasn't it? Why was he still here, worrying and fretting over a situation he'd done his best to resolve?

Because he was a damned fool. A damned childish fool. A passing carriage doused his boots with a splash of cold, murky water, but that was nothing next to the sudden dose of insight he was suffering.

He'd been shot—by a woman, no less—and the incident had triggered all of his old feelings of inadequacy. Jack knew he'd allowed the controlling, shadowy figure of Batiste to become mixed in his mind with his distant and disdainful father. But somehow he'd never understood that the idea of bringing Batiste to justice had become synonymous with justifying his choices, demonstrating his worth, proving himself a man.

Except that in trying to meet his father's standards, he'd betrayed his own. He'd forsaken logic and all rational thought. He'd acted like a volatile, scheming child, bent on achieving his own ends.

With a start, Jack realised that while his mind was treading new paths, his feet had taken him on the familiar route to Somerset House. On impulse he crossed the expansive courtyard and went in, travelling unerringly to the apartments of the Society for Antiquaries of London. He did not enter. Instead he stood in the corridor and delved even deeper into his soul, searching for the truth inside himself as he'd once sought knowledge inside those doors.

This place, together with his London rooms, had become his haven. Here he had come to find like minds, opportunities for intense study, and, most of all, respite from his father's contempt. But it was only more of the same, was it not? A place to build walls, to hide. He had arranged his entire adult life so carefully, manoeuvring neatly so he could avoid the harsh realities of his life.

Lily had opened his eyes, allowed him to see the extent to which he had secreted himself away. He had thought he had allowed himself to open up, but the truth was he had let her in and then slammed the door closed again. And at the first sign of trouble and heartache he had fallen right back into his old habits.

His quest to bring Batiste to justice had only been another barrier. He'd used it to keep from confronting his anger at his father and he'd used it to avoid the risks and fears that came with loving Lily too.

She'd been right. Oh, how Jack hated to admit it, but it was the truth. Even if Batiste had been in custody right now and on his way to the hangman's noose, all of his doubts and conflicts would still exist.

She was right about other things, too. It was time; time to grow up, time to let go. It was time and past that Jack Alden stopped hiding and fully entered the world.

Resolutely, he turned away. He left Somerset House, returned home and locked the door—and with blazing determination he did the single hardest thing he'd ever done in his life. He dropped his internal armour and let all of his suppressed feelings out. He allowed hurt, anger, fear and betrayal to wash over him. From childhood resentment, to his failure at the Egyptian Rooms, to the shameful way he'd left Lily Beecham, he examined scenes he'd laboured to forget and he faced his worst fears for the future. He ranted, railed and when he could contain himself no longer, he went back out into the streets and walked restlessly through the night.

With each step Jack beat his fury and frustration into the pavement. So long he had laboured to hide from the negative aspects of his life. But in reality all of those damaging emotions had burrowed inside him, fermenting, growing until there was no room for the affirmative, richer side of life. It was time he let them go. For hours he roamed the city, until his feet were tired and his soul felt empty and drained.

Then, at last, he returned home. He sat in front of the fire, watching the flames dance, and he tried to forgive, to allow peace and healing to take the place of hidden anger and thwarted longing. With all of his will and with the all of the yearning in his heart, Jack tried to become the man that Lily Beecham deserved.

Chapter Eighteen

'Enjoy your visit, dear.' Lily squeezed Anele's hand as they made their way up the short front walk. 'I've visits to make and these medicines to distribute. You'll have plenty of time for a proper goodbye.'

She smiled as Mr Bartleigh met them at the door and watched as Anele made her careful way inside. The separation from Matthew had been hard on the young woman. Lily's servants treated her kindly for Matthew's sake, but her tenants tended to view her with either awe or bland contempt. The local ladies had tut-tutted over the story of her ordeal, but had shown no inclination to invite her into their homes. Only with Mr Bartleigh had the girl struck up a friendship. Fresh from his own sorrow, he was sensitive to hers and he appeared grateful for the distraction. They had discovered that they shared a great love of music and spent hours teaching each other their native songs.

The first chords of the pianoforte followed Lily as she climbed back into her gig. She had several errands to run before they left for Portsmouth tomorrow. Matthew had written several times in the days since he and Jack had gone, but none of his letters had been more welcome to his wife than the one informing them of his new situation and asking her to join him there. There had been no word from Jack Alden at all.

Lily set off and told herself once more that it was best that way. A clean break was kinder, if Jack did not mean to return. Yet still she found herself fluctuating wildly between bleak despair and a vivid, uncontrolled hope. She tried not to pine as obviously as Anele, but she found herself eating little and sleeping less. As the days passed it became more difficult to keep from bursting into tears at odd moments. She sighed and sat straighter on the bench, eager to be done with the day's work. This trip to Portsmouth would be a welcome diversion.

It was evening before her visits were complete. Clouds gathered above, and the light was fading fast when Lily wearily turned the gig towards Weymouth once more. She had not travelled far when she came upon an abandoned farm cart alongside the road. Boxes and barrels were stacked in the cart, as well as other bulky goods covered by a large canvas, but she could see no sign of a driver. It wasn't until she carefully manoeuvred her gig past that she caught sight of the still form lying half in the ditch.

With a gasp she pulled to a stop and wrapped the reins. Looking helplessly up and down the quiet road, she scurried down and over to the fallen man. He breathed, thank goodness, but did not respond to her calling or nudging. Desperate, she shouted out, hoping someone would come to help.

No one appeared. She could see no sign of a wound or broken limb. He faced away from her, down into the ditch. It was impossible to tell who he was or how old he might be. Rather than roll his still, heavy form over, she scrambled around him, into the ditch. Her gown grew damp as she brushed his hair away from his face. To no avail. She had never seen him before.

She jumped as, without warning, his hand shot up and grasped her wrist where she touched him. Lily gasped in alarm and tried to withdraw, but the stranger reached over and captured her other wrist as well. 'I've got her,' he called, propping himself up on his elbows.

'Let go! What are you doing?' Lily struggled to get away. She hauled hard against him, twisting and trying to free herself, but the man's grip was iron, his expression implacable.

'Bring the rope,' he shouted.

There was a muffled response from the cart. Lily watched in horror as another man crawled from beneath the canvas and approached.

'Who are you?' she cried. 'What do you want?'

Neither answered. With grim efficiency the second man tied her wrists and hauled her from the ditch. He held her tight, despite her struggles, while the fallen man secured her ankles. No words were exchanged. Their unyielding silence and businesslike manner frightened Lily nearly out of her wits. Kicking, fighting, she screamed, as loud and long as she could, until her captor let loose the hand clamped over her stomach and clapped it over her mouth.

'Enough,' he growled.

'Where's the bottle?' the counterfeit victim asked.

'Still in the cart.'

'Dose her, then, and do it quick. You heard the orders. We've got to get back quick as we can.'

She panicked when the second man tossed her casually over his shoulder. She pitched and tried to throw herself off him, but he carried her to the cart as easily as he would a child. 'What are you doing?' she cried. 'What do you mean to do with me?'

And then she could see nothing as a thick white cloth came down over her face, covering her mouth and nose and eyes. A heavy, cloying scent stifled her until she was afraid she would choke on it. She strained, trying to rear back and away, but a hand held the fabric clamped firmly over her. Gradually her movements slowed, her limbs grew heavy and after a few minutes she had forgotten why she struggled.

Her mind drifted. Vaguely she felt a jolt as she was tossed into the cart and covered with the canvas. Shouldn't she be doing something? She concentrated. Oh, yes. She struggled to sit up, but the damp spots on her clothes distracted her. She felt the cold and discomfort intently, yet she felt strangely detached from everything else going on about her.

'She's a right tidy piece, that one,' she heard someone say, far away. 'Sure we can't delay the trip back a little?'

Someone else snorted. 'I busted a gut getting here in one day, and I'm turning about to make the same, damned miserable trip because Batiste said he wanted the girl in London before daybreak.'

Batiste, Lily thought idly. That name meant something…important. But her eyelids were so heavy.

'He didn't say nothing about leavin' her be,' came the sullen reply.

'Might be, but do you wanna mess about with a woman that he wants that quick and urgent? This is Batiste we're talking about. You do what you want, but leave me out of it. My bum might be swollen when we get back, but at least it'll be in one piece.'

The cart started up then, and the regular rocking motion lulled Lily, soothed her, until the blackness closed in and she drifted off to sleep.

'Be sure and tell the groom that I'm in a tearing hurry to leave. You know the address?' Jack passed his landlady's eldest son a coin and grinned at his eager expression. 'Tell him I'd like my rig here within the hour. Thirty minutes would better.'

The boy nodded and headed for the door. Jack watched him go, then turned to race back upstairs as quick as he'd come down. He'd slept the day nearly through, but he'd awakened feeling…light, eager. Perhaps even happy? More than ready, in any case, to get packed and on the way to Weymouth and to Lily.

'Mr Alden?' a hesitant voice called.

Jack turned and peered down over the railing. The street door had opened again and a man stood on the threshold.

'Mr Alden,' he said. 'Hello.'

'Yes?' The man looked vaguely familiar. Jack turned and started back down the stairs, but the gentleman had started up. They met on the first landing and Jack finally recognised him. 'Dr Arnott?'

'Yes,' the man said in relief. 'I'm glad you remember.'

'Of course! Please, come up and tell me what brings you from Greenwich.'

'No, sir, I do not mean to intrude and cannot stay. Two things, really, brought me.' The man carried a walking stick and nervously shifted it from hand to hand. 'I have to thank you so much for the donation that was made to our hospital. I know it came from your brother, but I also know you must have been behind it.' He reached out and shook Jack's hand. 'You must know we will put it to good use.'

'Of course, I expect no less. But tell me, how is Mr Crump? I hope he enjoyed the fruit I sent along?' Jack scrubbed a hand sheepishly through his hair. 'I confess, I've been meaning to come along for a visit before now…'

'That is the other reason I had to come. I'm sorry to tell you, sir, that Mr Crump passed on last night.'

Jack's heart fell. 'I'm very sorry indeed to hear that,' he said softly.

'I know he appreciated your kindness,' the doctor said. 'He thought of you, in the end. In fact, he asked me to pass a message on to you.'

'A message?'

'Yes.' The doctor frowned. 'He asked me to tell you that "He's back in London".'

Jack was puzzled. 'To be buried, you mean?'

'No, he was not referring to himself. That was the wording of the message. "He's back in London." I wondered if you would know who or what he meant.

Jack's heart stopped. 'Here?' he whispered.

'Mr Alden? Are you all right?'

Jack grasped the banister to steady himself. 'Batiste here? Now?' He'd finally unburdened himself, at long last let his past go, forced himself to recognise his obsession with Batiste as the avoidance it really was—and the man turned up now?

Frustration stabbed him, had him clenching his fists. He'd already kept Lily waiting too long. But this information could not be ignored. Batiste was still an evil, dangerous man and a real threat to Trey, Chione, Matthew, and who knew how many countless others. Jack's mind began to race. Much as he wished to, he could hardly leave London if Batiste was here.

Logic, long neglected, reared its head and kicked his grey matter into motion. He'd need to send the news to Devonshire straight off. Charles, he'd need Charles. The Admiralty should be notified straight away…

'Post!' A new voice, nasal and somehow familiar, interrupted his train of thought. The call echoed in the hallway and up the stairs. 'Did ye hear? This bloke's gone and ruined our surprise!'

From the shadows beneath the stairs stepped a

familiar figure. Jack stared. The swarthy man he had fought in the East End grinned up at him, a pistol aimed squarely at his chest. 'And I was so looking forward to breaking the news to ye, Bookworm.'

'Mr Alden?' The doctor's voice wavered and Jack followed his gaze almost directly upwards to the top landing. The giant Post glared down at them, a filthy bandage wrapped around one thick thigh, his cudgel in his hand.

'Don't ye worry none, guv. I'll forgive ye fer letting the cat out o' the bag,' the short one down below said. 'We been waitin' fer the chance to see yer friend again. It's him we want. Ye can just ease yer way down the stairs and out the door.' He gave a twisted grin, the pistol never wavering. 'Besides, I got me one more secret to tell.' He took a step closer to the bottom of the stairs, glanced about and spoke in a dramatic whisper. 'Batiste's got yer girl, Bookworm.'

A molten wave of fury twisted through Jack's gut. Logic died a final, painful death, swept away by raw hate and bleak determination. The thought of Anele and all that she had suffered ripped through him. By God, he'd almost ruined his relationship with Lily because of Batiste. There was no way in hell that he was going to let that bastard harm her further.

'Mr Alden?' Dr Arnott whispered again. He clutched Jack's arm and nodded his head towards

Post. The man's massive form was gaining speed as he advanced towards them down the stairs.

The time for thinking and rationalisation was done. The situation called for decisive, immediate action. He cast about, looking for an advantage, anything to help. Hours of studying the ancients and their battle strategies had to count for something. But the Romans had touted the advantage of holding the high ground, and his opponent held that. He watched Post moving determinedly towards him and something clicked in his brain.

He braced himself against the railing in the middle of the narrow landing. As Post turned around the corner at a clip, Jack reached out, not for the cudgel, but for the giant's nearest arm. He gripped the man tight and swung him forwards, following the advice of ancient Oriental warriors and using the man's own momentum to propel him unexpectedly towards the next flight of stairs.

He'd caught Post by surprise. The man stumbled, continued forwards, but caught himself at the very edge of the top step. As he teetered there, on the brink of getting himself under control, Dr Arnott grasped the situation. He poked the behemoth sharply in the back with his walking stick.

Post went over. His feet flew out from beneath him and he went tumbling head over heels with a grunt and a great deal of thudding and thumping. He hit the hall floor hard and lay there in a great, sprawling heap.

'Post?' the swarthy man said with low urgency. 'Post!'

Jack heard a querulous cry from his landlady's rooms. In a moment his other opponent would collect himself and more innocent bystanders would arrive to complicate the situation. He had to act now. And now *he* held the high ground.

He reached out, snatched the doctor's cane and, turning, leaped on to the banister. Without pausing for even a breath, Jack launched himself straight down. The swarthy thug below still faced his fallen companion. He caught sight of Jack out of the corner of his eye, but it was too late. He fell beneath the outstretched walking stick and conveniently broke the worst of Jack's fall. His pistol skittered harmlessly across the hall.

'And I'll have you know,' said Jack as he strad-dled the villain and pressed the cane threateningly across his throat, 'I learned each one of those skills from a *book*.'

His only answer was an indistinct wheeze.

'My God, are you all right, Mr Alden?' Dr Arnott called over the railing.

'Fine, Doctor.' Jack had to fight down a panicked

sense of urgency. 'Please come down here and retrieve that firearm before one of my landlady's children toddles out here and picks it up.' He did not wait for the doctor to comply, but turned to the man beneath him. 'Where is she?' Jack demanded.

The thug narrowed his eyes and grimaced through his pain.

Jack pressed the heavy stick tighter against his voice box. 'My brother is a viscount, did you know that, lowlife? Do you know what that means?' He leaned down to glare into his face. 'It means freedom. In short, I am free to do whatever it is I wish with you. I could shoot you now with your own pistol. I could cart you down to Brother Molly's and turn you over as the newest plaything for his particular clientele. No safe jail cell at the magistrate's office, no trial or chance for transportation. And no pesky questions or recriminations for me. Just you, and a permanent dunk in the Thames, should I so choose.'

The man's eyes had widened.

'Where?' Jack shouted. He eased up on the stick.

The thug snarled.

'Fine.' Jack gripped the staff with both hands and pressed it down mercilessly. 'Brother Molly's it is. But first I'm going to make damned sure you spend the rest of your short life as silent as your friend

Post. Molly won't mind the mess. It's not the front of you his clients are interested in, in any case.'

Beneath the stick, the man choked and nodded his head. 'Little Bure Street,' he spat out when Jack raised it.

The need to hurry, to get to Lily, overwhelmed Jack. 'Come over here with that pistol, Doctor. And please see if the landlady can find you some stout rope. You'll want them both restrained before our friend over there wakes up.' He crawled off Batiste's lackey and strode for the door.

'But where are you going?' asked the doctor.

'My cabriolet will be along shortly. Please take it and fetch my brother. The boy accompanying it will know the address. Tell Lord Dayle I'll need him and any reinforcements he can round up in Little Bure Street. I cannot wait.'

'But I…' Dr Arnott protested.

Jack did not wait to hear. He was on the street and summoning a hackney before the doctor finished his sentence. He'd allowed the idea of Batiste to waste enough of his time, and Lily's. Batiste might have finally made his first mistake in returning to English shores. He'd made his last when he laid hands on Lily Beecham.

Chapter Nineteen

The ever-increasing clamour of aching bones and throbbing muscles pulled Lily awake. She moaned and forced her eyes open—and was tempted to close them again and pray for the return of oblivion.

She lay in an ungainly sprawl on a dusty, wooden floor. Slowly and with much effort, she rose to her knees, and after several joint-popping, agonising moments, she climbed to her feet.

They'd left her in the dark. The only light leaked from beneath a door just a few feet away. As her eyes slowly adjusted, Lily explored the room, hands outstretched, step by painful step.

It did not take many steps. She was in a small room, empty but for a rickety wooden chair along the back wall. She tried the door, but it was solid and firmly locked. She had no idea where she might be or how much time had passed while she slept.

Thank heavens, though, she did not appear to be on board a ship.

Moving about eased her aches a little, and as her discomfort decreased, her thoughts began to churn. Her memory remained fuzzy, but she clearly recalled hearing her captors use Batiste's name. But what could he want of her? Perhaps to use her against Matthew? But if he had discovered enough to know of their connection, then surely he knew it was too late to prevent her cousin from bearing witness against him. Did he think to trade her for Anele? Or had he associated her with Jack Alden? Her head drooped in despair. Perhaps he only meant to kill her as an act of revenge against them both.

A scraping sound echoed in the small room, and with a start, Lily recognised the sound of a key in a little-used lock. Lily turned to face the door and tried to calm the frantic beating of her heart.

The door opened only wide enough for a head to poke in. It was the man who had lain in the ditch. Lily glared at him. He grinned and called out, 'She's awake.' Abruptly he shut the door once more.

Lily stood in the dark and fumed. She would *not* let her fear rule her. No matter what it was that Batiste and his lackeys wanted, she would thwart them in any way she could.

Mere minutes passed before the door swung

open again. Light flooded the tiny room as the same man entered, this time carrying another chair and a large candelabrum. He ignored her completely as he set the chair down and placed the light upon it. He retreated once more, giving Lily only a moment to contemplate how she could make use of the heavy thing before he returned. This time he carried another chair, and this time he did not return alone.

Lily studied the man who strolled so casually into her prison. It must be Batiste, based on his air of supreme confidence alone. He was surprisingly small of stature, and looked a little older than she had expected. He had the grim, severe expression of a man who has lived hard and seen much. He returned her perusal, standing with his hands behind his back while his eye traced a leisurely path over her.

His minion withdrew. The sound of the door closing carried a finality that was reinforced by the reptilian smile on Batiste's face.

It struck Lily that he clearly expected her to be intimidated—and that he was looking forward to her reaction with some anticipation. She folded her arms. Fine, then. That would be the first thing she denied him.

'I'm afraid there has been a mistake,' she said, lifting her chin and getting the first word in. 'Please tell whoever might be behind this ridiculously botched manoeuvre that they have taken the wrong girl.'

Batiste's smile did not fade. 'You are Miss Lily Beecham, are you not?' he asked calmly.

'I am,' she replied in the same tone. 'And I have neither money nor jewels to offer you, nor a rich husband or family to ransom me.' She sighed. 'I'm afraid that you have all quite wasted your time. And mine.'

He pursed his lips. 'Oh, I think not,' he said softly. 'Do you know, I have heard that you are quite an intelligent girl, besides being a beauty?'

He waited, but she did not respond.

'Can you not hazard a guess as to who I am?' he asked with an ingratiating grin.

She raised a brow and let her gaze wander over him. She made sure to pause at the queue at his nape, and again at his elaborately embroidered waistcoat, set off by the slightly too-long cut of his coat. 'Someone too attached to the fashions of his youth? Other than that, I'm sure I could not say.'

His face remained blank. He circled around the extra chair and sat down. Carefully, his eyes fixed on her face, he spoke softly. 'I am Batiste.'

Lily raised her brows. 'Indeed?' she asked. She waited a long moment until impatience showed on his expressive face. 'Batiste?' She frowned in concentration. 'Oh, yes,' she said, glaring at him accusingly. 'You are the one! You caused my cousin Matthew to lose his business in America!'

He leaned back. 'On the contrary, Matthew Beecham stole something of great value from me.' He paused. 'I wonder, do you know where she is?'

Lily stared. 'She? She who?' She waited just a beat. 'I knew it! I knew you had taken the wrong woman! Who was it that you *meant* to abduct?'

Batiste gaped at her. Then he scowled ferociously. He stood and began to pace back and forth in the tiny room. 'No, this cannot be,' he said, low and furious. 'Jack Alden is by all accounts a brilliant man—he came close to besting me, for God's sake! Surely he would not waste his time on such a—'

He stopped and subjected her to another long examination. Suddenly his brow lightened. 'Oh, but you are good, my fair one.' He laughed. 'Almost, you convinced me that I had made a grave miscalculation.' His expression hardened. 'But I have matched wits with greedy tribal chiefs and wily Egyptian *kashifs*. You, my dear, don't stand a chance.'

Lily stared. 'I do not understand you at all,' she complained. 'You speak in riddles.'

'Then let me explain.' His voice had grown hard. 'Your cousin may have made himself into a thief and an informer, but for all that, he is a mere thorn in my side. I crush men like Matthew Beecham daily, without trouble or remorse. But your Mr Alden, he has become a larger problem altogether.'

Batiste ceased his pacing and approached her. Lily fought to keep from cringing as he reached out and stroked a stray lock of her hair. 'For nearly a score of years,' he said in a near whisper, 'I have sought information about a treasure of immense value. So close, I came, to obtaining the key, the last clue I needed to find the Pharaoh's Lost Jewel. Mr Alden, it turns out, played a large part in keeping it out of my hands.'

He spun away. 'And if that were not enough, now I find that he was behind the ridiculously close call I recently had with the Royal Navy. For years I have gone about my business with my head down. A few coins paid to the right people here and there and I have been free to carry on without worry. No longer. Now I find my capture has become a top priority and that I have Mr Alden to thank for this as well.' He turned back to face her, his eyes filled with deadly intent. 'That is far more insolence than I have had to face from any man in a very long time. I have had enough. I have come back to England to cut the head off this snake that threatens my every step. And I shall at last obtain the information I need to seek out the Lost Jewel.' He smiled at her, and Lily felt the malice contained in him down to her toes. 'And you, my sweet, devious darling, are exactly what I need to achieve both of these goals.'

Lily cringed inside. The man was truly insane. Jack had been right all along. Batiste must be stopped. But how—

She stopped. A commotion sounded somewhere outside of the room. Not close, but loud.

Batiste had heard it as well. 'Joss!' he called. He strode to the door. 'Withers?' He opened the door, but Lily could see nothing except a darkened hallway beyond. The madman turned back to her and grinned. 'Come, my dear. The game has begun.'

The large purse Jack had tossed to the hackney driver had done the trick. The man broke every rule of traffic etiquette and caused at least one accident, but he got Jack to the East End in record time.

Jack asked to be let out a good way up Little Bure Street. The busy day was ending in the dockside neighbourhood. Fat, well-satisfied merchants strode along with burly stevedores and ink-fingered counting clerks, all eager to reach home or the local chop house or tavern. Jack brushed past them all. Unthinking, he'd carried the doctor's walking stick with him. He tightened his grip on the thing and wished he'd been carrying his knife when that pair of thugs had showed up. He vividly recalled his last trip to this destination, but this time a far greater danger than a wary Eli awaited him.

He approached the narrow alley with caution. The height of the surrounding buildings had cast it into near darkness already. Jack lingered a moment at the corner, straining to hear any hint of a sound.

There it was: footsteps, and a low murmur of voices. Jack braced himself, raised his stick—and slumped when two lightskirts emerged arm in arm into the light.

One of them, a garish redhead with a brightly painted mouth, eyed him and the cane up and down. 'If you're the business they turned us down to tend to, then we're well out of it,' she remarked.

Her companion, an older brunette with dark shadows under her eyes, sniffed. 'Still, they had no need to be hateful about it.'

'Sorry, ladies, I did not intend to frighten you,' Jack apologised.

The redhead glanced at him hopefully. He shook his head and she sighed. 'Come on, then,' she said to her friend. 'We got to find a bawdy house that'll take us.' She sighed. 'My feet hurt.'

'Just how many of them were in there?' Jack called quietly after them.

'Jest the two acid-tongued devils—leastaways, that's all that was in the front rooms.'

Jack watched as the pair turned towards the river. His mind ranged ahead, recalling the bare, cobbled courtyard that opened at the end of the alley. A diversion would be extremely helpful. What was it the ancient Chinese proverb said—something about starting a fire to rob a house? He shrugged. The ancients had not led him wrong yet today. He ran the few steps after the pair of prostitutes.

'Ladies!'

They turned around.

'I can't help you get into a bawdy house, but I'll give you each a fat purse and the chance to get your own back against those two, in exchange for a little help.'

The pair exchanged grins.

'It is not my fault!' screamed the redhead. She stumbled out of the dark alley and into the small open courtyard that housed Batiste's old offices.

''Tis, I tell ye!' yelled the brunette, following her. 'And that be my scarf ye've got wrapped round yer chicken neck—give it back!' She reached out and grabbed hold of the bright cloth.

'It's mine!' the redhead shrieked. She held on and the two of them engaged in a loud, raunchy tug of war. 'It's yer fault if 'tis anybody's—ye've got bags under yer eyes as big as rats—and twice as big as yer bubbies!'

'Oh, ye evil baggage!' A resounding slap echoed against the close walls. Jack, pressed up against the building that housed Batiste's old offices, tensed as the door opened and two men came out to watch the show. Laughing, they stepped out on to the small landing and leaned on the iron railing.

Jack flattened himself even further and crept up the stairs behind them. When he reached the landing, he swung the walking stick hard and knocked the closest man over the rail and on to the cobbled yard below. The two prostitutes screeched like harpies and fell on him, hauling his arms and legs behind him to be tied with the long scarf.

Jack was left to deal with the remaining lackey. This one did not seem the least perturbed by the fate of his comrade. He grinned evilly, and fists clenched, beckoned Jack to come on.

Jack obliged him. He gripped his stick tight and swung, trying to repeat his earlier success and knock his opponent down the stairs. But this adversary had more experience. He ducked under the swing and closed in, burying his fist in Jack's gut.

Jack dropped his stick. Bent double, he had no chance to acknowledge the pain. From inside the decrepit offices came a call, clear and heavy with a note of command. There was no time for any of this. Jack had to get to Lily.

But his opponent had heard the shout as well. It distracted him for the instant that Jack needed. Reaching deep, he drew on every lesson on fighting dirty his brothers had ever given him. He swung hard and true and delivered a crippling wallop to the man's kidney. The man gasped, and then turned just in time to meet Jack's next swing right on the jaw. His head jerked and he fell back, slumping slowly along the railing to the hard landing floor.

The lightskirts cheered. Jack flashed them a weak grin and shook out his hand. His newly healed arm screamed in protest of such abuse. 'Can you watch these two?' he asked, picking up the fallen cane.

'Aye, you go on.' The redhead nodded. Her mouth twisted bitterly. 'I'm good with knots.'

The last thing Jack heard, as he turned to enter the building, was her remark to her friend. 'Did ye know, in some houses they pay ye good to tie the blokes and beat them?'

Chapter Twenty

Batiste's grip bit cruelly into Lily's arm. He dragged her, slow and careful, into the hall. They travelled past several closed doors and turned left. Ahead, Lily could see dim light shining. The sounds of a scuffle grew louder as they approached the light at the end of the hall, and then the noise abruptly ceased.

'Quiet, girl,' Batiste said in a savage murmur. 'It would appear I am going to have to deal with this nuisance myself.'

He slowed as he approached the end of the hall, tugging her close as he edged into an anteroom at the front of the building. It was filled with only a broken table, a chair or two and the pervasive dust. But even as she gazed around the door opened and Jack Alden rushed in.

The sound of the cocking gun sounded eerily loud

in the small room. Lily gasped as the cold muzzle dug into her jaw.

'Good afternoon, Mr Alden,' Batiste said in politely formal tones. 'How very resourceful you are. I admit I fully intended to meet you again before the day was out, but these were not the circumstances I envisioned.'

'My God...' Jack faltered, seemingly shocked. 'You! It was you at the White Horse, chattering on about hearts' desires.'

'Get rid of your weapon, Mr Alden.' He shifted the muzzle of his gun so it rested directly beneath Lily's chin. She stared, terrified, into Jack's eyes.

He cursed and tossed a stout cane aside. It clattered to the floor a few feet away.

'Ah, thank you,' Batiste said mildly. 'Yes, I must also thank you for your frankness the other day. What a stroke of luck that conversation proved to be. I fully intended to grab you then and there, but I confess, I had worried that you would prove stubborn as well as resourceful. You've shown such tenacity in your pursuit, I feared that not even my men would be able to persuade you to give me the information that I want from you.' He smiled affably. 'But things worked out so much better than I had hoped. You gave me the weapon I needed to convince you. And now here we are—I have what your heart desires most and you hold the information I need to find what mine desires most.' He ran the cold steel along Lily's jaw in a revolting caress. 'Shall we trade?'

'Don't listen to him, Jack,' Lily said tightly. 'He means to kill you.'

Batiste gave her a shake. 'I will kill *her* if you don't tell me what Mervyn Latimer found in that coffer. Where is Treyford travelling to? Damn it—where is the Lost Jewel?'

An indescribable weariness washed across Jack's expression. 'I cannot believe that I actually owe you anything resembling thanks, Batiste, but it is true. What you said at the White Horse held more truth than you realise. I thought all I needed was to bring you to justice, but I was wrong. There is only one thing I need.' His gaze held Lily's and she knew. Despite the dire circumstances, her heart swelled and great, unshed tears collected in her eyes. 'I nearly walked away from it to follow a twisted obsession,' Jack said. 'I nearly turned myself into you.'

Through her watery gaze, she saw his attention turn back to Batiste. 'Let her go now. The Jewel does not exist. It is over.'

Batiste laughed, but it was an ugly, desperate attempt. 'It is *nearly* over, boy. The Jewel does not exist,' he spat. 'God, I hate to say it, but Mervyn

Latimer is a genius. He may have duped you, but I have laboured for nearly twenty years in search of the Jewel. Do you think I would give it up on the word of a besotted fool? It has been a long and difficult journey. I have been tested time and again. You—' He shook his head. 'You are the last obstacle I must breach.' He moved the gun to Lily's temple. 'Tell me!' he shouted.

Jack stared long and hard at Lily. His jaw clenched. In an agony of fear and longing, she stared back.

Jack sighed. 'It's in Devonshire,' he said simply.

'Jack, no!' Lily cried.

'Shut up, girl!' Batiste pushed her violently away. She struck the listing table, stumbled and fell.

Batiste turned the gun on Jack. 'Devonshire?' His voice had gone eager and unnervingly possessive. 'Do you mean that Mervyn has it already? It cannot be. Tell me what you mean!'

He advanced, but Jack merely spread his hands. 'The Jewel is not what you think. It is not a jewel at all, nor an ancient collar nor even a map, as has been theorised. It is something altogether different and unexpected.'

Batiste stepped closer. 'Yes, what—?'

He never finished his question. Jack's foot shot out and kicked the firearm from his grasp. Batiste's roar of rage was cut short as Jack's fist caught him in the nose.

The villain stepped back. He actually laughed. 'Fine, then, we'll do it the hard way. But rest assured that I will kill you slowly.' He pulled a curved blade from his waistcoat. 'I will carve you into pieces and there will be plenty of time for you to tell me what I want to know before you die.' Almost before he had finished speaking he rushed, his knife poised with deadly intent.

Jack danced back. On hands and knees, Lily crept along the wall, trying to reach the castaway pistol. Batiste must be stopped, before he harmed Jack, before he continued to destroy others in his self-serving madness. For all of their sakes, this had to end now—even if she had to shoot the bedlamite herself.

But Batiste had doubled his assault, fighting with the ease of long practice. Lily could scarcely credit how fast and cleverly he handled his blade. Jack was younger and quick on his feet, but unarmed and clearly at a disadvantage. Batiste surged suddenly forwards, delivering a vicious slash, low and quick. Jack staggered. Lily gasped as a thin red slice opened across his midriff.

Desperate, she turned again to find the gun. It had slid beneath an overturned chair. She strained to reach it, brushed the polished handle with her fingertips. There! She grasped it and pulled it free. With shaking hands, she held it tight and climbed to her feet.

But Jack had recovered. He stood his ground as Batiste pressed his next attack. He dodged a sharp thrust and feinted one of his own. Instinctively, Batiste lunged back, helped along with a well-timed swipe of Jack's boot. The villain lost his footing, tried frantically to regain it, and stepped squarely on the discarded walking stick. His feet flew out backwards; he crashed to the ground, automatically throwing his hands forwards to break his fall.

Batiste had not let go of his blade. Too late, he tried to rotate out of harm's way. Lily grimaced and closed her eyes against the sight as he fell straight on to his own knife, gave a massive jerk and died.

Jack's shoulders slumped. His breath came in ragged gasps and he struggled to regain control. It was over. Thank God, it was over at last. He pressed a hand against the cut on his belly and glanced over at Lily, hoping to share his elation and relief and sorrow. But her eyes were closed. She swayed on her feet, her complexion gone stark white against the subtle fire of her hair.

'Lily!' He leaped over to her, took the pistol from her shaky grasp and gathered her gently into his arms.

She clung to him. 'Oh, Jack—I am so sorry! You were right all along and I did not believe you, refused to understand—'

'No, no. All the apologies are mine to make. Hush now,' he soothed her as she trembled against him. 'Come, let's get you out of here and into the fresh air.'

Before they had taken a step a great noise rose up outside. Shouts and the echo of many footsteps rang loud in the courtyard. His heartrate ratcheting, Jack thrust Lily behind him as someone pounded up the steps and thrust open the door.

'Charles!' he exclaimed in relief.

'Fisher!' Lily exclaimed in surprise.

A multitude of footmen, groomsmen and a few men Jack had never seen before crowded behind the two. Charles took a good look around and then took instant command. 'Several of you search the back. Bring back anyone you find. The rest of you help the uh…ladies…outside with their burdens and keep anyone else from entering that damned alley.' He turned to his brother, 'You might have left us a sign. Do you know how many alleys there are off Little Bure Street?'

Jack scrubbed a hand through his hair. 'Sorry, this is not my area of expertise.'

Charles laughed. 'Little brother, judging by the

trail of criminals you left in your wake, I'd say you were an expert.' He sobered and nudged the body on the floor with his foot. 'Batiste?' he asked.

Jack nodded.

'Then I'd say you were an expert who's done the world a favour.' His voice gentled and he extended a hand towards Lily. 'Miss Beecham, our mother is waiting anxiously for you.' He chuckled. 'I nearly had to tie her down to keep her from coming along.' He took her hand and pulled her towards the door. 'I have a closed carriage waiting for you.'

'Thank you.' She sighed.

'I think I should warn you that word has come that your own mother is due in at any time.' He grinned. 'Let's just hope that you make it to Bruton Street before she does.'

'Oh, heavens, yes.' Lily took his brother's hand and allowed him to start to lead her away, but she cast a lingering glance back Jack's way.

'Wait,' he protested.

'Oh, I'll clean up your mess, Jack,' Charles said with exaggerated patience. 'You go along with her.' He shot Jack a pitying look. 'You've got some explaining to do.'

Jack stepped up to Lily's side. 'Truer words were never spoken.'

* * *

A considerable amount of time passed before Lily found herself settled into the carriage. There were a multitude of questions to be answered and assurances to be given. Hugs were exchanged, a few tears were shed, and she and Jack made a point to personally thank everyone who had been involved in Batiste's end and her rescue.

Now, at last, the two of them climbed into the coach. Fisher made a half-hearted protest, offering to send a footman along for propriety's sake, but Charles firmly shushed him and shut the door. With a clap on the side of the carriage and a shout to the driver, he sent them off.

It took only a moment for Jack to compose himself. Lily watched as he drew a deep breath. When he opened his mouth to speak, she held up a restraining hand.

'Wait. I have just one question.' She leaned forwards, suddenly terribly self-conscious of her dirty face, rumpled gown and dishevelled hair. But there was too much at stake to let such things stop her now. 'Is it true? Did you tell Batiste that I was your greatest desire?'

Jack laughed. 'Oh, Lord, Lily. Trust you to get to the heart of the matter.' He leaned in as well, until their faces nearly met in the centre. Lily breathed in the heady, masculine scent of him as his breath mingled with hers. 'Yes,' he said, looking a little sheepish. 'Yes, I did.'

Lily sighed happily. 'That's all I needed to hear.' She shuffled across to his side of the coach, burrowed under his arm and laid her head against his shoulder.

He lifted her chin. She was caught, mesmerised by the light, unburdened quality of his gaze. A great well of joy and gratitude swelled within her at the sight. Every moment of danger and fear, every tear and frustration—they had all been worth it. She would have endured far more to see such a shine in his hazel eyes.

He kissed her then, searing her with equal parts tenderness and fierce possession. She wrapped her arms tightly about him and abandoned herself to the slow, thorough pleasure of it.

She was not nearly ready to stop when Jack suddenly pulled back. 'God, that mouth of yours is irresistible,' he murmured, running a thumb along her lower lip. 'But resist I must, for, despite your generosity, there is more I find I need to say.'

Lily tried to draw him back down to her. 'Jack,' she protested. 'We'll be talking non-stop once we reach Bruton Street. Surely we can think of something better to do until then.'

Jack groaned. 'In a moment, minx.' He took her face in both of his hands, his expression grown serious. 'This is important. I want you to know I was on my way back to you when I found out that Batiste had taken you.'

She stilled, struck by what he had said, and then she smiled. He was right. It was a thrill to know that Jack had battled his enemy to save her, but the fact that he'd recognised his obsession for what it was and chosen life, love—and her—instead was infinitely more reassuring.

'Thank you,' she said with tears in her eyes. 'I know how incredibly difficult that choice must have been.' She gave him a tremulous smile. 'And it must have been doubly hard after the horrible lecture I read you when you left.'

'Horrible?' He gave an ironic chuckle. 'It was absolutely, in every way correct.' He settled back and pulled her in close. 'You were right all along. I harboured a seething mass of anger all those years, and a deal of sadness and resentment with it, but I couldn't acknowledge it.'

She placed her hand on his chest. 'So you built your walls to keep them out,' she said, trying to imbue her voice with all the sympathy in her heart.

'Yes. I used logic and rationality as bricks and mortar and I thought to keep myself safe. But instead of keeping the ugly emotions at bay, my walls only trapped them inside.' He squeezed her hand. 'Until you came along and demolished them.' He laughed ruefully. 'I thought I didn't know how to deal with so many feelings running amok, but the truth was, I was still clutching them tightly.'

'But you've let them go,' she said in wonder and absolute assurance. 'I can see it in your eyes.' She let her gaze drop to his mouth. 'And taste it in your kiss.'

'Yes, thanks to you, I saw that darkness for what it was, and I let it all go.'

She smiled. 'And how do you feel?'

'Empty,' he said, shifting beneath her. 'A little frightened. I nearly died when I heard that Batiste had you, Lily. Because I need you. I need you to fill me with light.' He turned towards her, holding her tightly. 'I thought I needed walls, but all I needed was you.'

The tears did fall then, as the enormity of all that he had done, for her sake, hit her. 'You've faced so much and shown such bravery,' she marvelled. 'But you've got something better than walls now, Jack. You've made a foundation.'

He wiped a tear from her cheek. 'Shall we build on it, then?'

Nodding emphatically, Lily pulled him down for a kiss. A kiss, and so much more. It was a promise, a vow, a vision of a future filled with contented days and passionate nights. For long moments they lingered, savouring passion, escalating desire, and the tantalising idea of a future faced together.

He broke the kiss and smiled down into her eyes. 'I'm afraid it'll be no easy job, being the keeper of my heart. It's not perfect. It's been neglected too long, and might still be subject to periods of surliness or need moments of solitude. But thanks to you, it is in better shape than it has ever been before.' His mouth quirked. 'Are you willing to take on such a heavy burden?'

'You know I will. You couldn't stop me if you wished to.' Lily reached up and ran a finger through his unruly hair, at long last taming it with her fingers. 'You should know, there was never any need for you to feel empty—for I gave my heart and soul over to you long ago.'

'That's all that has saved me,' he said simply.

She raised a brow at him. 'And you are already familiar with the burdens I represent. Along with me you'll get my opinionated mother, and assorted orphans, abolitionists and other charitable causes. Not to mention, I have a long list of requirements.'

He laughed. 'Requirements?'

'Yes, things that you will have to provide on a regular basis.'

He lowered his voice to a seductive whisper. 'Such as?'

Lily fought back a giggle as he buried his face in the nape of her neck. 'Oh, many things. Music, learning, travel.' She gasped as his hand climbed to cup her breast. 'Laughter,' she whispered, 'and kisses.'

'Like this?' He raised his head and brushed his lips, soft and clinging, across hers. His hands were busy with the line of buttons at her back.

'Oh, my, yes,' she breathed.

'And is that all of your requirements?'

She hunched a shoulder, helping him in his efforts to remove her bodice. 'No, I can think of so many more. More passionate interludes in libraries, for one.'

'And gardens?' he asked wickedly. He had her stays unfastened and pushed them wide.

'Definitely gardens.' She had to fight back a moan as his mouth traced a molten line down the column of her neck. 'And you must solemnly promise, Jack, that we will do this in the carriage, oh, at least once a week.'

'I promise,' he vowed right before he bent to suckle her through the thin fabric of her shift.

Lily closed her eyes and let her head fall back. 'So,' she eventually managed to bite out, 'will you agree to take me on, knowing me for the heavy burden I am?'

He raised his head and kissed her, long and hard. 'It's only fair,' he said.

Epilogue

The dining hall of the J. Crump School for Orphans had been transformed. Lord Dayle's wife Sophie had blown in like a whirlwind. In a matter of days what once had been a plain, serviceable room had magically become a beautiful desert city.

Actual sand covered the floor in strategic spots and ancient pillars created open-air rooms. Rich fabrics, earthy colours—it was a fitting setting for the first lecture and display on what was becoming internationally known as Lord Treyford's Lost City.

Scholars around the world had vied for tickets to tonight's event, along with a multitude of wealthy would-be patrons, but Lily made sure that tonight's festivities included those from every walk of life and level of society. Formal wear and gorgeous gowns rubbed up against brushed Sunday best, but no one made a peep of protest. They were all too caught up in the magic of the night and the wonderful array of artefacts and etchings that Lord Treyford's expedition had sent back to England.

'How long is Mr Alden goin' to talk?' a young boy whispered in Lily's ear.

'You know how he is,' answered another with a roll of his eyes. 'He talked for the whole class about what ancient Egyptians planted in their kitchen gardens.'

'Your turn is coming soon,' Lily replied softly. While the guests were sitting enthralled by her husband's brilliantly stirring history of the lost city and its rediscovery, Lily sat in the hallway outside, surrounded by students, attending to last-minute adjustments to hair and costume. As all the profits from tonight's event were going to help the combined school and orphanage, it was only fitting that the children should be a part of it.

'Missus Alden!' The quiet wail came from a girl with a drooping coiffure and a handful of hairpins. 'My hair!'

'Come, Daisy, I'll fix you straight up,' Lily reassured the girl.

Daisy pushed through and thrust the hairpins in Lily's hand.

'Turn around, now.' The girl obeyed and Lily was left holding the pins. She glanced around, and then ruefully set them on her well-rounded belly. She just had Daisy's hair repaired when a thunderous round of applause broke out in the dining hall. 'That's our signal, children! Line up, now.'

They all waited several minutes until the applause died down. 'All right. In you go!' She smiled universal encouragement over her group of performers. 'You'll be marvellous, I know it!'

Lily waited until the children were safely onstage before she followed them into the atmospherically lit hall. She kept to the back, lurking behind a pillar, glad to find something in the display rounder than she. She leaned against it, closed her eyes and allowed the simple beauty of childish harmonies to soothe her.

A draught of cool air across her cheek alerted her. She opened her eyes to find several seated ladies fluttering their fans and lashes. Smiling, she followed the direction of their gazes to find the handsome form of her husband approaching down the side of the hall.

'Your mother says you must sit down, and put your feet up if it can be contrived,' he said, his eyes running over her in a nearly tangible caress.

'She worries, bless her heart,' Lily said with patience. Casting an impudent grin at Jack, she asked, 'And what did my new father have to say?'

He grimaced. 'Your mother has improved Mr

Cooperage greatly, my dear, but some things never change. I don't care what he says about women in an advanced childbearing state, there is no way I would allow you to miss this evening.' He took her hand. 'But would you like me to find you a seat?'

She shook her head and leaned against him with a contented sigh. 'It was so generous of Lord Treyford to allow all of this.'

Jack laughed. 'Believe me, Trey is happy to miss all the uproar—especially since Chione finds herself in a condition similar to yours. There is no way they could travel home right now.'

'I know. I do not think it bothered her to miss this either, she sounded so completely happy in her last letter. I know just how she feels,' Lily said, gazing about at the spectacle. 'It's hard to believe, is it not?' she asked with a sweep of her hand. 'It feels as if we've built so much and come so far.'

Jack laid his hand on her belly, bent down and brushed her lips with his. 'It's easy to build, my darling wife, on a solid and beautiful foundation.'

* * * * *

HISTORICAL

LARGE PRINT

SCANDALOUS SECRET, DEFIANT BRIDE

Helen Dickson

Some call Christina Thornton spoilt, others simply call her beautiful. But one thing's for certain: she's a young woman firmly in charge of her destiny – or so she thinks! But when the dark-hearted Count Marchesi rides into town, it is to claim Miss Thornton as his bride. Her future is in the hands of this brooding Italian…

A QUESTION OF IMPROPRIETY

Michelle Styles

Diana Clare has had enough of London – the balls, the rakes you can never trust. Having returned home in disgrace, she is trying to forget what drove her from the *ton*. But rake and gambler Brett Farnham, Earl of Coltonby, seems intent on making Diana remember *exactly* what it was like to be seduced by the glint in your partner's eye…

CONQUERING KNIGHT, CAPTIVE LADY

Anne O'Brien

There is no way Lady Rosamund de Longspey has escaped an arranged marriage only to be conquered by a rogue. But Lord Gervase Fitz Osbern, weary of war and wanton women, will fight for what rightfully belongs to him. A warrior to his fingertips, he'll claim his castle – and just maybe a bride!

◉ MILLS & BOON®
Pure reading pleasure™

HIST0309 LP

HISTORICAL

LARGE PRINT

MISS WINBOLT AND THE FORTUNE HUNTER

Sylvia Andrew

Respected spinster Miss Emily Winbolt, so cool and cynical with would-be suitors, puts her reputation at risk after tumbling into a stranger's arms. Her rescuer is none other than Sir William Ashenden, a man of some distinction. He needs to marry – and Emily yearns to believe that he wants her not for her fortune but for herself…

CAPTAIN FAWLEY'S INNOCENT BRIDE

Annie Burrows

Battle-scarred Captain Robert Fawley was under no illusion that women found him attractive. None would ever agree to marry him – except perhaps Miss Deborah Gillies, a woman so down on her luck that a convenient marriage might improve her circumstances. Deborah accepted his pragmatic proposal – because she was already halfway to falling in love with him…

THE RAKE'S REBELLIOUS LADY

Anne Herries

Tomboy Caroline Holbrook is used to running riot, and can't imagine settling into a dull, respectable marriage. But her zest for life and alluring innocence draw the attention of Sir Frederick Rathbone – who is far from dull! In fact, he's the most exciting man Caroline has ever met. But should she resist the attentions of this rakish bachelor…?

 MILLS & BOON®
Pure reading pleasure™

HIST0409 L

HISTORICAL

LARGE PRINT

THE CAPTAIN'S FORBIDDEN MISS

Margaret McPhee

Captain Pierre Dammartin is a man of honour, but his captive, Josephine Mallington, is the daughter of his sworn enemy… She is the one woman he should hate, yet her innocence brings hope to his battle-weary heart. As the Peninsular War rages on, can the strength of their love conquer all that divides them?

THE EARL AND THE HOYDEN

Mary Nichols

Miss Charlotte Cartwright has never forgotten Roland Temple's contemptuous rejection of her hand in marriage. And she's not about to forgive, either – even if Roland, the new Earl of Amerleigh, is now older, wiser and ten times more handsome! But Roland is determined to right the wrongs of the past – and this time the hoyden will be his bride…

FROM GOVERNESS TO SOCIETY BRIDE

Helen Dickson

Lord Lucas Stainton is in need of a governess. The man is ruthless, rude beyond belief, and Eve Brody wishes him to the devil – but the position is hers if she'll accept… As sparks fly between Eve and the magnificent man of the house she learns that the dark-hearted Lord is carrying the weight of ruin on his broad shoulders. So she offers him a proposal…

MILLS & BOON®
Pure reading pleasure™

HIST0509 LP

HISTORICAL

LARGE PRINT

MARRYING THE MISTRESS

Juliet Landon

Helene Follet hasn't had close contact with Lord Burl
Winterson since she left to care for his brother. Now Burl
has become guardian to her son she is forced to live under
his protection. He has become cynical, while Helene hides
behind a calm, cool front. Neither can admit how affected
they are by the memory of a long-ago night…

TO DECEIVE A DUKE

Amanda McCabe

Clio Chase left for Sicily trying to forget the mysterious
Duke of Averton and the strange effect he has on her.
However, when he suddenly appears and warns her of
danger, her peace of mind is shattered. Under the
mysterious threat they are thrown together in intimate
circumstances…for how long can she resist?

KNIGHT OF GRACE

Sophia James

Grace knew that the safety of her home depended on her
betrothal to Laird Lachlan Kerr. She did not expect his
kindness, strength or care. Against his expectations, the
cynical Laird is increasingly intrigued by Grace's quiet
bravery. Used to betrayal at every turn, her faith in
him is somehow oddly seductive…

🌀™ MILLS & BOON®
Pure reading pleasure™

HIST0609 L